Fall 2003
ISSN: 0276-0045

THE REVIEW OF CONTEMPORARY FICTION

Editor
JOHN O'BRIEN
Illinois State University

Senior Editor
ROBERT L. MCLAUGHLIN
Illinois State University

Book Review Editor
TIM FEENEY

Production & Design
N. J. FURL

Editorial Assistant
TESSA SOMERS

Cover Illustration
SAMUEL BERKES

Cover Photos
BILL HAYWARD (Diane Williams)
MICHAL HERON (Patricia Eakins)
ELWIN HIGGINS (Aidan Higgins)

Copyright © 2003 *The Review of Contemporary Fiction.*
No part of this periodical may be reproduced without the
permission of the publisher. Address all correspondence to:
The Review of Contemporary Fiction,
ISU Campus Box 8905, Normal, IL 61790-8905 USA.

www.centerforbookculture.org
www.dalkeyarchive.com

The Review of Contemporary Fiction is published three times a year
(January, June, September) by the Center for Book Culture, a
nonprofit organization located at ISU Campus Box 8905, Normal,
IL 61790-8905. ISSN 0276-0045. Subscription prices are as follows:

  Single volume (three issues):
      Individuals: $17.00; foreign, add $3.50;
      Institutions: $26.00; foreign, add $3.50.

DISTRIBUTION. Bookstores should send orders to:

Review of Contemporary Fiction, ISU Campus Box 8905,
Normal, IL 61790-8905. Phone 309-438-7555; fax 309-438-7422.

This issue is partially supported by a grant from the Illinois Arts
Council, a state agency.

Indexed in *American Humanities Index, International Bibliography
of Periodical Literature, International Bibliography of Book
Reviews, MLA Bibliography,* and *Book Review Index.* Abstracted
in *Abstracts of English Studies.*

The Review of Contemporary Fiction is also available on 16mm
microfilm, 35mm microfilm, and 105mm microfiche from
University Microfilms International, 300 North Zeeb Road,
Ann Arbor, MI 48106-1346.

www.centerforbookculture.org

THE REVIEW OF CONTEMPORARY FICTION

BACK ISSUES AVAILABLE

Back issues are still available for the following numbers of the *Review of Contemporary Fiction* ($8 each unless otherwise noted):

NOVELIST AS CRITIC: Essays by Garrett, Barth, Sorrentino, Wallace, Ollier, Brooke-Rose, Creeley, Mathews, Kelly, Abbott, West, McCourt, McGonigle, and McCarthy

NEW FINNISH FICTION: Fiction by Eskelinen, Jäntti, Kontio, Krohn, Paltto, Sairanen, Selo, Siekkinen, Sund, Valkeapää

NEW ITALIAN FICTION: Interviews and fiction by Malerba, Tabucchi, Zanotto, Ferrucci, Busi, Corti, Rasy, Cherchi, Balduino, Ceresa, Capriolo, Carrera, Valesio, and Gramigna

GROVE PRESS NUMBER: Contributions by Allen, Beckett, Corso, Ferlinghetti, Jordan, McClure, Rechy, Rosset, Selby, Sorrentino, and others

NEW DANISH FICTION: Fiction by Brøgger, Høeg, Andersen, Grøndahl, Holst, Jensen, Thorup, Michael, Sibast, Ryum, Lynggaard, Grønfeldt, Willumsen, and Holm

NEW LATVIAN FICTION: Fiction by Nora Ikstena, Paul Bankovskis, Guntis Berelis, Arvis Kolmanis, Andra Neiburga, Rimants Ziedonis, and others

THE FUTURE OF FICTION: Essays by Birkerts, Caponegro, Franzen, Galloway, Maso, Morrow, Vollmann, White, and others

NEW JAPANESE FICTION: Interviews and fiction by Ohara, Shimada, Shono, Takahashi, Tsutsui, McCaffery, Gregory, Kotani, Tatsumi, Koshikawa, and others

Individuals receive a 10% discount on orders of one issue and a 20% discount on orders of two or more issues. To place an order, use the form on the last page of this issue.

RCF Call for Contributors

www.centerforbookculture.org/review

The *Review of Contemporary Fiction* is seeking contributors to write overview essays on the following writers:

Felipe Alfau, Chandler Brossard, Gabrielle Burton, Michel Butor, Julieta Campos, Jerome Charyn, Emily Holmes Coleman, Stanley Crawford, Eva Figes, William H. Gass, Karen Elizabeth Gordon, Carol De Chellis Hill, Violette Leduc, Olive Moore, Julián Ríos, Esther Tusquets.

The essays must:

- be 50 double-spaced pages;
- cover the subject's biography;
- summarize the critical reception of the subject's works;
- discuss the course of the subject's career, including each major work;
- provide interpretive strategies for new readers to apply to the subject's work;
- provide a bibliographic checklist of each of the subject's works (initial and latest printings);
- be written for a general, intelligent reader, who does not know the subject's work;
- avoid jargon, theoretical digressions, and excessive endnotes;
- be intelligent, interesting, and readable;
- be documented in MLA style.

Authors will be paid $250.00 when the essay is published. All essays will be subject to editorial review, and the editors reserve the right to request revisions and to reject unacceptable essays.

Applicants should send a CV and a brief writing sample. In your cover letter, be sure to address your qualifications.

Send applications to:

Robert L. McLaughlin
Dalkey Archive Press, Illinois State University, Campus Box 8905, Normal, IL 61790-8905

Inquiries: rmclaugh@ilstu.edu

Contents

Announcing
The Jane and Paul Bowles Society

The Jane and Paul Bowles Society was recently formed by several Bowles enthusiasts. The principal aim of the Society is to celebrate the work of Jane and Paul Bowles in academic venues. The Society will attend the MLA and American Literature Association annual conferences to present panels geared toward scholarly investigations of the Bowles' works. The Society will also provide resources on how to include the Bowles' works in university classrooms. The Society's newsletter, *Bowles Notes*, will be published twice a year and will feature reviews and criticism of the Bowles' works as well as news in Bowles studies.

For more information about the society or about becoming a member, contact:

David Racker
(dracker@temple.edu)

or

Anne Foltz
(a_foltz@msn.com)

Diane Williams

Laura Sims

Reading contemporary American fiction, one may assume that great innovators such as Donald Barthelme, Laura Riding, and Gertrude Stein, among others, have made a negligible impact on the form, which suffers undeniably from inertia. There persists the trend of telling "straight" stories, complete with richly drawn, psychologically complex characters, detailed landscapes, and plots that arc neatly, often predictably, into epiphany, then denouement. Of course it reassures the reader to know that she can still invest herself in a microcosm of The World, populated by Real People, that professes to explain some aspect of Life, Love, and Happiness. The promise of receiving that kernel of Truth is intoxicating; the mere reassurance of its existence in concrete, minable form extinguishes any desire to ferret out works that *don't* offer up that (illusory) golden nugget, those "full" characters, that "rich" psychological and/or physical landscape.

If anyone can alleviate the suffocating comfort and subsequent boredom of the aforementioned reading experience, it is Diane Williams. As one of the few true inheritors of the tradition of literary progress, Williams offers an enlivening alternative to the jaded reader. Her fiction "experiments" should not put off the reader (including me) wary of encountering one of the experiments-gone-sadly-awry that litter the premier avant-garde literary journals; nor should the diehard fans (including me) of "straight" narratives look the other way. Williams walks the line, constantly, between the world of elemental, sensual satisfaction and the realm of discomfort, in which her radical intellect sounds the depths to which our human existence is forlorn, our contact with the divine undependable, and our language obsolete. Her instinct and intuition guide her along this tightrope. The reader should look for no mere nugget when harvesting Williams's works; she should look instead for the adventuresome manipulation of characters, plot, and language itself, which entertains us, enriches us, and divests us of any precious ideas we may hold about what fiction is or should be.

What may sound like fiction of a very serious nature and intent comes across as rollicking, sly, and absurd on a first reading. Humor, an integral component of the stories, acts not as a glitzy sideshow, but as a gateway to the inner chamber of human emotions and situations through which our narrator leads us. It is her voice that crackles with wit and loony insight; she resembles an alien in her amused, detached observation of and interaction with humanity, although we feel certain she is human too. She lurks at the margins of her community and from this vantage point guides us straight to the wild heart of our civilization.

Williams's narrator strips off the surface layer of the everyday world and reveals to us what we often label inappropriate: our fierce lust for strangers or our own siblings; frank sexual encounters; misbehavior at a cocktail party. It is not merely the uniqueness of her narrator's perspective that marks Williams's work, but also the sense that these revelations of what lies beneath the material world set the narrator free—from the everyday, from family obligations, from social proprieties and expectations, all of which can stifle the soul. This, in turn, frees the reader; we can't help but stare at the marvelous world inside the world we know so well, even when the revelations disturb us deeply, even when the stories consistently deny us the closure we could easily receive from a more formulaic work of art.

Part of the charm that ensnares us is Williams's taut, electric language, which keeps us piqued and amused even when we are faced with the most troubling scenarios. Witness the first paragraph of "Spoon," from Williams's latest collection, *Romancer Erector*: "The person has no sanction for sucking. We had surprised her while she was in the act of sucking. She was a sucker who could make a variety of noises. She was spoony—we had thought she was easy to describe. I had thought she was a wallydraigle. She might not have been. Her hair was a moderate brown and it was aimed at her head. She was suffering from vulvovaginitis" (57). The short, almost staccato phrases of this paragraph, and of much of Williams's work, recall Stein's quest to pare language down to the bone. Each sentence lands with a dull thud, killing instantly any expectation we might have for the buildup to a thrilling, falsely revelatory conclusion. The language itself is the thrill; the exercise itself becomes the reward for the open-minded reader. The musical (and whimsical) repetition of as unlikely a word as *suck,* in various forms (*sucking, sucker*), clues us in to the unconventional tactics we can expect from this writer. The first few phrases circle around description, revealing in their circularity the difficulty of describing anyone. "[W]e had thought she was easy to describe," the narrator admits upon realizing the opposite. But Williams does not, in place of a fully formed, three-dimensional character, give us an ironic caricature of one, the usual "experimental" solution to the problem of characterization; instead she frolics, with great purpose, allowing us to ask, in her place: Is this woman "spoony?" Is she "a wallydraigle?" And why on earth does she have "vulvovaginitis?" But it is neither the urge to shock nor the urge to dispose of character altogether that fuels these lines—by the end, the narrator tells us, in cadence, "I have to put the worst of her into her," and with this the character, unreal and monstrous as she may appear to be, gains our sympathy (57). She does not stand for something else, we do not reach an epiphany via her presence in the story, but what is significant, remarkable even, is that Williams manages to move us even while she deconstructs "character" and "story" and likewise denatures language itself. Her explorations expand from one work to the next, repeatedly resisting contraction to a single, digestible solution.

Although Williams's work is hard to solidly define, falling somewhere between short-short fiction and prose poetry, it has been classified most frequently as sudden fiction or flash fiction. This "new" genre was first showcased in the anthology *Sudden Fiction: American Short-Short Stories,* published in 1986, whose editors, Robert Shapard and James Thomas, solicited the help of various writers in naming these super-short pieces, first leaning toward *blasters,* then, after the suggestion of Robert Kelly, deciding upon *sudden fiction. Sudden* comes from the Latin word *subire,* meaning "without warning . . . to steal upon. Unforeseen, swift," which seems to capture exactly what this fiction accomplishes at its best— a lightning-quick, though skillful and intricate attack, paired with a hasty retreat, which leaves the reader (usually pleasantly) stunned (Shapard and Thomas xvi). In this first of several *Sudden Fiction* anthologies, Shapard and Thomas selected stories that ranged from straightforward but severely truncated narratives (the majority) to the odd, truly innovative, disturbing "parables" of writers like Lydia Davis, Russell Edson, Robert Kelly, and Robert Coover, the common denominator being that each story does not exceed five pages, or about 1,500 words (Shapard and Thomas xiv). Williams, whose publishing career had just begun in 1986, was included in *Flash Fictions,* a later anthology edited by James Thomas, comprised of even shorter works, each a maximum of 750 words (Thomas, Thomas, and Hazuka 11).

In the first *Sudden Fiction* anthology, the editors acknowledge that these very brief prose concoctions are hard to define as a genre, spanning as they do the spectrum of fictional styles (Shapard and Thomas xiv). In an afterword, different writers and editors take stabs at defining them, revealing the lack of consensus on what this genre *is*; more conservative writers think the sudden fictions should be whole, small worlds, complete in themselves, merely shorter. The risk-taking writers, such as Robert Kelly, define sudden fiction as "neither poetic prose nor prosy verse, but the energy and clarity typical of prose coincident in the scope and rhythm of the poem" (qtd. in Shapard and Thomas 240), a definition that could easily be applied to Williams's work. Charles Baxter asks himself (and the reader), "Why these things, now? Well, who is notable for making plans anymore? Who feels like the hero of an epic? These are tunes for the end of time, for those in an information age who are sick of data. The future has narrowed, become so small a tunnel that no one feels like crawling into it" (qtd. in Shapard and Thomas 229). This idea of the future's narrowing fits perfectly with the form as defined by masters like Edson, Coover, Davis, and now Williams. There is no room, no ease of pace or mind for the long, drawn-out narrative of the past, although diluted echoes of the past continue to have a stronghold (stranglehold?) on today's fiction market. However contrived this sense of panic and hurry may be in the current age, there is no mistaking that the work of many innovative writers reflects the hectic pace of the times. Williams has answered the question about her own work's brevity with the following explanation: "I need thrills . . . quick thrills, satisfaction fast. . . . [I need to] get answers fast and get relief" (qtd. in Rosenberg). This statement reflects a personal urgency consistent with the times in which she lives and creates. In another interview, also from 1990, she expands on the previous statement by saying that "every moment is so boring to me, so hopeless, so dull, that if I can wrest from that moment some sort of bliss or enchantment, that's what I want to do" (qtd. in Hanson).

The editors of *Sudden Fiction* also remind us that "the name *short-short story* may be relatively new, but its forms are as old as parable and fable, myth and exemplum" (Shapard and Thomas xiv). This is something that resonates very strongly with Williams's own definition of what she does, of what her influences have been. She refers to texts that have influenced her as "testimony" or "crucial declarations . . . the mighty incantations, jokes and fables, prayers and psalms . . . parables . . . commandments . . . and prophesies" (qtd. in Enns 73–74). In keeping with such influence, many of her stories are strange little parables, and her narrator's highly dramatic voice mildly scolds, condemns mightily, or soothes, like an unpredictable deity addressing the large, recalcitrant crowd of humanity. Her issues and concerns resonate with the themes of these "crucial declarations" as well, namely, the timeless human questioning of why, how, where, who, and when, regarding existence.

The same questions can be more readily answered regarding Williams's biography (in appropriately miniature form). Born in

Chicago, Illinois, Williams grew up with two siblings in a neighborhood outside of Chicago, Highland Park. She attended the University of Pennsylvania, where she studied with Philip Roth, then moved to New York City, working first as a dance therapist in Bellevue Hospital's psychotic ward. Having trained as a dancer since the age of eight and having seriously considered becoming a professional dancer, Williams chose dance therapy as a way of continuing to use movement in her professional life. Her tenure at Bellevue was a short one, however, due to the traumatic nature of the work environment. During her years of dance training, Williams says she "loved choreographing and improvising," a statement that resonates with her written work as well as her physical artistry (qtd. in O'Brien 134).

After working as a dance therapist, Williams entered the publishing world as a secretary for Doubleday. At the time, women interested in editorial positions had to begin as secretaries; men started out immediately as editorial assistants. However unchallenging the daily administrative tasks were, the job provided Williams with the training she would need as a textbook editor and writer for the educational publishing company Scott Foresman, a job she secured after marrying and moving to Glencoe, a suburb of Chicago. As much as Williams enjoyed this work, she recalls the thrill she had on quitting when her first child was born; she had the initial sense of being released from perpetual work to long-term vacation. After a while, though, she began to sense that she was "disappearing," so she turned to fiction writing as a means to combat her own vanishing act. She began to write stories and publish them in journals of good standing.

Later, Williams studied with Gordon Lish, then an editor at Knopf, first briefly in a three-hour workshop in Detroit, then for two semesters in New York. Lish helped her become "conscious of how language can be manipulated to produce maximum effects" (qtd. in O'Brien 136). During this time she also recognized that the experiences she has called "anything in my life that I wanted to say no to . . . [everything that] was painful and terrifying," "personally dangerous material" (qtd. in O'Brien 137), would become the raw substance of her work. In many Williams stories, danger or dismay lurks just around the bend; the act of facing this terror, this nightmare, in writing or speech, becomes, as Williams says, a "healing" force (qtd. in O'Brien 138). Since there is "no pain that can't be made into an object and put up on a shelf," the act of writing can rescue her and perhaps others as well, by acting as an essential release for both writer and reader (qtd. in Rosenberg). Williams has often said of her writing that she feels like she is "singing for [her] life" (qtd. in Hanson). The "respectable" Diane Williams may not always approve of this function of her own writing—she may even turn away in disgust—but the artist Diane Williams looks it head-on, affirms it, and affirms that "this is exactly [her] business" (qtd. in O'Brien 140). Williams believes that the purpose of art is to "take no cover," and she feels a distinct camaraderie with other artists who work in the same way (Reading).

In a question-and-answer session with Syracuse University students following the publication of *Excitability,* Williams answered questions about the "controversial" nature of her work by saying that "literature is not necessarily the place for polite speech. . . . Our lives are permeated with occasions for polite speech and most of us suffer from that." She went on to tell the students that literature is "one realm for sanity and freedom," one place where we can escape our human burden of shame. In other interviews she has repeatedly refuted any sense of intending to be controversial or intending to be anything, for that matter, saying, "I'm trying to get myself . . . to not be a thinking person—I don't want to know what I know; I'm curious about what I don't know. I want access to that mysterious center" (qtd. in Hanson). This corresponds to the intuitive nature of her work.

Williams published her first book, *This Is about the Body, the Mind, the Soul, the World, Time, and Fate* in 1990. She had already begun co-editing the highly esteemed *StoryQuarterly* by this time, having started in 1985 and continuing as co-editor until 1996. In 2000 Williams launched a literary annual of short fiction and art-work, *NOON*; there have been four editions so far, each of which reflects her distinct sensibility. When asked about her predilections as a reader of fiction, in fact, many of the names she mentions are the names of people she herself publishes in *NOON*: Christine Schutt, Lydia Davis, and Gary Lutz, to name a few. Her work on both *StoryQuarterly* and *NOON* has provided her with an extensive view of the contemporary writing landscape; Williams has enjoyed this aspect of her editorial work as well as her exchanges with writers during the prepublication process (Personal Interview 5 Oct. 2002).

Having worn the editor hat and the writer hat, Williams has both given and received criticism. Because she is in the middle of her career, it is difficult to make an assessment of the entire critical reaction to her work, but up to this point, there has been a generally favorable response from diverse sources, ranging from *Entertainment Weekly* and *ELLE* to the *New York Times.* One of the most eloquent reviews, by Matthew Stadler, remarks on the "metaphysically uneasy speakers" and the "frequent exposure of artifice" at work in

Williams's second collection, *Some Sexual Success Stories* (21). Stadler calls her a "double agent," one who is "both a practitioner and an enemy of her craft. Beholden *and* hostile to the conceits of fiction, she takes to rooting around in them, like a clown at a carnival show." He also mentions her success in "conjur[ing] up an edgy, jagged state of mind, a lurching consciousness in a culture of speed and amnesia" (Stadler 21), a comment that hearkens back to the *Sudden Fiction* anthology and to Charles Baxter's declaration of the short-short story's formal alignment with the current age. A reviewer for *Entertainment Weekly*, in more current, pop-culture-centered lingo, similarly labeled Williams's work as "mental calisthenics for readers with MTV attention spans" (Mifflin 55).

Most reviewers have welcomed the chance to be confounded by Williams's "mental calisthenics," even when they use words like "infuriating" and "maddening" to describe the work (Rev. of *Some Sexual Success Stories*; Stadler). There are also reviewers who have not responded to her work or who have responded in part but cannot complete the journey, an unsurprising response considering the inventive nature of this fiction. One reviewer from the *New York Times* complains, after a full column of glowing praise, that "a succession of [the stories] can seem tiresome, even insubstantial" (McFall 23). Some readers believe that a collection of stories should be read like a novel, straight through, and, because these in particular are so short, as quickly as possible. Another reviewer, for *The Stranger.com,* notes that she "tend[s] to gulp, to guzzle" when it comes to short-short fiction. She says of Williams's volume of selected stories, *Excitability,* that, "like 'greatest hits' albums, this collection can create phobia and disorientation" (Kessler). The obvious solution to dilemmas of this type is for the reader to *slow down.* Williams's prose is as intricate, layered, and brief as most poetry; therefore it deserves the labored attention usually accorded automatically to poetry. Poetry affords none of the comfort and ease of a novel or a longer, more traditional short story, and Williams likewise affords neither the space, time, nor diffuse substance for a reader to recline and enjoy the passing scenery. Any collection of stories or poems would be "tiresome" if read straight through, and the tired mind may certainly find them "insubstantial."

Another criticism, first voiced in response to her first book, but continued in similar form and tone in reaction to subsequent publications, is that some of her stories, "in their extreme brevity simply do not work" (Rice D10). This is the complaint that some readers of Williams have expressed—that many of the stories seem to have been dashed out and then abandoned, and many of them fail to make a point or reach a destination. This complaint recurs more frequently in response to Williams's later books, which have become less and less "satisfying," causing a wider swath of the audience to feel frustrated. This very natural complaint has been countered and defused time and again by the work itself. The point of Williams's work is not to satisfy, cajole, or even to finish, at least not in the expected sense. The dropped-off endings, for example, could be considered beginnings; the question is this: Can we allow ourselves the freedom she offers of beginning at the physical end? Some readers may not be able to accept this and similar challenges inherent in Williams's work.

The reviews of Williams's latest book, *Romancer Erector,* have been largely favorable, if too few, in keeping with the overall reaction to her oeuvre. One reviewer notes that this volume of stories and novellas secures Williams's "position at the forefront of the avant-garde" (Sims 6). Matthea Harvey, reviewing the book for *BOMB,* appreciates the "giddying, unsettling effect" of Williams's stories, noting particularly that "the shortest pieces are little language Ferris wheels revolving obsessively around one subject" (Harvey 22). Stacey Levine, writing for *American Book Review,* argues her points eloquently, but fails to realize the potential of her own reading experience when she notes that "some readers may miss a sense of vulnerability in these experiments," furthermore implying that Williams's prose does not "resonate with inquiry, injury, and strangeness" in its quest to remain on the "surface of language" (Levine 9). Inquiry, injury, and strangeness form the very *core* of Williams's work; for all of Williams's concern with the texture of language, she never neglects, as many experimenters do, the heart of the matter. Beyond displaying language in "pure form," Williams seeks to explore what that form is, if anything at all, and its impact on our human means and modes of expression.

In the *North Carolina Review of Books* Mark Hornburg makes an apt comparison between Williams and Emily Dickinson. Williams, like Dickinson, "compresses and fractures the language . . . often to the point where meaning is lost" (16). This seems a more astute comparison than the one often drawn between Williams and Nathalie Sarraute. Sarraute, even in the relative brevity and disjointedness of the pieces in an early work such as *Tropisms* (1939), doesn't preface the playful, mischievous seriousness of Williams's prose. Sarraute and Williams do share a similar spirit of experiment—Sarraute, in her foreword to *Tropisms,* explains her attempt to capture in her prose the "movements, of which we are hardly cognizant, [that] slip through us on the frontiers of consciousness. . . . They hide behind our gestures, beneath the words we speak, the feelings we manifest" (6). Williams too deals directly as possible with those liquid "movements"; Sarraute's statement recalls Williams's desire for "access to that mysterious center" (qtd. in Hanson). Dickinson shared this objective as well, and in Dickinson we catch the same whiff of mischief we do in Williams. Like Dickinson, Williams is an original; in a perceptive, elegant article, "Reading Diane Williams," Brian Lennon applauds her for precisely the elements one finds in the best Dickinson poems: "the particular and the universal . . . joined without coercion, without force-feeding or pandering to habits of thinking, habits of knowing, habits of reading" (Lennon 5). In Williams we witness a distinctly Dickinsonian dwelling in possiblity, a "spreading wide [her] narrow Hands/To gather Paradise" (Dickinson 166).

This Is about the Body, the Mind, the Soul, the World, Time, and Fate

"Lady," the first story in this collection, serves as the perfect introduction to *This Is about,* which in turn serves aptly to introduce us to Williams's entire oeuvre. The first paragraph alerts the reader that she has entered a strange new realm, one very unlike the world of short fiction to which she has been accustomed: "She said *please.* Her face looked something more than bitter, with hair which it turned out was a hat, which came down over her ears, which was made of fake fur, which she never removed from her head" (3). The urgency of the woman's *"please"* is offset by the narrator's excruciating observation of her head, translated into a rhythmic string of clauses that suggests the beginning of a fairy tale, told in girlish, inaccurate bursts that lure us to join the adventure, even when the actual details of what has been confided suggest nothing like the start of a fairy tale at all. The reader, at this point, feels that she has stumbled into something very unlike the latest formula-story-of-the-week, and as the tale unwinds, her hunch proves correct. By the end, the narrator has "jammed [the lady] up into the corner with the jumble by the front door," and sums up her actions, and the whole story, by stating: "It hurt her more than it hurt me, to be a lady. Violence is never the problem. Love at first sight is" (5).

In this first collection the linguistic play is more familiarly "padded" than in her later works, and language likewise contributes more to the utilitarian advancement of plot, such as it is. Similarly, this first book, rambunctious and unorthodox though it may be, focuses on fairly familiar psychological and emotional themes that can be imperfectly summarized and generalized as the following: the comfort/confinement of family; the underbelly of human society;

human nature; sex and sexuality in contemporary life; the dynamics of male-female and female-female relationships; the power/impotence of fiction in accomplishing transcendence, control, and emotional or psychological release. It is how Williams manipulates this material that distinguishes her work. The lid on her unique version of Pandora's box begins to creak open in "Lady"; by the end of the collection it has been flung open, and will remain unhinged for eternity, it seems.

The woman who greets her guest at the door in "Lady," ushers her in, and ultimately assaults her, seems to remain our guide throughout the collection, maintaining a detached tone and perspective in her observations, with a few exceptions. The story "Cloud" epitomizes her role; she tells the story of a girl whose "body was in the world . . . in her little room or in *their* rooms . . . that she went through and through and through" (35). It concludes with a fairy tale-like summary: "And for the rest of her life, the girl, the woman, she never made a mark on anyone either that proved anything absolutely for certain . . . and this does not break her heart" (36). Neither shock nor despair accompanies this realization of the lack of proof for this girl's, like the narrator's own, existence. The narrator drifts through other people's rooms, untouched and untouching, commenting on the events in their lives. This holds true even when she herself or her loved ones are threatened with bodily harm.

In "Baby" someone is driving the narrator home from a party in dangerously icy conditions. The driver can't see, a wreck may be imminent, but the narrator coolly compares the experience to "being in one of those movies I have seen the previews for. It was like watching one of . . . those people who try to give you the willies. It was like that, watching her—while she tried to get us out" (34). She expresses no panic or fear, stripping her narration of emotion to highlight the difficulty, or impossibility, of faithfully rendering experience in words. The reader can never fully appreciate the impact of a terrifying fictional situation, so this narrator's voice mirrors our own emotional distance in an effort to reflect the truth. The experiment reveals the absurdity of realistic fiction's tendency to ignore such limitations, comforting as such voluntary blindness may be. But this is no cold-blooded exercise; it derives, rather, from love of language itself, from the narrator's need to express herself regardless of her success in so doing. This neatly corroborates what Williams herself has said about the necessity of raising her voice in an attempt to be heard, calling writing an act of "singing for [her] life" (qtd. in Hanson). The narrator, too, is singing, despite the odds stacked against a pure transmission to her reader via her distant, warm, and funny voice.

There are lapses in this detachment, although they occur rarely. The narrator becomes more actively engaged with the story in "Screaming." At a party, a man not her husband, who is also there, touches her unexpectedly: "someone was at my back, tugging at my hair. . . . I felt a mouth . . . on the nape of my neck. It was a kiss" (67). This is not a proprietary kiss, like the kiss of a husband would be, but a freeing one. When she looks at the man, "He [is] full of shame" (67). The man chooses to lock himself up in shame, our most primal human prison, but the narrator refuses to acknowledge any shame in the act. Her response to the kiss reveals that, although she may stand back and observe, she has been part of the human community all along, subject to the same attachments and subsequent confining obligations that bind her characters, leading her to harvest liberation from this unusual encounter. She says: "Thank God I did not know who he was. . . . I was praying he would do something more to me. Anything" (67). This misplaced affection provides nothing but relief and sensual pleasure for her, and she wants more.

These moments when the narrator allows herself to be directly affected are few and far between, perhaps because she uses others to stand in for her emotionally. There are in the stories numerous female characters who seem to act as her "twins" or "alter egos," who allow her to avoid the stickiness of the stories and lives she observes while she conducts their emotions and actions. A character usually emerges as a "twin" when the narrator identifies her as someone who could easily *be* her, for one reason or another. She fixates on the woman and on her comfy fit in the life to which the narrator also belongs, but awkwardly. Jealousy often taints and/or drives these relationships—the narrator wants to stand back, wants to avoid the particulars of "real life" by observing (i.e., channeling through these women), yet she covets those very particulars, or the outward signs of them, all the same. She wants to experience only vicariously the trials and delights of love, for instance, but then she envies the proof these women hold, whether in the form of a raccoon coat or diamond ring, of their desirability and beloved status, and sometimes she lashes out bitterly at these "sisters" of hers.

In "Forty Thousand Dollars" the narrator focuses in on one of these women, one whose "entire quality of . . . life is totally secure because of the size of" a huge diamond ring her husband bought her (37–38). In an effort to prove to this loved woman that she also is loved, the narrator secures a diamond ring for herself. But the attempt fails; *her* diamond "is stuck inside an old setting and cannot be measured" (39). Just as in "Cloud," when the narrator struggled and failed to prove her own existence, in this story she fails to produce concrete evidence of her "wantedness." In lieu of proving herself to be equal, the narrator seeks to fuse with this other woman, "to go along with her to wherever she was going" (39). This also fails, but not to the narrator's detriment. She chooses her own life, realizing that "the sense I had . . . that I could not possibly follow in my own footsteps, was gone" (39). The failure central to this story proves to be as liberating for the narrator as the stranger's kiss in "Screaming."

These pairings of women, whatever their quality or form, almost always take precedence over male-female relationships. Even in "My Female Honor Is of a Type," when the two women are rivals for the same man, what happens between the wife and The Other Woman is far more crucial to the outcome than what occurs between the man and either woman. The husband's infidelity has instigated the whole situation, but "It was between her and her," the narrator tells us (46). The only dialogue in the story passes between the two adversaries; the man, the instigator, remains silent and is nearly inconsequential. The narrator's father in "Glass of Fashion" has, in an entirely different situation, been rendered similarly passive and obsolete, even though he constitutes the heart of the drama. Instead of focusing on her father's imminent death, the narrator notes that "The doctor's hair was full and long and down, kinky and wavy and black. . . . I was admiring the doctor's body in her jeans. She had what I thought was a girlish and perfect form in her jeans, an enviable form" (48–49). A little later she admits that "What I was envying then were the doctor's legs in her jeans" (49). Sexual desire seems to play a part, but to what end? What follows is no consummation of desire, but her father's death, and the only physical contact is captured in the narrator's chilling remark that "Some of his teeth were the last things on my father that I ever touched" (50). In place of soft, sensual physical communion, the narrator gives us finger touching tooth: a hard, cold, unfulfilling moment, the only moment that breaks through the membrane created by the narrator's fascination with the doctor.

The sensual nature of her interest in the doctor at a time like this could surely be a form of displacement—the intimacy she desires but cannot achieve with her dying father she carries out in her head with the doctor. The doctor also acts as a more pleasing reflection of herself in this abject moment—she wants to be *in* the doctor's jeans—she envies "the doctor's legs in her jeans"; she wants to wear them, not just be in them sexually. Her father, however pivotal to the impetus of the plot (his sickness and death are why she's there), has been rendered silent and small: his "teeth had

never looked, each of them, so terribly small" (50). She almost succeeds in crowding out the terror she feels in response to her father's
death, but not quite. The image of his teeth pokes through, jabs us
at the very end. For Williams, who said that "for most of my life . . .
[I have felt] invisible, ignored, and dumbstruck; for me that's my
death and I want to make some noise and speak" (qtd. in Hanson),
the act of writing becomes an instrument of power, one that liber-
ates her from silence and passivity. In this light her dumbstruck
male characters assume the quality of men defeated in battle, but
this is a verbal battle for which the narrator has guaranteed herself
a triumphant outcome.

The narrator's tactic becomes clearer in "Hope," when she "ask[s
her] father a question after the doctors had rendered him positively
without the power of speech" (69). She feels "so incredibly nervy. He
was down in his bed. I was at the end of it. My father put his head
forward toward me, crazy to tell me the most essential thing I will
ever need to know" (70); then the story ends, in silence, and the narrator has essentially won. But what has she won? She has managed
to assert her voice, yes, but under very special circumstances: her
father is weak, dying, and dumb. Furthermore, and perhaps more
important, she has lost the chance to hear "the most essential
thing" (70). But within the context of this story, it may be safe to
assume that the most essential thing is the narrator putting forth
her voice. What seems to be a great loss of knowledge or enlightenment, then, is miniscule in the face of this accomplishment. Williams will find her "essential thing" wherever she chooses.

Williams's narrator manages to find her "most essential thing" in
another unlikely spot—not in temple or church as we might expect,
but at the doctor's, while having a cardiogram. Williams's relationship to religion has heavily influenced her work; she acknowledges
that she has been "devout" in the past—she attended synagogue as
a child and still writes under the influence of the gorgeous prose
and richly embroidered stories of the Old Testament (Personal Interview 5 Oct. 2002). Her stories demonstrate a fascinating mixture
of respect, awe, faith, and rebellion in relation to organized religion. All of these postures are undertaken with a wry, engaging humor, a cleverness that God himself would have to appreciate, at
least the God Williams conjures in her work.

The title, "Oh, My God, the Rapture!" alone is indicative of
Williams's irreverent recognition of religion's influence in our
lives. The subject of the story, a woman's achievement of bliss during a cardiogram, makes it even more amusing, but one cannot
miss the reverence inherent in the narrator's tone when she describes this awakening. She steps back to speak from the third

person, observing a woman who enjoys her cardiogram so thoroughly that she pays the nurse prematurely and tells her, "This was wonderful. This never happens. You hardly kept me waiting at all. You took me . . . just when you said you would" (88). Unlike the prophesied rapture, this visit was quick, efficient, and its messengers arrived on time, cause enough for religious ecstasy. Instead of finding the realm of science/medicine dry or sterile, Williams makes it a place for worship—she reinvents the very notion of transcendence. Without harping on the uncertainties of religious belief, she breaks ground in a new place where, if one looks in the right way, the spiritual rewards are sure and abundant.

This story, like others that challenge our notions of religion, spirituality, and the nature of faith, is marred neither by bitterness nor cynicism; Williams uses humor and the magnificent flight of her imagination to throw doubt on what we think we already know, in order to open new worlds for us. Her narrator's tone of childlike amazement helps achieve this; it would be hard to believe that this innocent showing us a strange new world could merely be mocking it, deriding it, and deriding us in the process. Williams brings to an old subject, the questioning of established religion, a fresh perspective in a charming voice.

She takes a similar approach to examining the institution of fiction, which could be considered the writer's "place of worship," questioning the dim outlines of the genre and her own authority as fiction-maker even as she continues to profess faith in and reverence for her craft, in both word and deed. In the aptly titled "Power," a woman's drive home in a taxi is interrupted by the entrance of a strange couple. The female partner's legs do not bend at the knee, as if both have been locked straight like a doll's. As the narrator ponders this problem, her mind snags on various logistical problems concerning sex: "How do they do it? She cannot bend her legs. Here I go, I must see him propping up her legs some way onto his shoulders, or with some contraption they have had to devise, or do they simply put a bunch of something under her hips, or does he get into her from behind when they are lying down?" (74). She is trying, as the dominant notion of the narrator's task dictates, to take these characters neatly from point A to point B and to draw certain insightful and/or instructive conclusions from this linear progress. But in the above quote she reveals her uncertainty—how do they do it? If she does not know, who does? We doubt her omnipotence even more when the couple is unable to direct the driver to their home. The narrator should be able to assist them, being the "driver" of the story, but she's powerless. When the couple has left, she reasserts herself; she knows how to direct the driver to her own home, at least, and imagines telling him, *"You listen to me! This is how you get somewhere!"* (76). She regains some control through the enactment of her own drive home, i.e., her own "plot," but what does it mean when she admits she cannot comprehend the significance of her own plot and turns to her audience to plead: "Somebody please tell me that this is all about something else entirely which is more important" (76)? Simply by asking for help she denies herself the power supposedly due a narrator; she begs for us to bestow on her wisdom because, "I could be a believer" (76). She has likewise implied that her story could mean *nothing at all*. As readers, we may be expecting a golden nugget of wisdom or truth from the narrator, our guide, that would clarify this story, unite its disparate elements into a coherent whole from which, perhaps, we could glean epiphany. The temple of fiction has historically provided its readers with possible answers to life's mysteries. In this case, the reader herself is asked to do the work so that the narrator can sit back and "believe." The narrator's passivity throws into doubt the whole idea of her omnipotence, which in turn leads us to doubt fiction's traditional justification for existence. Furthermore, what use is language itself if its master practitioner loses control? These doubts evoke chaos, but the hopefulness of the phrase "I could be a believer" persists. However violently she ransacks the overarching "temple of fiction," Williams suggests, through her narrator, that she *wants* to believe in fiction, and her own work hints at the emergence of a new form in which to believe, one more worthy of faith for its acknowledgment of the undeniable presence of the unknowable.

"Lifeguard" is one of several stories that illustrate how we can be a new kind of reader to complement a different kind of fiction. In this story a flood threatens the narrator's family home, and her father knows how to avert disaster but can't communicate his knowledge. This is another all-knowing male deprived of speech, and it clearly recalls the moment in "Hope" when the narrator loses her chance to find out "the most essential thing I will ever need to know" from her dying father (70). This narrator, struggling to understand his instructions for stopping the flood, says, "my father was telling me everything that we should do, even though I could not make it out, not the words, but I knew he was telling me how to stop the flood, if we wanted to" (103). The house of Williams's fiction, likewise, is flooded with linguistic playfulness, tangles of logic, and mysterious asides. There may exist a solution to the flood *inside the house,* but we, as readers, strain our ears for this answer to no avail. But what matters more than discovering the truth or a solution, both of which are of questionable value and existence, is our ongoing quest. Williams encourages us to continue and imparts in us the knowledge of the importance of our efforts at comprehension; desire, the search for *something,* maintains our vitality and our will to live. Perhaps this is why, at the end of "Lifeguard," she leaves forever dangling the possibility of her father "telling me how to stop the flood, if we wanted to" (103). We may not *want* the easy answer or solution. Instead of giving us a quick pill, her very own brand, to swallow for comfort, she prods us a little, hoping we choose the ongoing search instead of resolution.

This point is supported further in "The Nub," a story taking place on the significant occasion of a girl's bat mitzvah. A ceremony that has largely outlived its original practical applicability in contemporary society, it is nonetheless still considered a vital, sustaining element of the Jewish faith. Why do it? Why make the gesture? Isn't it merely a gesture of emptiness, as empty as worshipping in a temple or church, as empty as following the worn-out pattern of old-time religion? In other instances Williams seems to shun these long-established traditions and traditional scenes of worship, but this presents a slightly different take on the topic. One might ask, likewise, if we can no longer have the satisfaction of (believing we are) discovering "truth" in writing, hasn't it, too, become a useless endeavor? Why do it at all, if it will only be deconstructed, if the writer herself will destroy her own work while still in the act of creating it? Writing is merely an outdated gesture, a system of symbols referring to nothing, now that we have, in our postmodern wisdom, gleefully stripped signifiers of their signifieds and railed against reading below the surface. So why continue the ritual, either the coming-of-age or the ritual of fiction? Just for fun? In "The Nub" the Rabbi "had stood with the girl in front of the open ark with his hands on her. . . . He was staring into her eyes. She was staring into his eyes . . ." (105). Something passes between them, and we know from the language alone that it is something of deep significance, even if we don't understand. Some things slip past and surpass understanding, we find, and that is why making the gestures of both ritual and writing remain important. Something sacred abides in them, unreachable perhaps, but it is the gesture toward the sublime that gives the participant or reader a taste of *bliss.* Williams may embody a deconstructionist stance, but what distinguishes her work is that it juggles both gestures at once, tossing out literary conventions but poking at them, thus bringing the corpses back to life and welcoming them to a new life, a new world.

"Science and Sin or Love and Understanding," the last story of the collection and an impressive ending to this first book, is concerned, appropriately, with *power.* This relays the narrator's attempt to understand what moves her through life on earth, what moves her to cheat on her husband, what keeps her from knowing what her future actions will be, and forces her to equivocate, "I may or I may not cheat on him again" (117). What is this power, exactly, and shouldn't the narrator, within the context of the fictional world she herself narrates, be able to say *what* the power is? But Williams's fiction is unique in acknowledging the limitations of the written word, the written world. We can delineate, in words, what the power *makes us do:* "made me see things," and "turned [the husband] into the shape of a man wearing his clothes" (117). We can also acknowledge the presence of a power. But saying *what* the power is—whether it is the work of biological, chemical impulses or the sign of a transcendent existence—is impossible. It is even impossible for the narrator to self-analyze, something readers have depended on from fiction for years. When she looks back at herself in the moment of deciding whether or not to cheat on her husband, she says: "I see myself on the street, deciding. I am holding onto something. Now I cannot see what it is. This is no close-up view. I am a stick figure. I am the size of a pin" (117). *I have no answers,* the narrator tells us, I don't know why I cheated, I don't know what I'm "holding onto," not even in hindsight. This is, quite simply, human life—we are rendered small and insignificant by external powers and by our blindness to our own thoughts and actions—fiction, likewise, must be blind. Williams abandons the pretense to omniscient understanding of motive and meaning that most fiction continues to claim. Again the question: So why write at all, having acknowledged fiction's impotence? Because within this tiny story, there is contained something indefinable, unknowable, that has the power to make us "the size of a pin" (117), and it is important to be in the presence of such power—it is of vital importance to human survival to try to transcend, even if we are not successful and even if we cannot wholly translate the experience.

Some Sexual Success Stories, plus Other Stories in which God Might Choose to Appear

The title of this second book announces a more self-assured, almost cocky Williams who disarms us immediately with her blunt, ironic, often raunchy quips and commentary. But it would be a mistake to dismiss this intensified use of humor as gratuitous, meant only to shock or amuse. The humor highlights the seriousness of Williams's endeavor, which is as sincere and emotionally grounded as the first book's. This book is linguistically more streamlined and less concerned with the trappings of a specific environment; therefore it may be more successful in communicating the issues at hand. One feels keenly the difference in the writer's approach to her material, a sign that some transformation has enabled the emergence of this slimmer, physically lighter narrative. Whatever has shifted, this narrator, a kindred incarnation of the first book's, has broken free from the bonds of intimacy as surely as these stories have escaped physical place. She exercises freedom linguistically too—instead of pointing playfully to meaning, her language directs us almost relentlessly to the surface—to objects, light, to the words themselves. Despite this posture of superficial obsession, however, ultimately this collection illustrates the impossibility of escaping meaning. She tries to tell us, "I'm just playing around," but the work itself demonstrates the presence of heavy material, even if we can't discern its substance precisely. In spite of what a first reading may reveal, Williams reaffirms the unfashionable unemptiness of words.

To begin to explore this slippery substance she's created, it helps to ask, to *ask* at least, who is speaking? Who is guiding us through this text? As in the first book, the narrator's presence is obviously essential, but what remains obscure is *how*, or to what extent? *Is* the narrator our guide? *Is* she in control? Who is driving this story? The best place to start may be a story in which the act of driving figures prominently. In "This One's about (____)" the narrator's sister is driving with "a lame right arm and bad vision," and "she had forgotten to turn the car headlights on" (64–65). An accident occurs; the narrator is unharmed, but why does she so readily describe a life-threatening incident with such calm remove? She says, "Strange as it sounds, I still do not know how clear the danger was then. Speaking for myself, I felt then, This is an important drama. If I were the driver, I would be questioning what our alternatives were . . ." (65). It's hard to resist thinking, in response—you are the driver, of the story, aren't you? We are given no clear answer, but this story makes a stark contrast with "Baby" from the earlier book. In "Baby" the narrator is in a similarly treacherous situation, with a bad driver at the wheel and in icy conditions, but she remains passive. She doesn't even challenge the status quo verbally, with an "if I were the driver . . ."; she is clearly a *watcher*, and she observes detachedly while the driver "tried to get us out" (*This Is about* 34). In this second book she has left the cozy back seat, but she can't quite make up her mind about her level of control of the situation, or she doesn't want *us* to make up *our* minds. Is she driving or has she rejected the choice to be driver? That remains to be seen, but either way, she claims *agency*.

There are more stories in the collection where the narrator plays the fool, leaving us to wonder, as the ultimate fools, about her authority and motivation. In "Clunk" the narrator is watching people gathered outside; she notes, like a good traditional narrator observing people in a group: "there is some mobility in their faces, some nobility" (49). But she goes on to misbehave by saying, "I wonder why. I always wonder why" (49). "I always wonder why" ends the story; it's the final word. How can she wonder? Isn't it her job to *know* why? She makes us wonder at her nonchalance, and she makes us suspect that this befuddlement, however final, is voluntary, just as her position in "This One's about (_____)" reflected active ambiguity.

The dilemma intensifies in "They Were Naked Again," especially because at first the narrator is notably in charge. She begins by saying of her female character, "I'll get her into his bed" (37), and she continues for a while as an omniscient, third-person narrator. Then her own protagonist jumps ahead of her by speaking without the narrator's knowledge or permission to this man, her prospective lover. The narrator becomes a sort of rival to her own character, whining, "I would never say that to him . . . it is my time they are taking" (37–38). She is powerless in the face of their sudden independence, but still enraged. She tries to interrupt their discussion at one point, but acknowledges that "they cannot hear me" (38). In a last, pathetic gesture, like a teenage girl, she declares, "I'll threaten suicide!" (38). It's funny, of course, for a *narrator* to be saying this, but disturbing also. She makes one final attempt to regain power, by turning to the *reader* to command: "You—you think about a carpet" (38). As silly as this last-ditch effort seems, it may be effective. After all, we are reading her words, and at the mere mention of "carpet," most of us will inadvertently, obediently think about "carpet," in some form or other. She may have lost control of her characters, but she still has her captive audience in hand. This story gives us a clearer delineation of our narrator's role than the previous two stories have, although this sharper vision may not be comforting to us. Do we, as readers, want a narrator who controls *us* instead of the story and/or her characters? Like it or not, we have such a narrator here.

The first story in the book, "The Limits of the World," presents us with a different twist. This narrator at first seems akin to an unquestionable almighty. She talks about having "powerful powders" in her possession, one of which is called the "I command my man" powder, and we are told that "When I put this powder on my body, then I will command my man" (3). It sounds like this powder can only aid the narrator's acquisition of unlimited control, but there are drawbacks that throw her authority into question. After she uses the powder, her man "will be obedient and satisfied, whether that's what I want him to be or not. Nothing will ever take him

away, whether that's what I want or not" (3). We learn from this
that the power itself comes alive, relegating the puppet-master to
the sidelines, where she stands helplessly watching what she has
set in motion. As Mary Shelley's Dr. Frankenstein also learns, once
the power to create or manipulate has been exercised, the creation
takes on its own life. Williams's narrator here seems to embody the
agony of the artist; by the end, she has learned what the limits of
the world are. She has been put in her place, although she insists on
railing against these limits by telling us, "I can ask because I
asked" (4). She may no longer have true possession of those powders, because their effects will have outstripped her by now, but she
still has the power of the *word*, whatever its value or significance.
And here she exercises the right to *the last word,* perhaps the most
potent word of all.

Not all of the stories in this collection show the narrator at the
mercy of outside forces or the inside forces of character and plot. On
the contrary—in "Pussy," for example, the narrator dallies with her
own power while toying idly with her characters. She chastises her
protagonist by saying of her, "She could have understood sooner if
she had only tried . . ." (10). One can't help realizing that, yes, she
could have understood sooner if the narrator had stepped in to let
her understand. She stops making coy allusions to her power and
completely takes ownership of it at the end by declaring that the
woman "equals anything at all on my say-so" (11). Then we know we
have been manipulated right along with the characters, not only in
this story but in all of them, because this narrator is actually more
in control than most, not less. How is this possible when we have
noted her frustration and failure to rule in "The Limits of the
World," "They Were Naked Again," and "This One's about (_____)"?
She resembles the baby in the story "Naaa," whose "power is nowhere limited," the narrator tells us, because his "power is his renunciation of all power" (75). The narrator could be summarizing
her own technique in this second book: she brags about her power,
then ridicules it, denies outright that she has it, or at least acts like
she doesn't have it. She does all of this because she can, which
means she does, ultimately, have the power, she is driving the
story, just as all narrators drive the story (on behalf of The Driver,
The Writer), even if she is a fractured, splintered, joking, limping
trickster.

In the ultimate tricksterish move, the narrator of "Ha" joins
with the protagonist and her son to attempt to sabotage the story
from within. They are looking for a whistle, but "He knew he'd
never find one in their town. When you know how it will turn out,
you feel tired. So do I," the narrator finishes (98). The boy is tired,

the narrator is tired. What about the mother? "What would her boy's fate be? she wondered. Well, she decided, they need a victim. I need a victim. We all need a victim" (99). What mother sacrifices her son so languidly? Ultimately, the mother remembers at the end of the story that, "as a baby, [her son] had looked a trace displeased to be born" (99). The main subject of the story, we find, resents having been brought into being. All of these clever moves may simulate a backward erasure of the story, but the story still exists, undoubtedly, on the page, no matter what the narrator and characters do. Like the magical powders in "The Limits of the World," what truly has power is the stuff itself, not the creator or manipulator. These stories instruct us that the story is what matters, strange as it may seem for such unorthodox ones to be telling us so. In answer to the question of who's driving, then, Williams's innovative answer (the answer is in her innovation) is that the car is driving itself, in the end. If she says so.

The next logical step, after determining who is driving, would be to determine what, exactly, is being driven. In the case of Williams's work this is a dangerous endeavor. For clarity's sake, it is easiest to call what Williams does fiction, more specifically, short stories, even more specifically, short-short stories or sudden fiction, but in doing so, one must acknowledge the use of this singular genre as an ineffectual gesture. Even using a hybrid of two genres, such as prose poetry, proves inadequate; Williams's work asks not to be bound by such categories. Of course, this escape act the work performs only aggravates, thus encourages, the urge in us to label, put away, bury, and cover with dirt. We won't succeed with such slippery stuff as this, but because we are human we must ask, "what is it?" anyway.

The first and perhaps most obvious question for anything written without line breaks on the page is: Is it traditional fiction? In answering this, while remaining well aware of the quagmire of possibilities inside the realm of whatever is called traditional fiction, one can validly look for a few reliable traits: a plot that arcs relatively neatly from beginning to middle, then end; within that plot, a problem or conflict that arises and is resolved during the narrative, generally somewhere near the end; finally, characters that could be described as three-dimensional. These are the safest, blandest guidelines to use, but they by no means apply to all works in the "more traditional" category.

It certainly seems as though Williams has thrown plot out the window in this second book. For instance, in "The Band-Aid and the Piece of Gum," in place of a beginning, conflict, resolution, etc., the very first sentence tells us, "There was the possibility up until five o'clock—then there was no more possibility" (62). Short, sweet, and to the point. Or is it harsh, a severe blotting-out of the graceful arc of contingencies for this character? The narrator had, after all, woken up "cheered by the thought that maybe today, *today* would be the most important day of [her] life" (62). This leads us on as readers, leads us to expect something wonderful or something momentous at least. But the narrator's optimism becomes ludicrous after we realize her high hopes revolve around a man who gave her a Band-Aid and a piece of gum along with bits of silly pseudowisdom. In this case it's a relief to have known from the start "there was no more possibility" (62), her time was up from the very beginning, and perhaps that's for the best.

Nevertheless, we can discern the skeleton of a plot. First, "I woke up," a fairly typical beginning (62). Then something does happen— the narrator recalls Walter's gifts (Band-Aid, gum) and puts them to use. This counts as action, an important component of plot. These actions awaken memories of the narrator and Walter's last encounter, which could stand in for a conflict or obstacle: "he grabbed me around the neck . . . trying to get me to walk along with him" (62). What follows is a kind of resolution: "There was the possibility, perhaps, that we could both have toppled over onto his floor" (63). What makes this resolution different is the ambiguity; we know, by virtue of the verb tense, that nothing actually happened—it *could have*, but did not. On the other hand, she does not give us the literal ending, the words we desire; she does not say, "we did not fall." The journey toward resolution continues indefinitely; she goes on walking awkwardly with her lover-captor, and the threat of falling shadows her endlessly as well.

The ending she does give us, directly following the above description, is this: "That's it. Usually they start where a person was born . . . character traits . . . chronology, trauma . . . the obstacles . . . a centrifugal drama . . . plus summary statements made periodically throughout to sum up the situation at any given time" (63). Here we have it: what's missing from the story, in summary form. But because she has injected all these traditional elements into her own quirky story, even in list form, at the last minute, one could argue that they are not missing at all, because by invoking them in name at least she causes them to materialize. It is too simplistic to say that Williams rejects plot; this is a much more sophisticated and playful move, not entirely dismissive of the traditional elements of storytelling. She preserves tradition while poking fun. And even the "fun" is more complicated, directionally, than it could be; she teases herself while teasing us and the venerated story form.

Similarly, she simultaneously points a finger at herself and at the art of storytelling in "The Mistake," a tale permeated with threat, whose origin lies in "a girl . . . getting angry" (47). Something concrete does happen in this super-brief bundle of sentences, but instead of showing us the action, the narrator devours time and space by telling us she hears "telltale sounds" and by twice including the following sentences: "Stupid of me, but I am terrified. She is looking at me curiously. The natural thing is to act sympathetic" (47). In keeping with her role of the clueless narrator, she says: "I don't know which horrible thing happens next in my real bedroom" (47). She recognizes the "new carpeting . . . the bedspread . . . the room" itself, but that's it—otherwise all she remembers is "mystery, suspense, and adventure" (47). Once again, she eludes us by clouding over the details of the plot, while drawing in finer detail the inconsequential objects of her environment: carpet, bedspread, etc. She does admit at the end that "Even as I blot it out, I was dead wrong to summarize," which seems to acknowledge that "the mistake" is really her mistreatment of us, her readers, by denying us access to the "meat" of the tale. This would suggest there is value after all in filling in the details of a scene, in telling a straightforward story, even though Williams's work does nothing of the sort. The stronger proof is the story itself, not what the story (or narrator) says. In its undoing of form and convention, this story stands as testament to Williams's fictional credo. In fact, this story proceeds even farther down the path of unorthodoxy when the narrator tells us, "I blot it out," suggesting she is retracing her steps from the end of the story and erasing what she has written, therefore leaving us with a blank page. Just as in "Ha," this story remains in existence on the page despite the narrator's claim, but the gesture, likewise, remains a startling, unconventional one. At least two incompatible impulses co-exist in this tiny tale: the urge to tell a story straight and the urge to sabotage the straight story. It is impossible to say whether they co-exist harmoniously or not, but they do share the same crowded space. By ridiculing both her own method as well as the other, she obliterates both or lets them both stand, however you choose to see it.

Williams ventures further into unmarked territory by creating a work that seems to deny its own place in the historical progression of literary works, thereby calling into question the literary canon as a whole. In "A Progress in Spirituality" two women, one of them the narrator, compete for the same man. After the narrator defeats her rival, simply by "shaking her hand" (61), she proceeds to disavow, in a befuddled, seemingly harmless way, the historical precedence for this common motif: two women rivals clashing, with one emerging victorious. One sentence has already firmly grounded in antiquity this encounter between the narrator and her rival: "When I take her hot hand in mine, we could be the rivals dipped in stone, in the antique story" (61). But it goes on: "There should be a story. I don't know the story. There may be a story of them getting a grip on each other forever" (61). In the first sentence there is no question, there is simply "the antique story," but the narrator begins to doubt herself, and she is the voice for all of literature in this literary "moment." As we read the story, nothing exists outside of it; it is the world with which we are presented and the representative of all "story," like it or not. Thus, by doubting the antique story's grounding in literary history, she calls into doubt the very existence of the progression of literary works from antiquity to today. If this ancient precursor to many works never existed, as she suggests, then the many works themselves could never have followed. So, as the mischievous narrator asks, "What does that mean?" (61). Well, as she herself answers, "Nobody gets killed. I'm stuck with her. He's stuck with me. . . . It is already only a memory" (61). Even the loss of a place in history changes nothing; it is imaginary within the boundaries of the story itself, even inconsequential. What matters is that these particular characters remain where they are, that the story goes on. This, ironically, asserts the *continuance* of a literary progression—if the story goes on after this disavowal, so must the marching of time and the continued generation of literary history. Of course, the narrator reminds us in a final jab, "It is . . . only a memory" (61).

This trademark unconventionality extends, inevitably, to the realm of characterization. It should already be apparent that Williams's characters are not the full, three-dimensional creatures we come to know so well in, for example, the works of Alice Munro or Henry James. But unlike the characters in many experimental efforts, these are not cardboard creations, walking representations of an idea or theory. On the contrary, the narrator, who could be considered the main character of every Williams story, says charming things like, "Baby, I will miss you with your common sense, and with your blindness to psychology" (5), to start off a story. She also gives us keen, if funny and offbeat, insights into other characters, such as: "She's never really, really, really wished enough for anything in her life . . . but she had thought she should indulge herself somewhat, so she sort of did. She kept indulging herself somewhat, until she went broke" (17). This is intimate knowledge of a character, however oddly phrased and obscure. On the other hand, as she herself admits in "The Flesh": "Plenty has been missing here all along, in addition to most of the people's names in their entirety, more of what they were saying, also the overtones and the under-tones of their major statements" (30). She fills in the blanks with a one-line summary, and somehow it's adequate, acknowledging what her fiction supposedly lacks, but also expertly filling in her charac-ters' "blanks" with that very acknowledgment.

A story appropriately titled "Characterize" goes one step further, by showing the accepted notion of characterization to be insuffi-cient at best. In an echo of the Old Testament ("So God created man in his own image"), we are told that "The hostess," who makes tur-key-shaped cookies, "created them in their image" (50). What is so creative about that? We may likewise ask, what is so creative about making human *characters* in the image of living *humans*? That's the task most "realistic" fiction sets out to do, and is it successful? Are the cookies identical to living turkeys? No, not even close. There are also "two cooked, twelve-pound turkeys, no longer in those images" (50). These are "real" turkeys, but now that they're dead, they don't look like what they are. It is difficult, we find, if not impossible, to discern and then reflect the "real" image, the Truth. Yet by acknowledging this difficulty, Williams is not abandoning all hope of creating lively, alluring characters. On the contrary, she frees herself to characterize who and what she will as she pleases. By recognizing the limits of such a technique or tool, she exercises a more genuine power in delineating characters and likewise leaves them free to utter phrases like, "From where I sit on my toilet, the chrome soap holder, built into the wall, is looking great" (118). Something as kooky and seemingly irrelevant as this, Williams ef-fectively argues, is just as valid in developing character as detailing the so-called psychology of a character in a work of realist fiction.

This, paired with the other "proofs," seems to indicate that Williams's fiction is not "traditional." If we have decided that, can we then assert that it is a meaningless jumble of words? "The Meaning of Life" might help us answer yes, but no to this pivotal question. With such a heavy, portentous title as this, the reader can't help but expect some anecdote or phrase that holds The Key. What we get, instead, is the meaningless use of the story title in the story itself: "That's why I think the meaning of life is so won-derful. It has helped millions of men and women to achieve vastly rich and productive lives" (39). She speaks to us knowingly, as if we already know what the meaning of life is, but we do not. A reader bumping her head against this cheerfully vicious brick wall may be tempted to credit Williams with cruel irony alone. But is Williams gleefully highlighting the emptiness of fiction, words, more specifi-cally humankind's pet phrase, "the meaning of life"? Yes, you could certainly answer, but if that is the case, then in fact there is a "meaning" to the story after all; its meaning is that "the meaning of life" is meaningless. As Williams manages to do in so many of these delightful and tortuously constructed little tales, she contradicts herself while in the act of contradicting the original statement, idea, or line. Here she reveals "the meaning of life" to be an empty container while soothing us with the knowledge that this meaninglessness means something.

"I am tempted to not say anything more which could imply anything, because this is not literature. This is espionage," the narrator of "Meat" tells us directly (93). A greater outrageousness ends the story: "N.B. If you like, change all the words" (93). Her objective in this collection, it seems, has been to explore and sometimes escape the confines of genre, form, language, and meaning. As she tells us in this story, she doesn't want to "imply anything," but she does imply the arbitrary nature of language, words, narrative, etc.—and that, in itself, is an implication. "Espionage" is the perfect term for this coded language, although we know her purpose is to create a code that's unbreakable, and knowing that, ironically, means we have (to some extent) cracked the uncrackable code. This leaves us with a twisted formula of logic, which perhaps returns Williams from performing espionage to writing literature, much to her dismay.

In what is perhaps the most concise, eloquent statement of Williams's struggle for meaninglessness, "No, Cup" begins by commanding, "Get the family out forever, out from around the table" (82). This could represent a program akin to the first book's, of freeing the self from the confines of family and society, but here it becomes a move to eradicate the *idea* of the family from the pure, clean emptiness of *things*. In *Some Sexual Success Stories* Williams strives to free herself of significance—and what could be more significant than family? So she wants them *out,* wants meaning out; to achieve this, she struggles to focus on the surfaces of things, on the things themselves, such as "white paper napkin," "biscuits in the basket," and "white milk pitcher" (82), and to hell with the abstract. But she can't help herself—first a mention of "the children" slips in, then a greater slip: "allow for the possibility that both the lip of the pitcher and the napkin points express human aspiration, conceptually" (83). By the end, the attempt completely breaks down, and the narrator must chastise herself—her mind moves from "Cup" to "The shine on the cup" (more abstract) to "Light" (abstract!), back to materiality: "No, *cup*" (83). And finally, in a typically hilarious, clever move, she ends the story by calling someone, the reader perhaps, "you asshole," but even that is not the last word. "Defecation" is (83). Her better/lesser half removes us from the specificity of "asshole" to the broader term, "defecation." In this collection Williams seeks to escape rampant symbolism and signification. She struggles as fiercely to do this as she did to free herself from family/society; in these related attempts, the more she succeeds in letting go or in being let go, the more she finds herself embracing or embraced.

The Stupefaction: Stories and a Novella

This volume showcases the first of Williams's longer pieces, a novella called "The Stupefaction." Clark Humphrey of the *Stranger,* Seattle's alternative weekly, said after interviewing the author that Williams admitted writing the novella "to comply with commercial requirements for longer, more traditional narrative structures" (Humphrey 23), but other than length, there is no sign of such compliance in the piece itself. Williams defines "longer . . . narrative structure" in her own terms, seemingly regardless of market demands. Divided into forty-four minichapters, each one reminiscent of one of her microscopic stories, "The Stupefaction" distinguishes itself as a novella by the slow building of momentum and by the suspense that dangles us, almost absurdly neatly, from the end of one chapter to the beginning of the next. Williams has said that she wanted to imitate the kind of flat suspense of a Nancy Drew book, where one chapter ends with the sound of a key scraping in a lock, and the next begins with the door opening to reveal . . . a thief? A murderer? Her friend Bess? (Personal Interview 8 Nov. 2002). The novella does contain a sincere gesture toward suspense, but the definitive action (such as robbery or murder) to which the suspense directs us never materializes. The reader should no more expect a straight detective story from Williams's novella than she would expect the complexity of interactions and insight built into each moment of "The Stupefaction" from a Nancy Drew book.

The story starts out simply, with a man and a woman abandoning their everyday lives for what seems to be the ideal cottage in the woods; the narrator justifies their actions by telling the reader, "This heavenly life is not forbidden" (107). But the sanctity of their retreat is tarnished by an unnamable yet palpable threat from the very start and also by the insufficient foundation for the characters' supposed intimacy. "He likes it when she is acting as if she is nice and friendly, when he is imagining he wants to be with nobody else," the narrator explains (107). The romance goes smoothly only when both partners participate in a mutual delusion; many relationships stand on a similarly slippery base, yet stand the test of time. Will this one last as well or crumble away?

Much depends on the narrator's ever-increasing proximity to and involvement in the love story. At first she keeps her distance from the couple, but when she sees how successful the woman has been in "winning" this man, her jealousy rises to the surface. She moans, "Oh, why did I ever let her into the cottage?" (124). "She is nice, but she has aged" (125), she says to describe the woman, cattily, as if she hopes the man would hear this and reject his current lover (125). We, the readers, certainly "hear," but what good can we do her? Besides, as narrator, can't she change the path of the story at will? Yes, she can; her "spirit soared," she notes, when she "observed that [the man and woman] did not want to look at each other" (126). How triumphant can she feel, though, having narrated and manipulated this scene as she wished? And how sincere an obstacle is her "rival," if the rival was originally contrived by her?

In addition to creating the obstacle (i.e., the female character) herself, the narrator impedes her own progress by vacillating in her attitude toward the woman. Is she a rival or one of her very own pet characters? This confusion seems to stem from her own indecision about her role: Is she a human woman or is she The Narrator? At one point, for instance, she says nastily that the woman "is behaving as if she is a pleasant woman," and the next moment she says dotingly, "I think she is so beautiful" (134). Neither can she decide whether to inveigle herself into the story or remain an appropriate distance from it. One moment she's the official narrator, telling us, "I am impressed by what lies in store for them, which includes this current adventure of theirs, as well as another expedition" (134), and the next she's asking, "Will she miss it here as much as I do when I go away?," expressing her insecurity in a nearly whining human tone (147). In one stance she is in control, the narrator who is all-knowing and superior to her characters; in the other, she's one with them and as blind to the outcome of their adventures as they are.

By chapter 26, the vacillation and confusion abruptly end. The narrator has somehow managed to step through the looking glass, through the membrane surrounding the story, right into the story. She enacts her entry into the scene by having a ménage à trois with the couple: "I graze the back of her hand with the tail end of his penis. . . . When I sat down on top of him, having put his . . . penis up inside of her, everything was what I hoped it should be" (149–50). Instead of jumping in and wresting control of the romance, the narrator plays handmaid and humbly tells the man "that nobody could fill [the female character's] shoes" (150).

The narrator does not enter the story alone, though; a "you" has been dragged along with her. We, as readers, are implicated in this "you," because who else could have been paying such close attention? And of who else could the narrator say, "When you are inside of me . . ." (149)? This makes for a tantalizing scene, featuring a sexual relationship between the man and woman (the couple), between the narrator and her characters, and finally, between the narrator and "you," her reader. Then the narrator dumps her couple unceremoniously and focuses in on her relationship with you, a pairing that forms the real meat of the novella.

"I wish I lived here," the reader says, and the narrator responds, "But you do!" (160). This dialogue has been reported by the narrator, so it may be the realization of her own wish that makes "you" say that, but regardless, by the novella's end, you have become much more than a dutiful audience member or character; you have been coerced into being a collaborator. Coerced may be too harsh a term for the gentle yet unrelenting force the narrator uses, but the reader has no choice but to obey, whatever term we use. The narrator coaxes, "You could be the one who is all so certain about what somebody wants to do next . . ." (161), proffering her own power as a lure. Eventually she drops the pronouns "you" and "I" completely for "we," obliterating the boundary between you two. "We should be certain. We should have no doubt," she counsels, as though training you for her position (162). What makes this radical is not the collaboration itself, because writer and reader must collaborate to complete a creation, and what is written is always finished only by the reader's imagination, her willingness to "come with" (161). What *is* radical is the displaying of the silent, usually invisible mechanism at work; it has generally been taboo to show the cogs and wheels.

Soon, the narrator regrets the severity of her revisions, especially in having promoted you from reader to collaborator. She becomes paranoid, having awarded you the power to manipulate the ropes too. You have become a danger to her. "I want your assurance. I want your reassurance. . . . You don't speak to me," she says (163). Of course the reader doesn't speak to her, because the reader only reads. Nevertheless, the narrator worries that you "won't like [her] anymore" (166). She sounds more and more like an insecure partner in a relationship, and she even says, "Don't hate me when this is really all over. Do not go around saying crappy things about me" (167), as though she anticipates the end, the divorce, already. And well she should; the "divorce" will take place when the book ends. No matter how collaborative and friendly the relationship seems now, you will completely elude the narrator's grasp when you finish and put down the book. This may help us understand why the narrator is so desperate now, because we are only a few pages, physically, from the end. Once you close the book, you have the power to dismiss what you've read, forget it, and/or say "crappy things" about it.

But just when we think the narrator has sung her swan song, she informs us that "I get what I want when I want it. I have been, am, will be, well served" (168). This is tantamount to her announcing that she is still The Narrator, bold emissary of The Writer, and she retains the power to do as she pleases, make things happen as planned, and get what she wants. She also chooses, at this moment, to gesture to another audience: "They can keep remembering this—even if we do not" (173). She seems to be saying that there are always readers to spare; even if you disappear and/or betray her, the other readers "can keep remembering this," can keep the story alive indefinitely and perpetuate the reader-narrator marriage into infinity. The narrator relaxes with her control intact, and then the story ends for you. You have been dismissed; you are no longer needed. By engaging her narrator in inappropriate relations with both character and reader, Williams challenges the formal boundaries of fiction as a whole. What is a book that discards its main characters, along with their story, halfway through? And what is a book that dispenses with its reader at the end, instead of waiting, politely, for the reader to finish with *it?*

The short-shorts in this volume delve into related metafictional issues or explore those examined in the novella from a different angle. For instance, "The Stupefaction" features a narrator who seems eager to perpetuate the reader-narrator marriage, but in "O Rock!" the narrator treats our involvement as nothing more than intrusion, as if we were unwanted interlopers. "I am paying attention," she says, "Do *you* have to? I hate it when you're like this" (25). As readers, we have been led to believe our task is to insinuate ourselves into characters' lives; this narrator reveals to us the voyeuristic underside of reading, even though she has formerly encouraged us. She rejected us at the end of "The Stupefaction," dismissing us before we could dismiss her, but here she allows our continued presence while she taunts us. Given a choice between the two situations, we may choose the former over the latter, if only we could choose.

A character in "Careful" likewise has no choice, although she attempts to choose to escape from the story. The narrator of "The Stupefaction" dumped her characters midway through, but this incarnation of the narrator can't seem to function without her character firmly in hand—she can hope only that "Maybe sometime soon she will be destroyed" (51) as punishment, somehow forgetting that she herself could easily arrange that destruction. Without this character under her thumb, "We have nothing for—we have no plans for—we have no ideas for your—we have no wish to make you—we are—we—feel no—," the narrator mumbles incoherently (52). This meltdown sabotages the heretofore relatively smooth flow of the narrative itself. Finally, the narrator remembers who she is and re-asserts her authority: "there are other people . . . we could speak to," she recalls (52). Who needs any particular character when you can call up a new one at will? The narrative follows her confident lead, regaining its composure as well by returning to complete sentences and appropriate punctuation. Just as "The Stupefaction"'s narrator pointed out to us the audience waiting in the wings to replace us, this narrator gestures toward the characters just waiting to be "born," should this entirely expendable one wander astray.

The already complex network of relationships between the narrator and others in these stories grows more complicated when "Diane Williams" enters the story as a character. We know she is the author of the book, and we know the rule that prohibits blurring the boundary between the narrator and the writer. But what of the boundary between the writer and a character with the writer's name, whom we can't help thinking of as the writer herself? How does this affect the relationships between narrator and writer, narrator and reader, writer and reader, all of which ultimately determine the quality of the reading experience?

"For Diane" brings these questions to a head, abruptly and dramatically. The name Diane appears only in the title, but the story is reminiscent of a "Dear John" letter, one that the narrator has written to Diane Williams. We can assume, from this parallel, that the narrator is "leaving" Diane, and this is further confirmed when the narrator tells us she has "had it up to *here*" and that she has passed the reins of control to someone named Ira (40). Is this possible? It is if the narrator wills it so—she has told us that "Springtime will span the year because that's my decision," so we know better than to doubt her authority in regards to giving over her job to "Ira" (39). Diane Williams can do nothing at all to stop her, it seems; in other stories, the characters have rebelled against the narrator and vice versa, but now the narrator has managed to rebel against the Overlord, the writer herself. Why can the writer do nothing to stop her? Perhaps her impotence originates in the very injunction against reading the narrator as the writer; if the writer abandons her post in order to scold her narrator, she as good as abdicates her throne. If she shows us that she has a voice, she can no longer hold the reins behind the holder of reins, and then the illusion would crumble for good. Better to lose this ill-behaved character than her permanent position.

"The Helpmeet" also features Diane Williams, this time as a bona fide character. By entering into the story herself, she seems to have left her sword at the door, thereby putting herself at the narrator's mercy. The narrator starts out as Diane Williams's "handmaid," both in the figurative sense of facilitating the births of her fiction "babies" and in the literal, physical sense that ". . . Diane Williams wants me to hold her fucking ass" (69). This would contradict the claim that the writer has forfeited her inherent superiority, but then the narrator uses her symbiotic relationship with Diane to gain equal footing. She may serve Diane Williams, but Diane Williams needs her service, is dependent on it. "If I go away someday, I want to know how she will live without me," the narrator says (69). The narrator obviously also depends on helping Diane Williams because the story continues, which it cannot do without her voice. Even while she acts the role of the insubordinate servant, she reveals her need to be subordinated and her master's need to subordinate her, although we must always be aware that Williams has written these words and controls the whole game. In *The Stupefaction* Williams continues directing our gaze deeper into the shadowy regions of art and illusion in fiction. This, more than the length of the title story, furthers her provocative mission.

Excitability: Selected Stories 1986–1996

Excitability contains selections from Williams's first three books: *This Is about the Body, the Mind, the Soul, the World, Time, and Fate*; *Some Sexual Success Stories*; and *The Stupefaction*. Like most selected volumes, this one bears witness to the artist's development in concentrated form. This virtue of *Excitability* complements Williams's highly compressed prose and is especially useful because the first three books can be difficult to find. *Excitability* serves this practical purpose more than it showcases the highlights of a long career, primarily because Williams is still in midcareer. Of course, the access it provides is not unlimited. There is an excellent selection of stories, but some of the more interesting and unusual ones (some of which have been singled out in this essay for commentary) were left out. This includes "Good Luck!," "The Flesh," "Characterize," and "This One's about (_____)" from *Some Sexual Success Stories*; "Life after Death," "Lifeguard," and "My Female Honor Is of a Type" from *This Is about the Body, the Mind, the Soul, the World, Time, and Fate*; "A Shrewd and Cunning Authority" and "The Helpmeet" from *The Stupefaction*. Readers foraying into Williams territory via this collection alone will find their education incomplete. But as a supplement to a considerable prior education or as a preamble to more extensive exploration of Williams's oeuvre, *Excitability* is a blessing.

Romancer Erector: Novella and Stories

Williams obsessively returns to the same sites of exploration, relentlessly pushing at boundaries she has established in previous works. Her earlier works set the bar on exploration quite high; therefore her restlessness and advanced level of risk-taking are necessary. Williams seems as compelled by lust for the whys and hows of existence as by the energy and dynamism of the language itself, which is perhaps why some readers consider her more of a prose poet than a straight prose writer. Story and theme do not take precedence over language, as in most fiction; here, the language has an equal if not greater share of the writer's attention. But Williams herself questions the strict boundary that separates poetry from fiction, saying that "all that literature is is speech on the page," call it by whatever name you will (Reading). Likewise, whatever label for Williams you may choose, in *Romancer Erector* she further perfects her approach to linguistic and formal exploration, answering her own and our metaphysical questions by unanswering them—if not by tying herself and us into knots, then by unraveling the tight knot of imaginary logic at the heart of Story itself.

Again, the most compelling character of the collection is the narrator, who seems essentially unaltered even when she changes sex, situation, or surroundings. She acts as our jester, king, friend, lover, and enemy. Can all this be possible or even permissible? In the works of Diane Williams, no one grants or refuses permission but the narrator herself. In "Actual People Whose Behavior I Was Able to Observe" Williams serves up a God-like narrator, who says of the people she pretends to love, "I am so pleased to ruin them, you know" (39). She speaks carelessly of two people in particular who need "constant coaxing, intimacies," managing to sound dead bored with both of them and their needs (39). This is the Old Testament God, the one who rains down destruction on sinners without mercy. She tells someone named "Gor," a sidekick who seems to play the role of an archangel, "It will be as if they have never run around or as if they have never twisted upon their beds" (39). The language itself is biblical, reminiscent of the formal language of vengeance a God might use.

But then she reveals her own weakness, thus her humanity—she, too, is "tied down by [her] appearance," and she admits that "Someone must have told me to wear this" (40). Would the Old Testament

God have shared this with us? It's unthinkable. In place of respect, we feel pity and recognize that perhaps our awe was hastily awarded, that this is no God but merely a haughty housewife, one who is tired of caring for husband and child, tired of being reined in by appearances, of wearing "such a short skirt" (40). She reveals the extent of her ordinary life in the plain description that follows our rude awakening: ". . . I have to urinate frequently. It was warm enough not to dress warmly. This is what is in the refrigerator" (40).

The narrator of "Spoon" reveals no such vulnerability. She draws for us an unattractive character who "was too big," "was suffering from vulvovaginitis," whose belly was "a knob," and whose skin was "wan" (57). This character is encumbered by painful description, trapped in the physical world she so awkwardly inhabits. The narrator, although she never gives up her removed, Godly stance, does reveal that there are drawbacks to the act of creation, that her power is limited. Although she has heartlessly bestowed on her character a number of hideous aspects, she also tells us, at the end, "I have to put the worst of her into her" (57). In this short statement she reveals that what compels her to create such horrible details is a force outside of herself, beyond her control—she *has to* put "the worst of her into her"—she doesn't say "I put the worst of her into her" for the hell of it, nor does she explain why she *has to* do it, but merely states that she *has* to do it. However impervious she appears, she calls our attention to the master puppeteer hovering over her, pulling her strings.

Similarly, the narrator of "The Description of the Worlds" sounds more like a monarch than a God, one whose power is circumscribed by mortality, perhaps, or by her necessary submission to a higher being. Her own house betrays her mortal status, with its "Coves and console brackets on the bed of the ceiling remind[ing] us many monarchs lived here" (69). Seeing her as just one in a long line of rulers helps us, and the "queen" herself, recognize her limitations. She accepts tasks handed down from some higher power, not grudgingly like "Spoon"'s narrator, but in the open, straightforward manner of someone who expects orders and follows them. For instance, she has the formidable task of "sweeping away [her] neighborhood," something a narrator is surely equipped to do (70). There are also times when she does not comply, revealing that she does have some veto power. We learn this when she confides, "When I was asked to make a terrible mistake, I said I would not" (70). What is the mistake? What follows sweeping away a neighborhood—the destruction of the world, perhaps? Regardless, we feel certain that this monarch has chosen wisely in denying the Greater Power's command.

Another monarch (a prince, perhaps) narrates "The Duller Legend," a story whose title foretells the prince-narrator's discontentment with his fixed role in this most fixed of story forms, the fairy tale. At first we cannot understand why he should be discontent; he is a prince, after all, and the regal details of his life sound alluring. He has met a princess in "gorgeous clothing" who "clung to the curve of [his] faith"; he has "engaged in sixty-five battles" and seems like a valiant, courtly warrior of the highest order (44–45). Why, then, does he long to become the nameless, faceless girl character, of whom he says, "There is no item so common to us all as she is" (43)? He wants to "eat the girl's food as if it were [his] food" and "try to speak the way she speaks" (43) as a means, perhaps, of escaping the pattern he himself is charged with upholding as its narrator, ruler, and owner. Her blandness allows her to melt into the wall of the story, thus escaping it; his very extraordinariness ensnares him. He is tired of "owning" this patterned tale and tired of ownership in general. When he chases another girl in the story and wins her, he states blandly, "now I have her" (44). Likewise, he says of his "career—this so-called war—one always knows how these things are going to turn out" (45). And he is right: one knows that the "good" knight will defeat the "bad" knight and that the good knight will subsequently win the princess in the end. Williams's work makes a point of denying and disfiguring such patterns, and this story acts as the spokesperson for her own campaign against the expected form and content of a tale.

Another trapped narrator greets us in "There Are So Many Smart People Walking Around." She, like the princely narrator of "The Duller Legend," seeks escape, but instead of wanting freedom from the world's most strictly patterned, linear story, she wants out of a relentlessly circular narrative experiment. "When she started to eat me," she tells us, "I asked her if she was tired. She said yes. I told her to sleep. Then she cried. I brought her back . . . to eat me. She started to cry. I told her to sleep" (51). This unending cycle hinders progression—How can a narrator tell a story straight if the competing needs of a character's hunger and exhaustion must be simultaneously (impossibly) met? It is an impossible situation for the character, but an even more confining one for the narrator. She appeals to us, indirectly, for help: "What if the young person is as hungry as she is tired, how can I help out? Do I keep trying to feed it, and then do I keep trying to encourage the unreasonable thing to sleep?" (52). What can a storyteller do in this situation—Who wants to narrate for Sisyphus?

Well, Williams suggests, perhaps the narrator can continue to proceed circularly; perhaps the need to move in a straight line from

A to B is unnecessary, an old requirement that only further ossifies fiction as an art form. Isn't the narrator's plight just as interesting, and isn't the character being active, even if not in the expected way? Ironically, the dynamism of this story results from the static nature of its central drama and also from the compelling voice of the narrator-victim at the center of the so-called action.

Our help proved unnecessary for the previous narrator, but sometimes the narrator is truly in need of rescue, and we, the readers, are the nearest potential lifesavers. However, isn't it futile for her to cry for help, knowing her appeal will reach us only after the story has been written? Is it possible for a reader to rescue the narrator or the narrative after the creation is complete? This raises the question, when does the act of creation end? Many of the stories in *Romancer Erector* suggest that creation is an open-ended event in which all of us are active participants and collaborators. The act of reading and writing, according to what we have learned in Williams's oeuvre, is something quite apart from our preconceived notions.

"D. Beech and J. Beech," like a work of conceptual art, wants to actively engage the reader; however, unlike conceptual art, the narrator actually demands the reader's participation. Her urgency warrants our caution. Does she really want from us what she professes to want or need? She seems sincere enough. She confides that "Maybe I did not make it refreshing enough," and then tells us something we probably already know about fiction, as if she were training us for her job: "The whole idea is that there is the pattern" (37). This is true enough in traditional fiction—sometimes there is nothing at all to distract one from "the pattern": beginning, middle, and end, during which a crisis arises, then is resolved. Characters are fleshed out with descriptive terms, thoughts, habits, beliefs. But in this story, the characters are far too "off" to belong to any pattern. The man "has already had his best day," and the woman "has not yet" (38). In either case, they are not what they should be; they are not fully realized. Furthermore, "Both of these people have ears which are just wrong," and "their rough tongues seem to be merely pegged on" (38). There is something "tacked-on" about these characters—they show their joints and cracks instead of presenting to the reader a unified semblance of truth. As for the progress of the plot, it is nonexistent; it shows no evidence of beginning, middle, or end. Only glints of "action" appear: "She would put a coverlet on him and she would pet him and . . . kiss him. . . . [s]he must do as others do" (38). This is nebulous, dreamy "action" at best, and certainly does not "do as others do," namely, fulfill the requirements of the accepted pattern for a work of fiction.

The narrator, who is responsible for all this, says, "I hope you can restore [the female character's] beauty" because "She could well belong to a mythological landscape" (37). She flatly refuses to do the work—if we would like to fit these characters into a pattern, we will have to do it ourselves. And that is something we can do with the power of our imaginations, if it is what we would like or need. It is not a cry for help so much as it is a cry of revolt against reader needs, market needs, etc., that the narrator is voicing here. She doesn't really want or need our participation, it seems; she wants to teach us a lesson about what she does not want her story to be.

In "Tureen" the narrator softens, seems genuinely to need our help, but not with storyline or character development. She begins haughtily enough: "This is for me to say since the old times" (85). She claims the traditional storyteller's rights with this remark, but her control quickly slips away. In exchange for her telling us, "You are not going to say any of this. Good" (85), she assures us, "No, I won't tell them anything about you. I won't," thereby enacting a deal or bargain with the reader (86). Why should the narrator be so ill at ease? Perhaps because of essays just like this one—because, as the narrator admits, "Go up the stairs and you have gone quite beyond me. My room's on the first floor" (86). Once the words have been written, the narrator, the representative of the writer herself, loses control. The reader takes over and can read and judge and possibly then share her insights with others, as she pleases. So the narrator may be right to be paranoid—perhaps more narrators should be as nervous as she is. She may have been toying with us in "D. Beech and J. Beech," but here she reveals to us the heart of our power as readers and begs us not to abuse it.

The narrator has a little revenge in "Tony," when she addresses us as "my maker" (77). How is the reader the narrator's maker? The reader could be considered the narrator/writer's "maker" because she takes the raw material and makes of it, in her individual mind, what she can and will. The narrator turns to us coquettishly at the end and asks for some favors, because what else is a "maker" if not also a provider? "May I please have a bronze flower vessel, a vase with tiger handles, edged weapons. . . . May I please rape you?" (77). What starts out as a childish list of requests from a Santa Claus-like figure ends with a startling threat in the guise of a well-mannered request. Why would the narrator want to rape us, her "maker"? Well, it would give her a measure of control, wouldn't it? If we have been raping her work, she will try to rape us right back.

This latest collection is significant physically because there are three longer pieces, which, especially in the context of

Williams's microstories, could be considered novellas. The shortest of these three longer works may be the most successful and
interesting. In "Very, Very Red" the seemingly male narrator
takes care of a batch of girls, including one named, significantly,
"Diane" (13). From the very first the creator ("Diane" as Diane
Williams) infringes on the narrator's role and rights. "Remember
who you are. Remember what you do," Diane says patronizingly
(13). The narrator reciprocates by resenting Diane because "she
pities [him]" (13). Less harmfully, Diane also seems to blend in
with the other girl characters. "There are many imitations of
Diane here," the narrator tells us, "made of horn and rubber and
plastic" (15). And isn't that what a character does in many cases,
imitate the real thing, clone the creator herself? We could, then,
read the narrator as a caretaker of Williams's fictional world—he
keeps watch over and lords power over all the "girls" in the stories, including Williams herself, although she (via her representative, "Diane") also exerts power over him from time to time, reminding him of his place and the tasks he should be carrying out
in her name.

Later on we know that Diane is an automaton or at least a life-
sized doll. She may be the most successful of the "girls," but she is
not quite successful enough to be real—she is still artificial. The
narrator tell us, "He carried Diane back to the hiding place . . . ,"
also that "She can climb in, she can climb out of an automobile. . . .
She will do the cutest little trick" (17). Diane's failure in attaining
reality may well be the failure of all fiction to be "real." Williams
openly acknowledges the artifice of all art, and by doing so, she
gives herself, and her reader, a great deal of freedom and more
leeway for success than a work of "realistic" fiction gives itself.
Why should we expect fiction to be real, when it's impossible for
words on paper to achieve reality? Williams is not striving for reality, she lets us know, because it is a ridiculous goal. Why not reveal the artifice for what it is and see what doors open for us after
that? As we have seen, many doors open in Williams's work—the
revelations that issue forth are perhaps more vital, more important, and more truthful than ones we receive from realistic work,
because Williams admits that what she has been indulging in is
fiction.

The title novella, "Romancer Erector," is perhaps the closest of all
three longer pieces to what is traditionally called a novella. This
does not prevent the narrator from sabotaging the form from within,
though. How does she achieve this? For one, the sections grow
smaller as they proceed, instead of larger; because we have been
groomed to expect a story to build as it goes along, it is disturbing to

notice how this story physically wastes away. The content follows suit, beginning as more of a straight narrative, but unraveling to the last line of: "Okay, okay, okay, okay, okay, okay, okay" (143).

The narrator also helps to sabotage the progression of events by being uncooperative, as if she were engaged to carry out a task in which she has no confidence or belief. "So, um, what do I think our next step might be?" she asks herself, almost grudgingly (132). She also admits her own ineptitude for storytelling: "I have storyish ideas but no story in me. This is the row of empty marks. These are the signs of what is next" (129). And what comes next? Nothing. Or the Williams equivalent of nothing: "Don't I listen? We could get someone else to talk to me. Here is—well, well, here is—is it really one of you?" (129). The chapter ends with that question hanging in the air, with the reader incapable of making a satisfactory answer.

In the hands of a less gifted author, these maneuvers would merely confirm that the writer has resorted to playfulness to avoid her own failure as a storyteller. But in Williams's hands, the maneuvers are no more shields than they are gimmicks; they only reflect the earnestness with which Williams endeavors to move beyond the point to which previous fiction writers have journeyed in the past. But her adventurousness should not pigeonhole her work as difficult, labor-intensive fiction—not at all. There is discomfort, unease, paranoia, and a splintering of the accepted short-story form, but there are worldly comforts as well: good food, sex, sly humor, rich atmosphere, an alluring, if disconcerting, narrator, and familiar American scenes, all of which combine with the more challenging aspects to captivate an inquisitive reader.

Her work might be called a postmodernist's dream—hilarious and playful, profound, scornful of profundity, serious, scary, light as a feather, sumptuously textured, exasperatingly brief, intricate, simultaneously meaningful and meaningless. She takes the edge out of much of the experimental fiction that has been written and is being written today, much of which emerges as dry, formulaic exercises or tedious works of language play. Her work has a serious heart, even while it joyously denies that heart again and again. The challenges and ornaments of Williams's fiction alone create an unforgettable, remarkable body of work, but it is Williams's ability to let ambiguities stand and her determination to have ambiguous, even vexing fun, that classify her as one of our most valuable contemporary writers.

Works Cited

Dickinson, Emily. *The Complete Poems of Emily Dickinson.* Ed. Thomas H. Johnson. Boston: Little, Brown, 19660. 166.

Enns, Anthony. "Interview with Diane Williams." *Dominion Review* 15 (1997): 72–79.

Hanson, Liane. Interview with Diane Williams. *Weekend Edition.* National Public Radio 21 Jan. 1990.

Harvey, Matthea. Rev. of *Romancer Erector,* by Diane Williams. *BOMB* Summer 2002: 22.

Hornburg, Mark W. "Ladies' Nights." Rev. of *Excitability,* by Diane Williams. *North Carolina Review of Books* Winter 1999: 16.

Humphrey, Clark. Rev. of *The Stupefaction,* by Diane Williams. *Stranger* 24 Oct. 1999: 23.

Kessler, Rachel. Rev. of *Excitability,* by Diane Williams. *TheStranger.com* 29 Apr. 1999 <http://www.thestranger.com/1999-04-29/book_revue.html>.

Lennon, Brian. "Reading Diane Williams." *Context: A Forum for Literary Arts and Culture* 1 (Fall 1999): 5.

Levine, Stacey. "Dancing on the Borderline." Rev. of *Romancer Erector,* by Diane Williams. *American Book Review* 23.5 (July–Aug. 2002): 7, 9.

McFall, Gardner. Rev. of *Excitability,* by Diane Williams. *New York Times Book Review* 13 Dec. 1998: 23.

Mifflin, Margot. Rev. of *Some Sexual Success Stories,* by Diane Williams. *Entertainment Weekly* 6 March 1992: 55.

O'Brien, John. "An Interview with Diane Williams." *Review of Contemporary Fiction* 12.1 (1992): 133–40. <http://www.centerforbookculture.org/interviews/interview_williams.html>.

Rice, Doug. Rev. of *This Is about the Body, the Mind, the Soul, the World, Time, and Fate,* by Diane Williams. *Pittsburgh Press* 15 March 1990: D10.

Rosenberg, Stuart. Interview with Diane Williams. Chicago Public Radio. WBEZ 28 Feb. 1990.

Sarraute, Nathalie. *Tropisms.* New York: George Braziller, 1939.

Shapard, Robert, and James Thomas, eds. *Sudden Fiction: American Short-Short Stories.* Salt Lake City: Peregrine Smith, 1986.

Sims, Laura. Rev. of *Romancer Erector,* by Diane Williams. *Rain Taxi* 6.4 (2001–2002): 6.

Stadler, Matthew. "The Author Did It." Rev. of *Some Sexual Success Stories,* by Diane Williams. *New York Times Book Review* 19 July 1992: 21.

Thomas, James, Denise Thomas, and Tom Hazuka, eds. *Flash Fiction: 72 Very Short Stories.* New York: Norton, 1992.

Williams, Diane. *Excitability: Selected Stories 1986–1996*. Normal, IL: Dalkey Archive Press, 1998.

—. Personal Interview. 5 Oct. 2002.

—. Personal Interview. 8 Nov. 2002.

—. Reading and Question-and-Answer Session. The Raymond Carver Reading Series. Syracuse University 29 Sept. 1999.

—. *Romancer Erector: Novella and Stories*. Normal, IL: Dalkey Archive Press, 2001.

—. *Some Sexual Success Stories, plus Other Stories in which God Might Choose to Appear*. New York: Grove Weidenfeld, 1992.

—. *The Stupefaction: Stories and a Novella*. New York: Knopf, 1996.

—. *This Is about the Body, the Mind, the Soul, the World, Time, and Fate*. New York: Grove Weidenfeld, 1990.

A Diane Williams Checklist

This Is about the Body, the Mind, the Soul, the World, Time, and Fate. New York: Grove Weidenfeld, 1990.

Some Sexual Success Stories, plus Other Stories in which God Might Choose to Appear. New York: Grove Weidenfeld, 1992.

The Stupefaction: Stories and a Novella. New York: Knopf, 1996.

Excitability: Selected Stories 1986-1996. Normal, IL: Dalkey Archive Press, 1998.

Romancer Erector: Novella and Stories. Normal, IL: Dalkey Archive Press, 2001.

Diane Williams
Photograph by Bill Hayward

Aidan Higgins

Neil Murphy

*That time, that place, was it all your own invention, that
you shared with me? And I too perhaps was your invention.*
—Aidan Higgins,
Helsingor Station and Other Departures

More than thirty years ago Aidan Higgins indicated that all of his
work followed his life, "like slug trails . . . all the fiction happened"
(Higgins, "Writer in Profile" 13), a comment that implies much
more than autobiographical admission. In his earliest fictions, *Felo
de Se* and *Langrishe, Go Down,* his birthplace, Springfield House,
Celbridge, is a recurring setting, and Higgins was also to later acknowledge in his trio of autobiographies that the sisters in
Langrishe were actually he and his brothers in fictional drag. *Balcony of Europe* is largely based in Andalucian Spain, where
Higgins lived in the 1970s. *Scenes from a Receding Past*'s fictionalized setting of Sligo seems suspiciously like the Celbridge of his
youth, and *Bornholm Night-Ferry* and *Lions of the Grunewald* re-
visit the northern European landscapes where Higgins lived during the early 1980s, partly under the benefice of Deutsch
Akademischer Austauschdienst (Berlin). The fascination with autobiographical detail is obviously more overt in his travel writing
and autobiographies as well as in the numerous short autobiographical sketches that he has penned throughout his career. The
travel book *Images of Africa* recounts his journeys in South Africa
with a marionette theater company, while the twin texts *Helsingor
Station and Other Departures* and *Rhonda Gorge and Other Precipices* gather together many short fictions and straight autobiographical pieces. More recently, the author, still "consumed by
memories" (Higgins, *Donkey's Years* 3), embarked on a trilogy of autobiographies: *Donkey's Years: Memories of a Life as Story Told,
Dog Days,* and *The Whole Hog.* Everywhere in the work Higgins's
life finds expression, but in such a way that the distinction between autobiography and fiction gradually grows to mean less and
less, and in some respects the final part of the autobiographical
trilogy, *The Whole Hog,* reads like a fiction. This is because the traditional demarcations between fiction and reality are constantly
confronted in Higgins's work, and much of the significance of his
writing finally rests on his deeply troubled response to the means

with which we grapple with a life that so often refuses to be named, either in writing or in living.

When viewed in retrospect, the work of many writers reveals characteristic interests that are revisited throughout their writing lives. One of Aidan Higgins's primary recurring epistemological concerns has always been with how the past is reshaped by memory and imagination, ensuring that the events recounted in his texts are rarely as poignant as their aftermaths. Furthermore, the fascination with the autobiographical past repeatedly takes thematic shape in dissolved or dissolving love affairs, absent or lost lovers, and a persistent struggle to make sense of the meaning of love. Hence, the defining thematic concerns of love and the past are never absent in Higgins's fictions and are usually present in his travel writing and autobiographies. More significant perhaps are the formal implications that emerge as a result of his fascination with love and memory, both of which, as exemplified by Higgins's various heroes, are intricately related to a range of epistemological issues that are the defining components of his work. The past in Higgins's fictional universe is a deeply problematic concept, replete with puzzlement at its inaccuracy and dismay at its irrevocable passing and the essentially dreamlike status that he finally accords to it. The pastness of the accounts of his narrators' various love affairs have a resounding impact, so much so that most of Higgins's mature fiction seems consumed with the problem of how to locate a form to accommodate the strangeness of a life that is frequently incomprehensible, forever on the point of departure, but always somehow anchored by bright moments of love, however brief. Thus *Scenes from a Receding Past* and *Balcony of Europe* initiate Higgins's lifelong defiance of linear narrative and use instead spatial narratives, more familiar to the visual arts, in the hope that some sense can be communicated by building extraordinary images from which networks of binding associations can emerge. Similarly so with *Bornholm Night-Ferry,* in which Higgins maximizes the particular advantages of the epistolary novel to evade the limits of sequential narrative and conventional characterization. This persistent desire to locate some kind of narrative structure that manages to contain, without distorting, the author's vision of life is what is most intriguing about Higgins's work on a formal level. His most recent novel, *Lions of the Grunewald,* revisits familiar subject matter, but fashions it in a way that is reminiscent of, though not as extensive as, the self-reflexivity of Calvino or Nabokov. In addition, the novel is structured around a series of seemingly disparate elements, like dream sequences, historical detail, digressions, and imagined conversations with real figures, all of which are tentatively held in place by the narrator's troubled, but playful, consciousness. Ultimately, Higgins appears intent on exploring what consciousness means in terms of its relationship to the events we call life. The extraordinary factor that underpins all of Higgins's work, finally, is the belief that his own reality is already an elaborate fiction, and thus the traditional distinction between fiction and reality is itself a ruse, a polarized game with which most writers seem to be engaged. If reality is already a fiction, a fluid, extraordinary one, how does the artist respond? This seems to be the defining question in all of Higgins's work, and the pitch of the question intensifies as the work matures.

The primary focus of this essay is Aidan Higgins's fiction, an aim that is complicated somewhat by the enormously significant contribution to his work that his autobiographical writing represents. In addition, Higgins has reissued, relocated, and revised much of his writing in several ways, something that poses significant difficulties to serious readers of his work. For example, the first collection of stories, *Felo de Se,* was originally published in the U.S. as *Killachter Meadow* and later reprinted as *Asylum and Other Stories.* Some of the material from *Felo de Se* is included in *Helsingor Station and Other Departures* (most notably the stories "Killachter Meadow" and "Lebensraum") and in the collected fiction and prose, *Flotsam and Jetsam. Ronda Gorge and Other Precipices* contains many autobiographical echoes of *Bornholm Night-Ferry* and also includes a reprint of *Images of Africa,* the early travel book. Many of the short fictions and prose pieces of *Helsingor* and *Ronda Gorge* are reprinted in *Flotsam and Jetsam,* and the stories of *Felo de Se* again reappear, though they are renamed and revised. Almost all of the material in *Helsingor* and *Ronda* continually echoes the novels. All of this is not to suggest that Higgins simply recycles his work. He has continually revised, added new material, and even renamed some of the shorter fictions and has, as he says in the Apologia to *Lions of the Grunewald,* tended to transplant "fugitive *Ur*-fiction" into its "proper context, relocated from embryonic themes" (vi). The *process* appears to be all to Higgins.

Forced by necessity to choose one of the "versions" above the others, I have selected those that appear in their "proper context," which generally means in the final versions of the novels, though in the interest of mapping development I have focused on the earliest versions of the stories that appear in *Felo de Se.* No doubt, however, a certain degree of revisitation is inevitable in work as integrated as Higgins's. For this reason, I do not offer close analysis of *Helsingor* and *Ronda,* both of which are almost entirely comprised of work, or versions of it, that is found elsewhere in the novels and stories. Similarly with *Flotsam and Jetsam,* which is essentially a collection of short fictions and prose pieces that have all appeared elsewhere, though again, many have been revised.

Felo de Se

Aidan Higgins's first work of fiction, *Felo de Se,* depicts a series of characters that are variously situated in Ireland, England, South Africa, and Germany. While the plots are relatively plausible, and place names and indigenous factual detail locate the events in recognizable landscapes, there are numerous factors that undercut the illusion of realism. Translated as *felons of ourselves, Felo de Se* details episodes of struggle in a world that always evades comprehension, revealing Higgins's deep epistemological uneasiness from the outset of his fictional oeuvre. Eddie Brazill, the main protagonist of "Asylum," is an emigrant laborer and factory worker in a world indifferent to his toils, so indifferent that it nudges him toward destitution. Mr. Vaschel, of "Nightfall on Cape Piscator," an unsuccessful antiquea dealer, suffers from an advanced state of lethargy that utterly confounds him: "By the sea Mr. Vaschel walked alone with his troubles, though what these troubles were he could not say" (*Felo de Se* 183). The recurrent refusal to accept the "responsibility of feeling" (43) is the characters' outstanding felony.

The stories of *Felo de Se* generally use the conventions of realism. Higgins creates recognizable, if not well-defined, characters that suffer from credible human shortcomings, and he constructs familiar social and historical landscapes. However, chronological sequence is subverted by the construction of spatial narratives in order to painstakingly focus on vibrant moments, which might radiate meaning in a nontemporal sense. Hence, Higgins's creations frequently appear to exist in a static vacuum. Patrick O'Neill claims that Higgins's characters typically "emerge abruptly out of nowhere, are subjected to a portrait painter's penetrating scrutiny, and disappear again into the darkness from which they came" (95). O'Neill's assertion implies that Higgins's creations are instances of the author's art rather than realistic characters. The primary motivation behind O'Neill's view is the density of language used by Higgins. Unlike O'Neill, Roger Garfitt views this as a narrative weakness: "the external world of experience is accurately perceived, but it is rendered into a dense, highly subjective linguistic structure which becomes finally a bulwark against the experience itself. Reality is internalised" (225). He proceeds to contrast Higgins's "linguistic structure" with John McGahern's "bare style," asserting that McGahern's approach is more courageous because it allows "experience" to have the last word. Or the illusion of experience perhaps? Because Higgins wishes to imprison his readers, as well as his characters, in moments of inertia, he creates dense, linguistic constructs, much as Conrad does in *Heart of Darkness* in his efforts to emphasize Marlow's problems with comprehending his unfamiliar landscape.

The stories of *Felo de Se* represent barren, passive conditions by presenting dreamlike, linguistically dense fictional worlds. The foregrounding of such elaborate, subjective language reveals that the plots themselves, although obviously important constituent parts, are subservient to the act of telling, and thus reality is knowable only insofar as it is possible to express it. This is a central epistemological concern with which each succeeding Higgins novel has since grappled. In fact, it can be argued that much of Higgins's fictional direction is hereafter energized by a crisis of knowing, and much of his technical innovation is directly related to this crisis.

Higgins's "realist" *Felo de Se* is also subverted by an implicit artificiality in some of the short stories. For example, one of the four sisters of "Killachter Meadow" is absent from the narrative. The narrator refuses to inform us of her whereabouts, instead tersely stating that "She is not in this story" (13). Effectively, the illusion of reality is disturbed. She is not of relevance to the narratorial emphasis of the text and is simply omitted, rendering the fictional ontology superior to any imagined "reality." Similarly, Fraulein Sevi Klein of "Lebensraum" actually fades out of existence once her function within the narrative is complete: "He watched her evaporating, crawling into her background, not declining it, deliberately seeking it, lurching away from him to stumble into a new medium (a way she had), beating down the foreshore. . . . [F]or an instant longer she remained in sight, contracting and expanding in the gloom, and then was gone" (50). This deliberate assertion of narratorial authority and affirmation of the primary significance of the fiction over a potential mirrored reality is reminiscent of Nabokovian or Beckettian postmodern fictional play, but Higgins retains more than a passing embrace of realism, a characteristic of his writing that never disappears. The strangeness, the overwhelming sense of transience that he discovers everywhere about him, is very much a condition of life itself, and hence his work remains in perpetual argument with the ways in which one tries to know the world. The stories contain the genesis of his later work in that the characters evoke the author's vision of transience. Irwin Pastern, the primary figure of "Tower and Angels" informs us, "Perhaps nothing ends, he suggested, —only changes" (167). Higgins's characters fade in and out of his stories and resurface again and again in different guises. That his characters may have a basis in reality is secondary to their relevance for his artistic intent.

Higgins's short fictions, especially "Killachter Meadow" and "Lebensraum," suffer from the sheer weight of their own ambition, because the medium is simply too brief to embrace the range of themes with which he grapples. Sam Baneham has suggested, with good reason, that the stories cannot contain their characters: "Indeed it is a feature of Mr. Higgins' short stories that, while all of the characters compel attention, some through their originality burst from the constraints of the form and seem in search of a novel" (171). In fact this is what transpired with at least two of the stories, "Killachter Meadow" and "Lebensraum." Anticipating *Images of Africa,* Higgins's first travel work, "Lebensraum" explores the theme of travel through the character of Sevi Klein, who "had travelled all her life and would probably continue to do so until the day of her death . . . so that she would always be out of reach" (*Felo de Se* 39). "Killachter Meadow" also prompts further development and finds greater expression in Higgins's first and most critically acclaimed novel, *Langrishe, Go Down.*

Langrishe, Go Down

As with the embryonic story, *Langrishe, Go Down* retains the big-house themes of decay and inertia, and much of the imagery powerfully evokes the collapse of a class. The brief love affair between Imogen and Otto in "Killachter Meadow" is now a tempestuous relationship that stands at the center of the novel and radiates much of the text's significance. Higgins also constructs a tragic tale of the dissolution of a culture, depicting the anguished passing of Ascendancy values into the modern world. In fact, Higgins's attempt to evoke the plight of the Langrishe family gains some of its impetus from this traditional genre of decay. However, he avails of the genre only in a formal sense. There are many layers of significance in the novel that resonate far beyond the traditional theme of decay, as Vera Kreilkamp has convincingly argued by suggesting that Higgins redefines the form and reinvents it. Kreilkamp also accurately suggests that the author is ultimately concerned not just with his own birthplace, but with history itself: "In its most painful moments *Langrishe, Go Down* is about the loss of historical memory, and even more painfully, about living in a world where history itself has been transmuted into the debris of civilisation. For Stephen Dedalus, 'history is a nightmare,' for Helen Langrishe, history consists of the dead monuments of a dead culture" (30).

The big-house genre, a powerful symbol of transience, is used by Higgins as an extended metaphor that reaches beyond the social and historical. For example, Helen's memory constructs an ordered movement that leads to her present situation, a movement in which little changes, "variations apart (the passing of her parents, the death of Emily), in the immutable order of events" (23). This is the source of her ultimate tragic disintegration. Her memories are sterile, and thus she has almost nothing with which she can sustain herself. Imogen's musings on Helen, after she dies, elucidate the sad condition of her life: "And is it not strange, most strange, that a life which can be so positive, so placed, going on for years, seemingly endless, can one day go; and, which is strangest of all, leave little or no trace?" (259–60). Thus Higgins's positioning of his characters within the big-house framework allows him to approach the deeper epistemological concerns that always inform his work: the significance and unreliability of memory, the difficulty of knowing one's existence, and the flood of transience that challenges such attempts to know one's life.

Higgins's fascination with the nature of memory and transience is mirrored in the novel's structure, begun in medias res and followed by an analeptic account of Imogen and Otto's doomed and torturous love affair, allowing us to witness the grim reality of a fading life, half-lived-out through clinging to frail memories. Again, this emphasizes the centrality in Higgins's work of the relationship between memory and the historical past. Richard Kearney, in analyzing what he calls the postcritical novel, a tradition to which he asserts Higgins belongs, registers the problematic nature of this relationship: "Once this distinction between word and thing was deconstructed by Joyce and Beckett, the distance between the narrator's subjective consciousness and the historical world— which motivates the narrator's quest for meaning in the first place—was greatly diminished" (*Transitions* 98). Higgins registers the "distance between subjective consciousness and the historical world" throughout *Langrishe, Go Down* and in doing so creates the tension that lingers at the core of the novel: "The memory of things—are they better than the things themselves?" (70). Imogen believes so: "Of that time, what do I remember now? What can I recall if I try? Was he good to me? Yes. He was good to me; good for me; kind and considerate" (58). In part 2, when Imogen's narration is superseded by an anonymous narrator, the more objective rendition of Otto's behavior indicates quite a different tale, revealing that Imogen's subjective consciousness has greatly refashioned historical actuality. During one of Otto's typically sensitive moments, he addresses Imogen: "You're so soft, Otto said, staring before him with a vindictive face. Some soft spineless insect that's been trodden on. I can feel you beginning to curl up at the sides" (227). The memory of things for Imogen is surely better than the things themselves. By depicting the difference between the actuality and the mind's conception of it, Higgins implies the necessary consolatory nature of memory, which functions as a kind of automated panacea for human consciousness. Reality is relativized by the human imagination not simply in the act of telling, but in the act of self-preservation.

The past in Higgins's novel is an evasive entity. It may affect the present, but it cannot be captured, and thus the lessons it can teach are indistinct at best. Patrick O'Neill incisively evaluates Higgins's approach: "However, for Higgins, the big house theme is clearly not just a realist portrayal of the decline of a passing age of grace, beauty and culture—though it certainly is that—but also a symbol of the inevitable dissolution of all order, all form" (98). O'Neill's analysis contains the kernel of Higgins's endeavors. *Langrishe, Go Down* acknowledges that the lines of communication are down between word and thing, between the individual and his or her past, between perception and reality. It also accepts the artificial nature of human ordering systems and registers Higgins's allegiance to flux. O'Neill extends his view of *Langrishe, Go Down* to include such matters: "This suggestion of the immutability and indifference of things, the essential existential irrelevance of human beings and their concerns, is repeated through the narrative in the attitudes of the Langrishe sisters" (99). The bleakness of Higgins's vision finds utterance in the meaningless lives of most of his characters, who plod desperately onward. They exist on the periphery in a modernist, Godless, loveless universe, where all those things with which humanity comforts itself are absent, except memory, to which they cling tenaciously.

Langrishe, Go Down acknowledges the inheritance of Beckett and Joyce, and it accepts the frailty and transience of human ordering systems, but ultimately it evokes a message of hope, however meagre, for humanity and its ability to communicate. All of these aspects are constituent parts to a multifaceted fiction that always retains a power to generate discourse. Its value lies in the fact that it has the power to communicate the demise of a major cultural occasion and tells a moving and often sympathetic account of the lives of the Langrishe girls, Helen and Imogen in particular, while also acknowledging that order and the act of recapturing the past are problematic concepts. As such, the text attempts to fuse two seemingly paradoxical arguments. It accepts and assimilates the critical heritage of Joyce and Beckett while attempting to retain the act of representing the world. The central significance of such an approach is that the limitations of knowledge and communication must be named, but history cannot be discarded, flawed though it may be as a representative act. Higgins, all too aware of Beckett's reductionist tendencies, refuses to abandon an engagement with reality despite his foregrounding of the intellectual modes and communicative methods with which we construct that engagement. Thus with *Langrishe,* Higgins still maintains dialogue with his world and yet takes as his primary emphasis the instability of reality, both in terms of human consciousness and in the forms we construct to contain our experience.

Balcony of Europe

Balcony of Europe represents a crucial moment for Higgins's literary reputation. A novel that the author refuses to allow to return to print, *Balcony* has commanded much respect while also attracting quite severe criticism, largely fixed on the rather tired cliché of highly promising artist turned profligate. For this reason and because it represents seven years of the author's work at a time when much was expected, the novel requires close attention. In the sprawling fiction, we are presented with a complex tapestry of moments that are repeatedly submitted to the narrator's, Dan Ruttle's, interrogative eye. Beginning in Dun Laoghaire, Co. Dublin, in 1961, we observe Ruttle's parents in the bitter throes of social decline. After his mother's drawn-out demise, Ruttle and his wife Olivia relocate to Andalucia, where much of the novel is situated and where we are swiftly informed of the author's extramarital affair with Charlotte Bayless, a young married American Jew.

  Balcony of Europe is a reconstruction of Dan Ruttle's experiences, largely in Andalucia, and thus the problems of memory and communication are foregrounded from the outset of the narrative retelling. Of his early life, Dan is uncertain: "All that seems to have happened, if it ever happened, long ago, belonging to someone else's past, not mine" (43). Dan's awareness of his essential separation from the past is clear, but he is, like all of Higgins's protagonists, ineluctably drawn to past events, which proves to be the source of much grief in the novel: "That which is past is past; that which is wished for may not (cannot) come again. Certain scents imply: *a longing for what cannot come again*" (160). The closest one can be to one's past, it is implied, is through the incidental things: scents and longings.

  Ruttle's elusive past is but a part of his difficulty. His ability to communicate is also tenuous: "I had no means to describe it, the world, myself, the world before myself" (45). The linguistic medium is problematized, and this, added to his difficulty with memory, conspires to form a very uncertain base from which to reconstruct his past. Dan's response to this essentially modernist epistemological problem is to conflate memory and imagination. The past, as he sees it, is a fiction and hence can only be knowable as such. Reconsidering his early difficulties, Dan grows to understand that memory is not actually lost; rather it is transformed, inevitably and necessarily so. Richard Kearney isolates the central theme of *Balcony of Europe* as "the attempt to wrest imagination from the vortex of memory" ("Crisis" 401). The text thus does not simply represent an account of Ruttle's experiences, rather it probes the very condition of their creation. Memory is initially questioned and then accepted, but only as a fluid entity forged from imagination. Crucially, the reality from which the memories originally spring is also offered up as an imagined construct. The nature of this primary thematic concern has obvious implications for the way in which the narrator's account is structured, giving rise to what Joseph Frank among others (Vidan) has termed spatial fiction, or the "simultaneity of perception" (Frank 87).

The form of *Balcony of Europe* has been the focus of much negative criticism. Many have hastened to dismiss it unconditionally, with one critic rejecting it as "an intelligent tourist's notebook jottings" (Lubbers 242). Similarly, John Banville asserts that the form of *Balcony of Europe* is its major flaw: "So much fine writing is blurred and even lost in the formlessness of the book. . . . Mr. Higgins has no sense of form" (18). Banville is, however, cautious enough to admit that form is an "elusive quality," citing Joyce's *Ulysses* as the famous precedent. Alternatively, Rüdiger Imhof, comparing Higgins's writing to that of Proust, is clearly impressed: "its curious collage form is not least the result of its fundamental *raison d'être*: a ruminating narratorial consciousness trying to come to grips with the past, one that in the process of recollecting makes use of everything that comes to hand—impressions of people, places, events, biographical detail, Epiphanies; semantic play . . ." (258–59). Imhof proceeds to suggest that the aim of such an approach may be to transcend the Proustian recherché heritage "in the direction of what may be termed a 'total book'" (259). Robin Skelton too claims that there is a cohesive power in *Balcony of Europe* that lends to the novel an intricate unity: "Higgins creates connections and correspondences, a web of echo and allusion which run underneath his novels. They are part of the sensibility of the narrator, whose mind, whose mirroring mind is composed of so many fragments of myth, of poetry, of learning, and of experience; they

are also, however, the mind, the consciousness of the novel itself"
(35). If Skelton's evaluation of Higgins's novel is even relatively accurate, then there is something of rare quality in *Balcony of Europe*. What Skelton names the "consciousness of the novel itself"
suggests that Higgins has achieved what Imhof calls the "total
book," but how well this consciousness adapts to the possible psy-
chosis when imagination blends with reality, or the reality of
memory, is central to the success of Higgins's endeavors.

Higgins claims of the novel, "I wanted to dispense with plot, do
it that way: tenuous associations that would ramify, could be built
upon, would stay in the mind better than the plotted thing—all
lies anyway" (qtd. in Beja 163). So the author, rejecting sequential
plotted narrative for spatial narrative, defined by Vidan as "a composition dominated by the recurrence and juxtaposition of verbal
motifs, operative words, and key themes" (437), refuses chronological order in an attempt to surpass the intrinsic inaccuracy of
that order. From an early age, Dan Ruttle is aware that the remembered past, or reality itself, cannot be an ordered structure:
"the Jesuit fiction of the world's order and essential goodness,
stretching out ahead like the white guide lines. No" (43). Higgins's
fiction strives to a form, but not to an order. One of the hidden epigraphs to *Balcony,* by Edmund Husserl, provides an indication of
intent:

> This world now present to me, and every waking "now" obviously so,
> has its temporal horizon, infinite in both directions, its known and
> unknown, its intimately alive and its unalive past and future. Moving
> freely with the movement of experience which brings what is present
> into my intuitional grasp, I can follow up these connections of the real-
> ity which immediately surrounds me, I can shift my standpoint in
> space and time, look this way and that, turn temporarily forward and
> backwards; I can provide for myself constantly new and more or less
> clear and meaningful perceptions and representations, and images
> more or less clear, in which I make intuitable to myself whatever can
> possibly exist really or supposedly in the steadfast order of space and
> time.
>   In this way, when consciously awake, I find myself at all times, and
> without ever being unable to change this, set in relation to a world
> which, though its constants change, remains one and ever the same.
> (460–61)

Higgins's spatial narrative aims to realize Husserl's state of perception, and Dan's lover, Charlotte Bayless, acts as a focal point for
many of the associations and implications generated in the novel.
That she is an American Jew is central to the spatialization of the
text. Dan, caught up in the throes of his obsession, allows his

imagination to roam freely through history. Within a few lines of initially mentioning her, Dan likens Charlotte to the American gangster Dillinger (because of her childhood nickname, Dilly), refers to her Jewishness, and observes that she has high Slav cheekbones and a Byzantine nose. These flashes of experience coalesce in Charlotte, who "comes from the dark plains of American sexual experience where the bison still roam" (77). Dan, of tired "forty-six Christian Old World years," marvels at Charlotte's "bright twenty-four Jewish New World years" (78). In her, many moments of history meet. Dan's imagination tries to visualize Charlotte's past by dreaming up many scenarios: "She might have ended her days as a Jewess in Auschwitz. As a child holding on to her mother's skirt, an actress from an old silent movie" (289). He proceeds to juxtapose history, the present, and film to form a vibrant image of her. Her character, salvaged from Jewish and Polish heritage, Auschwitz, America, and Spain, becomes for Ruttle a symbol of historical reality itself. In her the past converges, and he imagines that he can witness her as such: "She speaks from the back of the throat, the epiglottis, a complex human being's speech, made up of all her ancestors and past" (78). The narrator conjures up a kind of history by gathering diverse fragments from many areas. He imagines a past life for Charlotte and in doing so creates her: "I dreamed her as she dreamed me . . ." (390). Charlotte exists in the novel only in this way, not as a character in conventional terms. All her movements and dialogue, filtered through Dan's imagining memory, are imbued with associations that generate a kind of superreality throbbing in his consciousness.

The collage of history that emerges in Dan's account of Charlotte resonates in other ways throughout the novel. For example, the figure of Baron von Gerhar, an ex-Nazi with whom Dan drinks on one occasion, powerfully lingers in the fiction as a constant reminder of the atrocities committed against the Jews. Although not a central figure in the narrative, the Baron symbolizes a whole era by his presence. Dan's direct discussion about the Jews, concentration camps, and Hitler and his choice of imagery do much to charge the incident with significance: "fixing me with his red-rimmed killer's eyes, he put it point-blank" (110). All this occurs while U.S. fighter aircraft slice the skies over Andalucia, Ruttle's mind acting as a focal point for past and present. From the aptly named Balcon de Europa bar, Dan's vision emerges. There are numerous other incidents that contain associations that knit the fiction together without availing of temporal sequence or a recognizable arrangement of cause and effect, so much so that many of Higgins's critics are unable to perceive a form to the text. The only real constant in the fiction is Ruttle's mind, which eagerly brings these strands of meaning together, and his mind does not always work in familiar patterns. Imagination, it is implied, generates its own order and has little in common with conventional ordering systems.

Dan's love for Charlotte forms the central plotted impetus of the novel. She initially rejuvenates him, and this is the part of their relationship that matters most: "Being with her, I felt lifted out of my lethargy and sloth, from the banality that encumbered my life; this small bright-faced person had that effect on me" (126). Because of this new enthusiasm, Dan's imagination is freed to re-create her in the context of his dreams and impressions. Through the very process of recollection, however, he realizes she is utterly lost to him: "Two dead actors, a cinema that no longer existed in a narrow street so changed I hardly knew it, as dead and non-existent as my own youth. Non-existent as any touch I ever had with her . . ." (120). In the realm that is Ruttle's mind, the past is transformed into a vague image, directly informed by cinema and dead actors. The past may be reclaimed, recollected, vivified by imagination, but essentially it is nonexistent. It remains like the blurred images on a cinema screen, remote and unreal despite what it might whisper to us in moments of nostalgia or longing. Dan learns that once those images are accepted *as* images, transformations, then one's epistemological grasp of actuality is forever altered. Primarily through Charlotte, Dan responds to this understanding: "She had pale Polish eyes. She is there. She is my opposite, yet part of me. She who appears so permanent, is transitory—a souvenir" (290). The past teaches us that living is transitory as are all the moments that contribute to that life. Dan learns that there are no constants, only impermanent flux. Armed with the lessons of his youth, he realizes even when the affair is being conducted that Charlotte is not a fixed shape: "So she would always escape me, changing shapes, changing clothes as she changed her lovers, changing her style as she changed her admirers . . ." (203). The imaginative power of his account of Spain is powerful, but ironically, late in the text, everything of that time has evaporated: "I thought of the time in Spain: those transient friends which events bring and events take away" (455). The former intimacy of those dissolved days is cast aside by the passing of time, just as with all his past. Life, then, is emphatically shown to be a volatile construct, a narrative mediated through one's imagining consciousness, and as such the spatial narrative constructed by Higgins represents an attempt to achieve an accommodation with the very fluidity that he presents as life.

Life is not an ordered construct for Dan, but a fluid series of beginnings. He finally realizes that his experiences exist only in his

mind, claiming of Charlotte, "You had existed as a part of the semi-
nal substance of the universe that is always becoming and never is:
and now had disappeared into that which produced you" (239). Life,
Dan tells us, must be accepted as such: "There are no fixtures in
nature. The universe is fluid and volatile. Permanence is but a word
of degrees. Our globe seen by God is a transparent law, not a mass
of facts" (352). *Balcony of Europe* registers the essentially chaotic
nature of humanity through its amassing of historical detail and
impending wars, coupled with the account of Dan's failed love and
acute awareness of his own transience; it is ultimately a lament for
what Higgins sees as the unavoidable disintegration of order. However, although a lament, *Balcony of Europe* suggests, in its optimis-
tic moments, that impermanence is not necessarily a destructive
element. If one accepts transience and the true nature of memory,
then our present lives may become bearable or at least comprehen-
sible. During a meditative moment near the close of his account,
Dan considers the folklore of Aran: "Aran, it is said, is the strangest
place on earth. Sometimes for an hour you *are*, the rest is history;
sometimes the two floods culminate in a dream" (446). The present
and the past converge, and the dream born from such a union constitutes life in its fullest sense. The past is knowable only through
our present discourses, and it is from this perpetually shifting vantage point that we inevitably reconstruct our pasts. This is the vision of existence that *Balcony of Europe,* as a textual reconstruction, strives to be.

The complex patterns of association woven into *Balcony of Europe* combine to evoke Higgins's major themes: the transience of living and the chaotic state of human existence. But these very
themes contain intrinsic implications on another level. Patrick
O'Neill suggests that the novel operates on two levels: "it is also,
and overtly, a highly modernist text, a way of presenting that world
and a way of presenting its own discourse" (101). Any account of
past events that raises the problematic issue of memory invariably
challenges the validity of its own writing. Higgins's particular response to memory directly conditions the nature of his fictions. If
the universe is in a state of flux, if life is ephemeral and refuses to
be imprisoned by humans' powers of communication, then the act of
writing must respond accordingly. Not only do events alter in one's
memory, but so too does the mind that remembers. Dan informs us
that "Everything is only for a day, both that which remembers and
that which is remembered" (239). Thus if both the present and the
past are in flux, then how is it possible to transcribe events or
states of feeling? Higgins's fiction insists that it is not possible to
transcribe life: "To seek to paint that which cannot be painted—the

Deity's human form—was considered by the wise Ancients to be human imbecility" (166–67). This is the artistic principle upon which this text is built. Dan's recollections accept, as part of their process, the true nature of memory and in doing so refrain from realist portrayals. His account assumes, as a constituent part of its process, the flux that he believes to be a condition of memory. Therefore, the text must be constructed in a way that implicitly rejects the traditional realist novel. Higgins declares his attitude toward realistic fiction openly in the novel: "The rule of desire for realistic possession: *to hold a great power within a small volume*" (325). The role of realism in fiction is a possessive one, a diminishing of life. *Balcony of Europe* seeks to redress that situation in its formal construction of a fictionalized landscape whose order is, arguably, defined by the ever-shifting actuality of existence that the author sees all about him. Thus the author constructs an image of the world that evades all such attempts to name the world with certainty.

Balcony of Europe registers a connection with the real world, even if not in the same way as realist fiction. The novel attempts to invent a new type of discourse, within which the author can speak of human existence. One of the ways he does so is by rendering the novel self-reflexive. Richard Kearney views the epigraphs to be of major significance in this regard: "they render the novel 'self-reflexive': the epigraphs turn the writing back on itself, they mirror the attempt of the novel itself to write back itself, against time" ("Crisis" 401). The rejected epigraphs are especially significant because, although discarded, they are printed at the rear of the novel and thus form part of the available text. Already quoted is Husserl's visionary epigraph, which mirrors Higgins's formal aim. Here is Kafka's epigraph on the past: "Nothing is granted to me, everything has to be earned, not only the present and the future, but the past too—something after all which perhaps every human being has inherited, this too must be earned, and it is perhaps the hardest work. When the Earth turns to the right—I'm not sure that it does—I would have to turn to the left to make up for the past" (461–62). Kafka's sentiments translate directly into the forging of *Balcony of Europe,* and in its most despairing moments, when Dan grapples with the ghosts of his past in an effort to reclaim them or earn them, Kafka's words ring through. The sentiments that the epigraphs contain, writerly or historical, turn the writing back on itself and render it self-reflexive, and in doing so, Higgins earns his own past; he learns to comprehend the meaning of his past. By foregrounding the textual nature of his account, partly through the use of the epigraphs and partly by dwelling on the epistemological issues of memory, language, and human modes of perception, the author emphasizes that the intellectual comprehension of one's own past must be accompanied by a transfiguration of the events that make up that past.

Balcony of Europe is a composite of many associated elements. It questions communication, history, the transience of living, memory, and the meaning of human perception. Combined with these powerful elements, it questions the process of its own formation. Its own discourse becomes one of the primary subjects of the text itself. This doesn't destabilize the fiction, except perhaps to subtly alter the reader's perspective. There are no overt statements concerning the nature of art in the novel, which remains, as with all of Higgins's work, essentially about life. The nature of the medium simply demands that some response must be made to the problem of memory and what it means. Higgins allows his artistic motivation to unfold within the narrative itself and in doing so creates a novel that addresses the condition of living which is echoed in the formal design of the text. Each aspect complements and reinforces the other, and it is for this reason that *Balcony of Europe* is a truly important novel. It insists on working on two levels, refusing to operate in the highly problematic realm of the mimetic novel and refraining from the excesses of some extreme postmodern novels which deconstruct their universes of dialogue to the point of nihilism. Hence, in *Balcony of Europe* the seemingly intractable epistemological problems that beset postmodern fiction are rendered into suitable material for fiction, rather than being the reason for endless prevarication.

Scenes from a Receding Past

With *Scenes from a Receding Past,* the autobiographical web spins backward in time to the pre-*Balcony of Europe* years, on occasion even to prenatal times. Dan Ruttle is resurrected, as are his parents, siblings, and wife, as is Molly Cushen, with whom Otto Beck has an affair in *Langrishe.* Not only do fiction and autobiography collide, so too do fictional worlds themselves. In *Scenes from a Receding Past* the treatment of the past is similar to that in *Balcony of Europe,* and the author also returns to the big-house genre. In many ways *Scenes from a Receding Past* regroups many of Higgins's previous concerns, particularly memory, and expresses them in another way. The epigraph from Richard Brautigan is a telling foretaste of things to come:

> I do not long for the world as it was when I was a child. I do not long for the person I was in that world. I do not want to be the person I am now in that world then.

I've been examining half-scraps of my childhood. They are pieces of
distant life that have no form or meaning. They are things that just
happened like lint. (10)

In an attempt to understand the nature of transience, Dan attempts to reconstruct his youth by means of spatial narrative, re-
creating images of the past via a selection of ostensibly random vignettes. This reconstruction hinges on generating resonant images,
like the chilling account of his brother Wally in a mental institution, a fate shared by his mother. What emerges through this kind
of arrangement is a profound sense of despair, dissolution, indicat-
ing a deep sense of pathos in the face of human suffering, and,
above all, the gradual drift of time. Later, when Dan meets Olivia,
the reality of his lost youth is clearly expressed in contrast with his
sense of her life: "Her past, obscure enough, had become more real
than my own" (192). However, through his desire to possess his
wife Olivia, he learns the insurmountable difficulties of communicating past events: "From my own imperfect memory, from no notes,
from distractions and places, from my love of her, from her own re-
tellings, emerges this rigmarole: her past that is more real than my
own" (156). Or so it seems, and yet it too is a fabrication synthesized
from all the means he has available to him. Through Olivia, the as-
sumptions of traditional realism are exposed: "That was her past,
part of it, as she told it to me, as I remember it, or what I remember
of it" (167–68). Olivia's past is qualified three times, questioned
three times. Her version is a qualification, as is his memory, as is
the selective nature of his memory. The inability to locate the past
is a cause of grief to Dan, but nevertheless he continues piecing together the hazardous shreds of memory. In doing so, he demonstrates how his attempt to write her biography is essentially a work
of imagination. The veracity of Dan's account is thrown into disar-
ray by his insistence on re-creating exacting landscapes from
Olivia's Past: "That place, your home, I can't imagine it. You lived
there in a house I cannot quite see, walking in an overgrown garden
in the heat" (157). He can't imagine it, yet proceeds to build elaborate scenarios. The implications that such a pursuit have for the reconstruction of his own receding past are clear. From the author's
opening note, which refers to, "those gentle times, those guileless
gossoons, [which] are now consigned to oblivion" (10), the realistic
aims of the narrative are intentionally deflated. Furthermore, the
nature of the narrative itself, first-person present, creates the possibility of unreliability. Does an eleven-year-old boy think in terms
as exotic as those espoused by the child Dan?: "Overhead huge
white clouds are piled up, vasty citadels, white castles loom" (37).
But *Scenes from a Receding Past*, like *Balcony of Europe*, is not a

realist novel, rejecting as it does temporal sequence and causal logic in its attempt to say the past.

For example, when Dan is first absent from his home, Nullamore, he imagines it to be a source of unchanging order: "I miss Nullamore. I think: The place that never changes" (107). However, as with much else in the text, time dismantles the cosy certainties of his home: "It's vacation. Nullamore seems to have shrunk" (107). Dan's education begins here. That first certainty, familial security, fades, or rather Dan's imagining mind dreams Nullamore into a kind of superreality that the actuality cannot match. His desire for certainty is frequently evident in the text, as is his dismay when he cannot achieve it. Discovering a fixed reality in a photograph, in the midst of change, he is astonished: "Nothing can change or disturb her. She is perfect, naked and coolly regarding me. Her expression does not change. She watches me" (77). This much-cherished certainty is not to be found in reality, but the desire for order finds its mirror image in an awareness of chaos. By the conclusion of the novel, acute awareness of disorder has forced Dan to an accommodation with impermanence:

> Hold onto nothing; nothing lasts.
> Long ago I was this, was that, twisting and turning, incredulous, baffled, believing nothing, believing all. Now I am, what? I feel frightened, sometimes, but may be just tired. I feel depressed quite often, but may just be hungry.
> All but blind
> In his chambered hole
> Gropes for worms . . . (204)

The closing image of a blind mole groping for worms suggests that Higgins's accommodation is far from joyous, and the bleakness of his vision is clear. The author burrows deep into the past in an effort to comprehend his life and in doing so confronts the opaque reality of memory. All but blind, he understands the volatility of life and records it as such.

Higgins's major themes of transience, memory, and decay emerge once again, although *Scenes from a Receding Past* responds to the issues of memory and transience in a more direct way than its predecessors, because it is less restrained by their concessions to form, however innovative. Fundamentally, *Scenes from a Receding Past* is a fictionalized autobiography that foregrounds and formally illustrates the essential problems associated with reconstructing the past. In formal terms it is less strictly literary than *Balcony of Europe* or *Langrishe, Go Down* in that the author seems less concerned with interweaving binding associations and images. Higgins presents much incidental detail, including lists of boarding-school requirements, cricket scores, and much particularized geographical data. The only binding force is the narrator himself and the images that emerge in the telling, like Proustian madeleines. George O'Brien also comments on these qualities in the novel:

> All that Higgins unrhetorically intends to claim, it seems, is that certain materials insist on presenting themselves—memories, vignettes, moments, quotations, gossip, arcana, rage, pleasure, boredom, love. . . . Higgins seems to say there is only the world, the other; the writer, clerk-like (attentive rather than subservient), takes—rather than raises—its stock. He proceeds in the direction of that nakedness which is more familiarly the painter's objective. Simplicity and directness unveils while leaving intact. . . . (90–91)

The author allows the randomness of reality to reveal itself. Much is omitted from what might constitute a life story. Thus the form of the novel depends on the interrelation of the moments presented. The threads of association are not strong, and beyond Ruttle's selective consciousness, there is little in the way of unity—there are only "Impressions" which "offer themselves, focus, slip away" (200). Is this sufficient to bind a work of art? In a rare moment of overt self-reflexive advice, the narrator reveals himself: "Do as I tell you and you will find out my shape. There are no pure substances in nature. Each is contained in each" (200). The essential unity in nature, he implies, is the source of his shape. The artist who allows landscapes to reveal themselves, rather than attempt to interrogate their meaning, lets the chaos of the past life and the universe seep into the fiction. Freeing itself from the formal restraints of the novel genre, *Scenes from a Receding Past* aims to be just what its title suggests, scenes, and not a life bound together by illusory sequential narrative or the imposition of synthetic structures in search of order. In *Scenes from a Receding Past* Higgins begins to remove the frame from his pictures, a precarious activity, considering the essentially formal nature of fiction writing. He clearly attempts, in *Scenes,* an escape from the novelists' guild, from the technical strategies with which the world is transformed. It is of little surprise, therefore, that Higgins takes an even greater technical risk with the novel that immediately follows and writes an epistolary novel, hardly the genre of choice among late-twentieth-century novelists.

Bornholm Night-Ferry

In *Bornholm Night-Ferry* love is again the central focus from which all else emanates. Elin, a Danish poet, and Fitzy, an Irish novelist, conduct an illicit five-year relationship (though they spend a total of just forty-seven days together) primarily through the medium of love letters, resulting in a highly charged linguistic universe in which the conditions of memory and language are consistently interrogated. The epistolary novel depicts both narrators roaming freely across almost limitless imaginative landscapes, declaring love, jealousy, rejuvenated love, interest, hatred, and ultimately rejection.

To suggest that Higgins turns the same literary sod each time is not altogether untrue, but his understanding of his piece of soil is more refined with each new visitation, and he continually experiments with new forms to house his concerns. In a fiction comprising sixty-five letters and a few short diary pieces, the issues of language, imagination, and remembrance form one sustained dismissal of traditional narrative and attempt to formulate a unique way of focusing on the world. *Bornholm Night-Ferry* is a highly self-reflexive fiction, because it directly informs us of the process of its creation, and what more forceful means are there than letters between lovers/writers who struggle to keep their love, an almost exclusively linguistic one, alive?

The love letters essentially map the progression of Elin's and Fitzy's responses to memory and language. Elin distinguishes between the words she uses and the actuality of their time together: "Not forgotten in words but in action. The sensual memory of you is going to disappear, replaced by reflections" (17). She knows that outside of the actuality, of her fading sensual memory, there are but "'figments of the imagination,' monologues" (18). Thus the epistolary love affair is conducted solely in their respective imaginative reactions to both memory and language. Furthermore, because they speak different languages, they grapple with each other's tongues in an effort to create a love-language. Initially, Elin responds to the barriers between them by gleefully pursuing her imaginative explorations: "We don't know each other, no. We exited to a high degree each others' dreams. We don't know each other, we are dreaming. Everything depends on if we are clever enough to dream. And believe in our dreams. And realize our dreams so fervently we are able to" (21). She plunges into a landscape of dreams wherein the constraints of time, language, and geography are diminished, but retained. Any other reaction is doomed to failure. However, the dreaming proves to be unsustainable because the actuality of their relationship must be registered. Elin pleads with Fitzy to confront this: "Please, my beloved let us save our dream by naming the reality, let us say awfull [sic] things so the rest can be true. The ghosts grow and grow when you never face them" (92). Fitzy responds to this plea by refusing to accept a distinction between the dreams and

reality: "As to dream (perhaps the only word we cannot put quotation marks around) and 'reality,' whatever that may be, well they
are for me one and the same" (93). The lines of communication for
him provide only a dream reality. "Doesn't a child," Fitzy asks,
"who knows nothing, invent the whole world?" (94). It is questionable whether Fitzy's vision of reality constitutes a separation of
imagination and reason in favor of imagination or is a true marriage of both. The reality principle, however, must remain a constituent part of the imagination and vice versa in order for coherent dialogue to exist. Ultimately, Fitzy falters: "It has been going
on for some time. I am dreaming it, or it is dreaming me, for some
time, particulars forgotten" (174). Reality dissolves, the pure
dream remains, and dialogue between the lovers ultimately ends,
or at least the struggle to articulate the actuality of their affair
ends. Fitzy falls silent and Elin is consigned to some out-of-reach,
extralinguistic universe.

Elin refuses to dissolve her reality principle into pure imagination except in moments of extreme longing. She never loses sight of
the rational, allowing herself to dream while constantly reminding
herself that she is dreaming. She warns him, "I tell you Fitzy, I
imagine you so you would die from it if you were here" (68). Her vision of him is excessive, but she knows that the actuality cannot
compare to it, cannot hope to compare to it. This distinction pre-
vails in Elin's letters, and her lack of sensual experience leads to
her estrangement. The "unreal correspondence" (146) cannot satisfy her as it can Fitzy. She learns to see the difference between
them from this perspective: "You never divide hope from reality,
and you are not a happy person. I always divide hope from reality
(try to) and am not a happy being. You refuse to see reality and I am
hoping wrong hopes. This goes on: Wrong moves, failured [sic] gestures. Will it ever change?" (153). Conducted in a linguistic medium, their love cannot survive the rigors of two opposing visions.
Being separated, writing in a love-language and imagining each
other, they need hope. However, for Fitzy, hope, imagination, and
reality all converge and express themselves in a linguistic dream
world. Elin's last letter doesn't even conclude the relationship,
meaning has long since been lost in a sea of imagination and language, and finality is a forgotten concept.

The alternate poles that Elin and Fitzy come to represent correspond to the self-reflexive discourse of the novel itself. Conveniently,
the two narrators comment on each other's letters, and the novel itself becomes a commentary on the nature of fiction and the imaginative process. Initially, one experiences, with all the attendant
difficulties, then remembers, and then transforms. The two lovers

lose sensual memory and conjure up many desperate methods to regain it: "If I cannot have you all in one piece, mail me bits of you. *Du*" (73). Such ploys are little more than futile love games. Soon they grow to rely on memory with all its consequent vagaries and imaginings. Inherent in this is the suggestion that any attempt to apprehend life linguistically must conform to these principles. It is what one does with such knowledge, within a problematic linguistic structure, that is central to *Bornholm Night-Ferry*.

Bornholm Night-Ferry is one of Higgins's most overtly self-reflexive novels because it directly confronts its own medium and in doing so interrogates the meaning of memory and the limitations of language. Furthermore, it openly exposes the hazardous transformative process that is art. Elin and Fitzy create fictions forged from their imperfect memories, their language, and their different responses to these things. The presumption of a fixed reality vanishes in the creation of the letters. Elin registers the inadequacy of the reality principle in one of her letters: "Your memories of us are too full of 'unreliableness' but mostly more true than the reality" (65). Reality is expressed as a collage of moving surfaces rather than a static, empirically attainable actuality. The actual expression of this fact is the transformative agent. Thus reality is raised to the level of Fitzy's and Elin's imaginings via memory and language. In this way *Bornholm Night-Ferry* comments on its own formation and its own relationship to Higgins's "reality."

Despite his obvious acceptance of the artificial nature of man's linguistic medium, the author also acknowledges that a breakdown in dialogue is directly related to overreliance on imagination. The affair falters and dies because the "real," the sensual, is forsaken and replaced by a world comprising language, memory, and imagination. Humanity cannot survive in such a nonsensual ontology. *Bornholm Night-Ferry* accepts that human communication is at best problematic because there are many chasms which render communication hazardous: between word and thing, memory and actuality, thought and gesture. The linguistic lovers interrogate these chasms, but the gaps prove too great and communication ultimately falters. Communication is always difficult, perhaps even impossible, in absolute terms, but if the true nature of the web of human dialogue is comprehended then perhaps communication can evolve. For this reason, Higgins's self-reflexive epistolary novel is valuable. Life, it is implied, is a fiction that must be interpreted (or imagined) in conjunction with one's sensual experience and not a mass of exactitudes that we can simply name with synthetic modes of expression. The epistolary novel form allows Higgins to confront the primacy of experience without the formal constructs of linear narrative and narrated characterization. Elin and Fitzy instead emerge via their respective collages of recollection and expressions of love and loss, allowing the author to generate fictional ontologies that are limited by language, but not by time and space. In keeping with the technical achievements of *Bornholm Night-Ferry, Lions of the Grunewald,* Higgins's first full-length fiction in a decade, provides yet more evidence of the author's aim to develop an aesthetic shape that might accommodate the complexity of living.

Lions of the Grunewald

Lions of the Grunewald is situated on mainland Europe and peopled by Dallan Weaver, drunken writer, and his wife Nancy. Like *Balcony of Europe*'s Dan Ruttle, Weaver conducts a dramatic extramarital affair that acts as the primary narrative movement in the novel. Weaver and Nancy live in Berlin at the expense of DILDO *(Deutsche Internationale Literatur Dienst Organisation)* and mingle with persons real and imaginary, including Peter Handke, Max Frisch, Sir Kenneth Clarke, and a host of others. Beckett gets a mention (and an unanswered telephone call), as do Jack Lynch and Günter Grass, while Weaver drunkenly cavorts through Berlin days and nights, mostly oblivious, occasionally intensely sensitive, a potent recipe for disaster and heartache.

Lions raises some questions concerning Higgins's Berlin, where the author lived for a while. Is his besotted and bibulous hero a caustic self-portrait? Did the riot of events, situated circa 1968, really happen? It seems likely, but in the end it doesn't really matter. With Higgins there really is very little difference between the "Instant fictionalisation" technique that he reputedly used in the writing of *Balcony of Europe* (Share 162) and the "reality." The actuality of experience always lingers in his work, the only question being how he orders that experience. Within Higgins's ordering structure in *Lions,* the love triangle traced out among Weaver, Nancy, and his lover Lore is initially treated with much irreverence, but gradually, as the sequential plot dissolves, the author's voice surfaces to reveal Higgins's familiar themes: love and its transience, the pain of the past, and ultimately, how one apprehends and lives with such strangeness.

Higgins's epigraphs to *Lions* are indicative of his intent. The first, taken from John Cheever's *Journals,* tells of when the lions escaped from the zoo during the last days of the war. Not only does this indicate the relevance of the zoo imagery prevalent throughout, but it also tells of nightmarish days of a "world that has outstripped our nightmares,/our subconscious" (xiii), the kind of days that the novel maps. A sense of desolation pervades all, extending even to the frantic coupling of two homosexual lovers in subzero snow, prior to one of them leaping into the uninviting, freezing Spree River. Alice Munro's epigraph, from *The Progress of Love,* speaks of the obvious wrenches and slashing that accompany the parting of lovers, and this predicts the marital chaos about to ensue. The final epigraph, taken from Nabokov's *Speak, Memory,* Nabokov himself a habitual frequenter of Berlin, is especially telling: "In the evening there, in little *cul de / sacs,* the soul seems to dissolve" (xiii). Higgins's Weaver, the dominant character in *Lions,* does indeed seem to dissolve when confronted with the impasse of naming the life he has lived. Berlin, fittingly, becomes a ghostly presence in his, and the narrator's, consciousness, until ultimately, Weaver effectively merges with Higgins's own voice or that of a narratorial substitute. The dissolution is intensified by a disintegration of the linear narrative into a rush of half-memories, dreams, and random observations. At the core of this life is Lore, with her teasing name and symbolic role as metaphorical expression of love.

In this, Higgins's most complete fiction, love is an essential ingredient, not just for its thematic attractions, but for the associations it generates. It is the sense of impermanence that is dominant, rather than any sentimental cry from the heart of lost love. However, Weaver's painful awareness of transience is coaxed to a heightened peak because it is love that is lost, not just life. Love itself, with its frightful joys and acute pains, is presented as the central image of loss within which the author allows his other themes to take root. This is not to suggest that Lore is merely a functional image within which the author bemoans the loss of the past. Rather, love is presented as a way of seeing, so valuable and sacred that its loss is all the greater. Weaver, rephrasing Proust, claims that "love is time and space the heart can catch . . ." (198). Love is a state from which one can witness existence outside of the mad swirl of life. Time spent with Lore is, for Weaver, like "a morning outside of Time" (196). As an extended epiphany, love becomes a means of comprehension, of consolation, a kind of imaginative intensity which allows him to redeem life from that state of ineffable confusion within which he is frequently lost.

Late in the novel, everything radiates from Weaver's, or by now Higgins's (the distinction grows increasingly unclear), memory of love, even the geography of Berlin: "The other day I was thinking of you; or rather of *Nullgrab,* that quartered city you love so much, which amounts to the same thing. When I recall *Nullgrab* I remember you, or vice versa. Go quietly, the ghosts are listening" (274). A part of the past cannot simply be recalled, unimpeded by the vastness of all else connected to it. It is saturated with people, none more pervasive than old lovers who, inevitably, are impossible to rescue from the past, a point not lost on Weaver: "Is it even possible to think of somebody in the past? Are the memories of things better than the things themselves? Chateaubriand seemed to think so; and now he too belongs to that past" (274). The past is Weaver's primary difficulty, yet he ultimately accepts its foibles with a kind of grace that comes only with an intimate understanding of its mesmerising transience. The only pain he expresses is in gentle moments of sadness at the loss of Lore, whom he places at the nucleus of all that is gone. Metaphorically, she finds powerful expression as the power of art, replete with its imaginative associations. Weaver somehow retains the essence of her in his poetic imagination, despite the onslaught of time: "I say things but I may mean times. I say things and times but I may mean persons and places, or may be just thinking of you. Your name at the end of the world" (274). Love, for Higgins, is the key to the past, possibly the only one. It doesn't gain power over the unassailable power of the past, but it does make it more manageable, more visible. Your *name* "at the end of the world," he tellingly writes. None of Higgins's best fiction functions without the presence of love and its complicated rituals, its communicative problems, its instability, beauty, and transience. A tragic note of lost love rings through, both as a lament for the loss of such a wonderful state and also as a celebration of that state, that way of seeing which, in its finest moments, releases the imagination from the burden of reason.

The sexual act is one of Weaver's overriding fascinations. Everyone, it seems, is coupling with someone. So insistent are Weaver's tales of sex, one feels the act itself emerges to symbolize Berlin in the author's imagination. Like a latter-day Sodom or Gomorrah (without moral overtones), Berlin's sexual permissiveness is presented as a frantic survival urge that, for Weaver and Lore, ultimately yields no child (Lore has an abortion). Furthermore, their frantic lovemaking grows steadily more frenetic as their parting becomes imminent. It clearly doesn't need the retrospective eye to confirm the passing of an extraordinary love. Weaver, because he recognizes the visionary nature of being in love with her, likens their separation to death: "So they sat together on the top step in the gloaming and sipped vodka and tasted the ice and fire and no doubt entertained (if that is the word) some considerations of those Final Things that must in time come to us all, to be recorded with all the ones who had gone before, all set down in the Great Book of Numbers" (235). He strikes up a connection between death and the passing of love, because love makes death remote and the passing of love is a chilling reminder of how quickly and mercilessly one hurtles to that final moment. "[L]ove is time and space the heart can catch . . ." (198), Weaver tells us, but inherent in such a state is the reality of its transience and thus the tragic nature of the consciousness, which seems so dependent on love as a way of seeing. None of Higgins's love "stories" end in joy, and it is the sense of tragedy that this failure lends to the works that helps to create the profound sense of impermanence at the center of all his work. But these are no simple, tragic love stories. Lions tells not just of the passing of Weaver's one true love (his great love for Lore happens to coincide with the demise of his once great love for his wife, Nancy!). For Weaver, it is the sense of life that love affords him that is so valuable: "It was another language of another world; you took me there. I couldn't follow you; but I followed you" (276). Love is a way of defeating the undefeatable, a way of arresting time, of intimately knowing a place and finally knowing how to rediscover the gleam of one's past life. For Weaver the key to existence is love, Higgins's potent, enduring symbol for the imagined life, the poetic memory.

Love is the most powerful image in Higgins's Lions. It not only binds the narrative, but it acts as the focal point through which everything else radiates. Weaver doesn't simply inform us that love is a way of seeing, of apprehending, he allows us to sneak a glimpse at the world that he apprehends. In a sense, here the problems begin. Lions differs from its immediate predecessors because the narrator's overt concerns on the opening page are similar to those at the end. In short, there is a coherent plot that doesn't entirely disappear along the way. There are moments, of course, when Higgins's narrator digresses to trawl through Berlin's troubled history and places various historical events beside the microcosm of Weaver's own troubled life. The effect is dizzying and sometimes hazardous to the cohesion of the novel. However, within the philosophical framework of this particular text, this process justifies itself. Higgins expresses his understanding of history very clearly in one phrase that acts as a refrain in the novel: "All days are different; all days are the same" (175). Repeated several times, it emphatically communicates Higgins's perspective. Life, history, one's being—these things don't change, only the way we see them changes. Life is recurrent, events are basically the same, but the mind that apprehends can change, and thus everything changes.

In a sense, the plotted events that comprise Lions are secondary and yet deeply integrated with the most important and striking aspect of the novel, how the tale is told. Everything that happens is directed by the feasibility of Higgins's narrative form. Love, the most powerful image in the text, is likened to a way of seeing, a way of imaginative apprehension. Furthermore, the pastness of the tale means that the narrator must somehow create structures through which the past can be communicated. Like Joyce, Higgins crams his tale with topographical detail, allusions, historical references, and real people, but unlike Eliot's or Joyce's high modernist work, *Lions* does not possess a mythic order as the author struggles to allow chaos to define the form of the text.

Higgins uses many different techniques to articulate the mess of experience, which must be forced into coherent form and simultaneously evade such coherence. Initially, the narrator toys with overt self-reflexive play by using theatrical stage directions: "Quick curtain here to indicate the Passage of Time" (116). Such devices are more playful than disruptive. More technically familiar is the way that Nancy's character is constructed. As in *Balcony of Europe,* Nancy's character is partly revealed by certain key phrases that she repeatedly uses. This type of characterization results not in any meaningful revelation, but contributes to Higgins's wraithlike two-dimensional characters. It is as though the narrator does not trust himself with any more expansive description.

Weaver is the only character who is fully realized in the novel. He is frequently liberated from chronological sequence when his imagination roams from Berlin to Russia (where he's never been) and to Dover and Hamburg. Anecdotes tumble forth from his imagination, suggestive of a life he shared with Nancy. Sequential narration is abandoned as insufficient, and the result, although disturbing, is a relatively intelligible passage through Weaver's troubled consciousness. As the novel progresses, this becomes increasingly erratic, and the third-person past tense, sequential narrative of part 1 grows more reliant on alternative methods to reveal the meaning of the past and, by implication, life itself. Although the plot is initially subverted by self-reflexive comments ("The truncated metropolis hereinafter designated *Nullgrab* is of course very much our own invention and figures and descriptions may be more aromatic than exact. An odour of pines pervades all" (12)), the basic sequential narrative remains intact until near the end of part 1, when the narrator presents fragmentary dreams by both Nancy and Lore as a chapter. Another chapter follows, which relates a tale about the Berlin poet Gottfried Benn, with little obvious connection to the plot. Part 2 develops into an increasingly anecdotal account and offers little in the way of significance to plot. The binding consciousness, Weaver, loses what few reservations he has, both in terms of his extramarital affair and his digressive consciousness. Part 3 confirms the radical disintegration of the sparse sequential narrative that existed at the beginning. Lore's and Weaver's relationship falters and they separate. This is the time of the Munich Olympic slaughter, and when Weaver's wandering mind tires of Munich, he recalls a trip to South Africa. The plot remains, but is no longer the dominant ontological base, the digressions now forming the authoritative center of the imaginative world.

The final stages of the novel reveal Weaver's consciousness via his reminiscences, especially of his relationship with Lore, in the collage chapter of past moments, "The Other Day I Was Thinking of You." Furthermore, the distinction between narrator and author dissolves, to be replaced by a series of letters and a short account of an imagined meeting between Günter Grass and Max Frisch. Finally, the voice that remains has not resolved the meaning of his past life—acceptance perhaps, but this doesn't necessarily anaesthetize the knowledge that much of that life has evaporated. Nearing the end of this patchwork of memory, history, comedy, and above all imaginative apprehension, the disconnected voice asks, "Of all that remains, what residue is there, I ask you, trapped in vertiginous Time?" (301). Nothing remains except the author's telling exhortation: "Stir it up" (301). Just as he has done.

Higgins's sobering perspectives on time are supplemented by his commentary on dreams, offering a valuable insight to the novel: "In dreams there is no time, no ages; just a seamless, tireless state of the sleeper's drifting fears. It had been a time of dire portents in Jo'burg. . . . To remember it or have it evoked in a nightmare was to make that heart bleed again . . ." (258). He instinctively likens memory to the dream state, and his narrative structure clearly aspires to such a structure. With *Lions,* Higgins has finally found a narrative structure that will accommodate his vision of existence. Form and content rest easily together. The widely held desire for an ordered life, he suggests, is less important than the evoked memory, the dream state, and since memory, like dreams, operates in an unsystematic way, so too must his fictions.

Much of Higgins's energy is directed at creating powerful images, almost visual in their bright intensity, and these images seek to compensate for his abandonment of sequential narrative form. Dermot Healy recognizes this aspect in Higgins's writing: "The key to Higgins is the *image*—for him storytelling stopped there—If you told what was there visually the story would inevitably follow" ("Travel Guide" B10). This accounts for the narrator's reluctance to flesh out authentic characters. We are thrown a few morsels, probably "real," a few resonant phrases, and a kind of life must emanate from there. The surface must somehow radiate meaning, as it must

in life. There are no cheap symbolic frameworks or rigid characterization in Higgins's *Lions,* because such things belong to the inven-
tions of artistic form and not to life. The challenge, of course, is to
allow the fiction to accommodate life.

Life is presented as a swirling mess of complexity, tenuously ordered only by the mind that perceives. And, of course, the order
that Weaver's mind conjures up is itself a fiction, a vision of life
that insists on remaining aloof. When Nancy, once an object of love
and the mother of his child, can be expressed primarily by external
utterances, how, then, can one ever know one's own life? Added to
this is the author's retrospective telling, which complicates everything even more. As Aidan Matthews has succinctly put it: "So the
fable becomes a fiction about fictions, about the fantasies of 30
years ago" (B12).

Since *Langrishe, Go Down,* Higgins's achievement is uneven. Although his works don't deserve the lack of critical attention they
receive, *Langrishe, Balcony,* and *Bornholm* are, prior to *Lions,* his
most complete works because, while operating within the novel
form, the author has managed to confront the major dilemmas of
the twentieth-century novelist. Higgins's works are never comfort-
able fictions; they never seek to ingratiate themselves with a public
that demands the luxury of recognizable conventions. Higgins is
clearly aware that all the mind apprehends is a fiction, and he has
perpetually striven to articulate that knowledge in the way all
great writers express their ideas, through stories. That his fictional
journey has frequently drifted into autobiography is indicative of
his aesthetic conceptions of art and life. *Lions of the Grunewald*
adopts a poetic suggestion that life and art share much more than
one might assume. Art is not simply a transformation of "reality,"
because, for Higgins, life is already story, lacking the complex ordering strategies of art, but story nonetheless. Higgins's life has
been used as material for his art before, but in *Lions* his life isn't
simply availed of as material for fiction, it is that fiction. It is apparent that the author believes that the life he led all those years
ago in Berlin was as much a dream at the time as it is now. People
and places merge with memory or Higgins's poetic imagination to
suggest a story rather than to tell it *as it was,* itself a great literary
fraud. The life described is itself as near to a "story" as a life can get
with its endless complexity and contradictions, all of which evade
order. The telling of events from one's life amounts to an act of possession. Unfortunately, in the act of possession life is transformed
by the conventions of art. Higgins tries desperately to avoid this
wilful possession. In losing a coherent narrative of his own life, he
paradoxically claims it.

Autobiographies

Although this essay is mainly a consideration of Higgins's fiction, the nature of his frequent conflation of fiction and autobiography demands that his trilogy of autobiographies is offered some brief consideration, because, as he says, "stories . . . make up my life and lend it whatever veracity and purpose it may have" (*Donkey's Years* 3). In his trilogy of autobiographies, *Donkey's Years, Dog Days,* and *The Whole Hog,* Higgins effectively abandons the transformative conventions of the fictive mode and writes what Dermot Healy calls "a straight narrative" account of the first half of his life ("*Donkey's*" 46). Because Higgins has always blurred generic differences between the novel and autobiography, he knows, of course, that there are technical differences between the masking process of autobiographical fiction and his autobiography, in which certain events "have become my own stories again" (*Donkey's Years* 324). However, the author's subtitle to *Donkey's Years* reveals his continued unwillingness to render that difference absolute: *Memories of a Life as Story Told.* This implies much, as does his description of *Donkey's Years:* "this bogus autobiography, bogus as all honest autobiographies must be" (*Donkey's Years* 325). In fact, Higgins, having reclaimed his "own stories," seems gleefully unwilling to allow them conventional autobiographical status, embedding, as he frequently does, slyly subversive comments throughout the trilogy, as in *Dog Days:* "Reality is concretness rotating towards illusion, or vice versa, arsyversy; illusion rotating towards concreteness" (202). Again, of course, it is not as simple as a rejection of the possibility of representation. For Higgins, the story must be told, but as precisely that, a story. And it is all about stories: local folklore, private yarns that act as belief systems, rumors, "the greatest of all whores" (*Donkey's Years* 325), and how people are sustained throughout their lives not by accurate and true versions of reality, but by conceptions of themselves, stories of themselves. People live in narrative, play out their public and private conceptions of themselves in various narrative models. For example, the Bowsy Murray, local hero, is here described by Higgins with irony and humor: "The act of throwing a stumpy-booted and gaitered leg athwart the low saddle was a grave gesture both ceremonial and heraldic, man and machine (wrapped in symbolic flame, suggesting Mercury) emblazoned on some obscure escutcheon invoking Subordinacy, Humility, Obeisance, Homage, Destiny, *Victualler!*" (*Donkey's Years* 47). The world and its inhabitants come to us as creatures who live by their own conceptions of themselves, often informed by ready-made models, like the heroic Bowsy, and

Higgins's ever-discerning eye witnesses a kind of prolonged story in the process of unfolding. It is his job to communicate a sense of the grand charade. And he does so with tenderness and sympathy.

Much of the material in the trilogy is familiar to readers of Higgins's fiction, though certainly not the same. The autobiographies sometimes elaborate on or explain incidents in the fictions, offer fresh nuances, and add further "real" detail. Higgins's youth, in various stages, throughout all three volumes, generates many connections with the early fictions, while *The Whole Hog* clarifies some of the events in *Bornholm Night-Ferry* and *Balcony of Europe*. Much of this is interesting to Higgins's readers, but doesn't really explain the curious power of the texts. The final volume in particular is immensely powerful, partly due to the delightful variety of writing styles, formal arrangements of material, and darkly comic undertow. *The Whole Hog* is a composite of intimate letters, lists, anecdotes, diary entries, imagined reconstructions ("Borges and I"), farewells to departed friends, inscriptions on cemetery headstones, observations on Karen Blixen and Djuna Barnes, among others, and a variety of curious takes on history. That the author manages to retain intelligibility is testament to his enormous gifts as a storyteller.

The curious texture of these most unconventional of autobiographies reminds one yet again of Higgins's uncompromising writing. Consumed by memories, Higgins has sought to offer up a powerful sustained gaze at the life of Rory, as he calls himself in the trilogy. Predictable in his insistence of writing it as he understands it, sees it, the autobiographies are no mere accompaniment to the fictions, no simple gesture of clarification. Instead, the trilogy, autobiographical in name, paradoxically convinces one of Higgins's masterful narrative craft and reminds one of his recurring insistence that life is already a fiction as one lives it. The implications for the genre of autobiography are clear.

Passing, as it does, through various developmental phases, Higgins's work inevitably challenges simplistic categorization. In *Langrishe* and *Felo De Se* he bears witness not simply to Irish history and his own experiences, but to the demise of a culture in Europe, informed as much by the world wars as by the decline of the Ascendancy in Ireland. It is all connected for Higgins. In addition, his writing has always responded to modernist epistemological problems, especially those of memory, language, and perception. No doubt he learned valuable lessons from the modernist identification of language with experience and has perpetually sought to locate a fictional medium to frame his vision. However, in his quest to discover a framing narrative, the author has sought to avoid the mythic structuring devices preferred by modernism and rarely uses archetypal framing stories in his work. He has also generally refrained from highly stylized linguistic constructions like the dramatic interior monologues of Joyce or the informing symbolism of Woolf. There is, of course, a cost when one seeks to dispense with recognizable narrative order. Gradually, his work has blurred the generic differences between the novel, autobiography, and travel writing to the extent that it challenges the view that narrative points of recognition are necessary for the preservation of human discourse.

Ultimately, Higgins's work suggests that one can write about one's experiences without freezing them in some fixed order. The human reception of experience is an intensely complex phenomenon, and literature must confront that fact. Reacting against Joyce's stylized example of *Ulysses,* Higgins is certainly influenced by Beckett's desire to accommodate the fragmentary nature of life, but again, Beckett's example is only partially accepted. Where the world is an apocalyptic memory to many of Beckett's heroes, Higgins's characters are always situated in recognizable social landscapes. His characters and plots almost always have corresponding "real" referents, while those of his illustrious predecessor don't.

However, Higgins's work does display some of the technical characteristics of postmodern fiction. His epigraphs, allusions, overt epistemological questioning, and direct addressing of writerly matters are all self-reflexive acts. The flaunting of artifice gradually increases in Higgins's work until in *Lions* the text draws attention to its own textual nature to such an extent that reality ostensibly becomes a product of the artistic mind, and while this represents Higgins's primary fascination, it is also the source of the doubts about his final worth as an artist.

Admired by writers as varied as Beckett, Dermot Healy, Annie Proulx, John Banville, Harold Pinter, Nuala Ni Dhomhnaill, and Thomas McGonigle, Higgins is also the winner of the James Tait Black Memorial prize (*Langrishe, Go Down*), the Berlin Residential Scholarship, the American-Irish Foundation Award, and the Irish Academy award, and he was short-listed for the Booker prize (*Balcony of Europe*), as well as being a member of *Aosdána* and a recipient of grants and bursaries from the Irish and British Arts Councils, all of which suggests a career that has been offered due recognition. Unfortunately, Higgins remains something of a peripheral figure in the literary world, or as Annie Proulx has observed, "Some pair him gingerly with Joyce and Beckett, some accuse him of not having yet

written the Total Book, or of untidy endings, of density and melan-
choly, of abrupt stops and over-portrayal of frustration and *accidie"*
(7). Higgins's uncompromising artistic adventures partly account
for such floundering neglect, because while book reviewers frequently cannot but acknowledge the extraordinary beauty of his
prose, many appear simultaneously puzzled by the abrupt shifts in
time and space and the perpetual retreat from linear narrative. In
addition, his reputation in Ireland has not been helped by the frequent abandonment of Irish landscapes, and it is unsurprising that
Langrishe, with its deeply Irish landscapes, remains his best-
known novel in Ireland, despite him having penned a dozen books
since then. Even the grand master, Joyce, planted his experiments
in an Irish setting.

In Higgins's writing human experience is already a fiction in the
living (and remembering) of it. He does not, finally, differentiate between life and fiction, because life, once apprehended, is already a
fiction. The question is how to communicate that apprehension. In
refusing to avail of recognizable literary conventions in communicating his vision, Higgins effectively breaks the coded agreement
between reader and writer, and in doing so, he erases many points
of recognition necessary for the reader. In this, Higgins has always
been uncompromising, illustrated by his chosen artistic direction
after the commercially successful, and relatively accessible,
Langrishe, Go Down. Above all, *Langrishe* proves that Higgins is,
and has always been, more than capable of erecting formal structures. More important to the author is the need to construct a form
that will accommodate his conception of a life that is characterized
by fragmentation, transience, and unpredictability as much as it is
by moments of illumination, love, and the residual effect of the past
on people's lives. Traditional narrative forms generate too much order to accommodate such a vision, and modernist artistic order essentially replaces one system for another. Thus Higgins risks inco-
herence in his writing in order to speak of a fragmentary life.
Ultimately, his success depends on one's conception of the purpose
of art. Does art impose ordered structures upon human experience,
metaphorical, social, or otherwise, as acts of consolation in the face
of disorder? The very essence of narratology implicitly suggests
this. If Higgins, like Beckett in this, refuses to construct consolatory narratives in the face of uncertainty, does it mean he has failed
as an artist? I think not. In his effort to articulate what he sees as
the essence of human life in narrative form, he does what all important writers have done: he finds a form that is appropriate to his
vision. To berate Higgins's work for refusing a transformative ordering system neglects to value his efforts to strike up an honest and

meaningful dialogue with his experiences, surely the mark of all important writing of integrity. The success of his formal arrangement of his material is dependent on the author's vision, and surely the act of reading is not simply an act of recognition—it is also an act of exploration during which we discover rather than simply recognize. Ultimately, this is the challenge that Higgins has offered us, a challenge to which, I suspect, many more readers will eventually rise.

Works Cited

Baneham, Sam. "Aidan Higgins: A Political Dimension." *Review of Contemporary Fiction* 3.1 (1983): 168–74.

Banville, John. "Colony of Expatriates." *Hibernia* 6 Oct. 1972: 18.

Beja, Morris. "Felons of Our Selves: The Fiction of Aidan Higgins." *Irish University Review* 3.2 (1973): 163–78.

Deane, Seamus. "The Literary Myths of the Revival: A Case for Their Abandonment." *Myth and Reality in Irish Literature*. Ed. Joseph Ronsley. Waterloo, Canada: Wilfred Laurier UP, 1977. 317–29.

Frank, Joseph. "Spatial Form in Modern Literature." *Essentials of the Theory of Fiction*. Ed. Michael J. Hoffman and Patrick Murphy. Duke: Duke UP, 1995. 85–100.

Garfitt, Roger. "Constants in Contemporary Irish Fiction." *Two Decades of Irish Writing—A Critical Study*. Cheshire: Carcanet, 1975. 207–41.

Healy, Dermot. "*Donkey's Years*: A Review." *Asylum Arts Review* 1.1 (1995): 45–46.

—. "A Travel Guide to the Imagination." *Sunday Tribune* 23 April 1989: B10.

Higgins, Aidan. *Balcony of Europe*. London: Calder & Boyers, 1972.

—. *Bornholm Night-Ferry*. London: Allison & Busby, 1983; London: Abacus, 1985.

—. *Dog Days*. London: Secker & Warburg, 1998.

—. *Donkey's Years*. London: Secker & Warburg, 1995.

—. *Felo de Se*. London: John Calder, 1960.

—. *Langrishe, Go Down*. London: Calder & Boyars, 1966.

—. *Lions of the Grunewald*. London: Secker & Warburg, 1993.

—. *Scenes from a Receding Past*. London: John Calder, 1977.

—. "Writer in Profile: Aidan Higgins." *RTE Guide* 5 February 1971: 13.

Imhof, Rüdiger. "Proust and Contemporary Irish Fiction." *The Internationalism of Irish Literature and Drama: Irish Literary Studies 41*. Ed. Joseph McMinn, assisted by Anne McMaster and Angela Welch. Buckinghamshire: Colin Smythe, 1992. 255–60.

Kearney, Richard. "A Crisis of Imagination." *Crane Bag Book of Irish Studies* (1982): 390–401.

—. *Transitions: Narratives in Irish Culture*. Dublin: Wolfhound Press, 1988.

Kreilkamp, Vera. "Reinventing a Form: The Big House in Aidan Higgins's *Langrishe, Go Down*." *Canadian Journal of Irish Studies* 11.2 (1985): 27–38.

Lubbers, Klaus. "*Balcony of Europe*: The Trend towards Internationalization in Recent Irish Fiction." *Literary Interrelations: Ireland, England and the World*. Tubingen: Gunter Narr, 1987. 235–44.

Matthews, Aidan. "A Rush through the Vagaries of Berlin Life: Review of *Lions of the Grunewald*." *Sunday Tribune* 21 Nov. 1993: B12.

O'Brien, George. "Goodbye to All That." *Irish Review* 7 (1989): 89–92.

O'Neill, Patrick. "Aidan Higgins." *Contemporary Irish Novelists*. Ed. Rüdiger Imhof. Tubingen: Gunter Narr Verlag, 1990. 93–107.

Proulx, Annie. "Drift and Mastery." Rev. of *Flotsam and Jetsam*, by Aidan Higgins. *Washington Post Book World* 16 June 2002: 7.

Share, Bernard. "Down from the Balcony." *Review of Contemporary Fiction* 3.1 (1983): 162–63.

Skelton, Robin. "Aidan Higgins and the Total Book." *Mosaic* 10.1 (1976): 27–37.

Vidan, Ivo. "Time Sequence in Spatial Fiction." *Essentials of the Theory of Fiction*. Ed. Michael J. Hoffman and Patrick Murphy. Duke: Duke UP, 1995. 434–56.

An Aidan Higgins Checklist

Fiction, Autobiography and Travel Writing

Felo de Se. London: John Calder, 1960; rpt. as *Asylum & Other Stories.* London: Calder & Boyars, 1978; Dallas: Riverrun Press 1978.

Langrishe, Go Down. London: Calder & Boyars, 1966; London: Paladin, 1987.

Images of Africa. London: Calder & Boyers, 1971.

Balcony of Europe. London: Calder & Boyers, 1972; New York: Delacorte, 1972.

Scenes from a Receding Past. London: John Calder, 1977.

Bornholm Night-Ferry. London: Allison & Busby, 1983; London: Abacus, 1985.

Ronda Gorge & Other Precipices. London: Secker & Warburg, 1989.

Helsingor Station & Other Departures. London: Secker & Warburg, 1989.

Lions of the Grunewald. London: Secker & Warburg, 1993.

Donkey's Years. London: Secker & Warburg, 1995.

Flotsam & Jetsam. London: Minerva, 1996; Normal, IL: Dalkey Archive Press, 2002.

Dog Days. London: Secker & Warburg, 1998.

The Whole Hog. London: Secker & Warburg, 2000.

Aidan Higgins
Photograph by Elwin Higgins

Patricia Eakins

Françoise Palleau

Walking the wrong way, I necessarily fall behind not only the vanguard but the army of its imitators. Already I have walked past the prostitutes, trailing the army in rags and rouge. I am gleaning with the naked, scabby beggars behind them, scraping the dirt, pawing for scraps, trying to put together a soup from shattered stones, sucking the shards for unwritten runes.
—Patricia Eakins, "In That Case, What Is the Question?" Colloquium for Original Voices, Brown University's Festival of Innovative Women Writers, 11–13 November 1993

To introduce Patricia Eakins's work, what comes to mind first is the delight her style provides for the reader. Eakins is a craftsman and works with language to give a unique flavor to her stories and novels, with tongue-in-cheek sternness, irony, and playfulness, but also with incisiveness and anger at times. She is into displacement, by which I mean that she deftly displaces her stories and settings and our readerly expectations of what the characters should say or do next. Slight variations in language will transpose us into an odd re-creation of eighteenth-century literature in her latest published novel, for example, with certain shifts and subtle changes that manage to surprise us and unsettle our sense of what a decorous use of the eighteenth century might do. Or, as she puts it, "The truth is that I don't work in traditional forms. I work in re-invented traditional forms" (qtd. in Palleau, "Conversation" 85).

So far, apart from uncollected writings, she has published only one collection of stories and one novel, both of great intensity and masterful craft in her use of language. She is an archetypal victim of her commitment to noncommercial literature or, to put it differently, a born resistant. She is not, however, a difficult read and mostly follows a fairly straightforward story line. The odd displacement is what she calls "a side-ways scuttle" (qtd. in Palleau, "Conversation" 86) and does not in the least obscure her work. She is simply and powerfully a teller of tales who gives us something to chew on once the book is closed and also, a writer whose use of English gives us the odd notion that we may be discovering a new language, or a new usage of a language "we did not know we knew," to misquote Robert Frost.

Biography, or How to Connect

Eakins was born in Philadelphia in 1942 and was raised in Birmingham, Michigan. When asked about the languages she learned at school, she mentions a dead language that is not part of her direct family heritage: "I studied Latin for four years in high school and in some ways it was my favorite subject, though I was a lazy student and took advantage of my own facility. Latin gave me the delicious sense that I could read a language of the elegant and remote dead, a language of kings and priests and poets, not a language like Swedish that would smear me as a parvenu ('right off the boat') in the Anglophile bourgeois town I grew up in. Latin was a language of cosmopolitan freedom" (E-mail to author). For Eakins, delving into the etymology of English words gives a writer the freedom of playing with language, as she dramatizes in her story "The Shade Man," in which the narrator, who is also a writer indexing her own story, inserts rare words in the texture of her sentences, thereby working out as she writes her program of "redeeming etymological possibilities" (97). The Latin word *regeneratrix* is inserted in italics, and the sentence structure is disturbed in syntactic havoc: "the way **regeneratrix** save pennies or string or every fortune they ever **page 7** the wreck of **unwordable, page—** comma, comma, coma—please!" (97). This writer, who seems to have gone wild with the cut-and-paste function of her word processor, takes erotic delight in articulating words, all the more so if they are rare, long Latinate ones and unexpected in context (as argued in *Reading Patricia Eakins* (Palleau-Papin, "Patricia Eakins" 80)). As Eakins explains about her high-school Latin: "I had no idea that for centuries it was the language of instruction for liberal arts and thus for elite education, but I savored the ability Latin conferred to understand the meaning of many English words by breaking them into parts. Latin transported me forward through neologism, and backward, where it allowed me to read the otherness of the past" (E-mail to author). This limited incursion into Eakins's high-school curriculum is as telling about her writing as the many more official degrees and awards that came subsequently.

Just as a "dead" language connects her indirectly to a great heritage of linguistic history, to Latin mythology, and to a wealth of storytelling, she evokes her family history as a convergence of many historical trajectories to which she feels connected: "My father's family came from Ireland and Scotland before the Civil War. They made the archetypal American journey from Pennsylvania to Colorado in a covered wagon and lived for a while in sod huts—my great-aunt's was still part of her wooden house in Pueblo when I visited at the age of ten, though my father's parents' had disappeared, its location by then a corn field. Knowing this history from my earliest years gave me a sense of connection to the larger-than-life characters of movie Westerns and made them seem real to me" (E-mail to author). Eakins is particularly observant of how we come to turn our lives into mythology, how we turn people to "larger-than-life characters." She does not set out to condemn this human tendency, but shows its process and its purpose. Thus her complex mythologizing of the past is also an intricate way to make sense of experience and to understand the self. She goes on about her mother's side of the family, insisting on the family tribulations under religious persecution, explaining that their identity was threatened to the point of changing the family name, and although Eakins herself does not draw the comparison, I would liken this, with due respect to the difference, to a slave's Middle Passage with a name change and a sense of dispossession in the passage:

> My mother's father's family came to the United States at the turn of the century. In Sweden, they had been iron-workers; giants at their forges, like Thor with his hammer. I was an adult before I fully understood that they had been Walloons who migrated to Sweden from what is now Belgium the year after the Revocation of the Edict of Nantes. The family name, which had been La Mange, was changed to Osbeck. Growing up, I had only the dimmest sense of all this. . . . I think many Americans have the sense that their history has fallen away with the generations and the passages over sea and land. (E-mail to author)

This is much more than an original-sin syndrome reflecting the whites' sense of historical guilt, but a common experience of dispossession. She does not draw the comparison, and, needless to say, she is acutely aware of the privilege of white immigration over the exploitation of slavery; yet her sense of her Huguenot ancestors' flight is resonant with the incomparably more tragic history of persecution and suffering in the slaves' experience; it anticipates her obsession as an artist with the question of how one reconstructs a sense of identity that has been fragmented, if not erased. In the way many of her stories offer a reinterpretation of the past and renewed creation myths, Eakins sets out to connect, to reestablish a link with the past or, rather, with a recovered past, having come to terms with guilt, with anger, and with the harshness of history. She adds:

> All these stories of struggle with harsh conditions were part of the texture of the life I knew growing up, as were my parents' stories of the struggle to survive and be educated during the Great Depression. My parents moved house fourteen times in their life together and between them lived in most parts of the United States! Seen in that light, my

own peripatetic stories, while far from the psychological subtlety of Chekhovian fiction that we call Mainstream, are both very American and very close to many traditions of worldwide storytelling—the stories of people on the move, putting the past out of mind, "tricking to stay alive," as one Appalachian storyteller put it. Much is left behind. Outlines remain. And then they are lost. (E-mail to author)

Eakins prepared for college at Walnut Hill School in Natick, Massachusetts, and received her B.A. degree from Wellesley College in 1964. After graduate studies in theater history at Wayne State University in Detroit—and we'll see how theater-oriented her work gets—she took the M.F.A. in the original Goddard College Creative Writing Program (Plainfield, Vermont) in 1977 (the writing program is now at Warren Wilson College, Swannanoa, North Carolina). At Goddard, Eakins studied first with Rosellen Brown and then with her principal mentor, the experimental fiction writer George Chambers, whose motto, "Where there are words there is hope," she says she has adopted.

Those words are not to be taken lightly, in the face of Eakins's personal experience in the early years. In her essay "Manifesto of a Dead Daughter," written in the 1990s about events that took place in the late 1960s and early 1970s, she explains the difficulty of her first marriage, emblematic of her struggle with her upbringing and of her commitment to the Civil Rights movement. In her twenties she married "a black man whose experience of the world had been hard": "my new husband had been a burglar, a con man, a brawler. . . . Yet his poems were richly musical, courtly and controlled in their rhythm" ("Manifesto" 4). She lived in "Detroit under martial law after the assassination of Martin Luther King" and was disowned by her family, who pronounced her a "dead" daughter, not wanting "nigger grandchildren" ("Manifesto" 2). The violent and open racism of those days, when white supremacists fought against the people demonstrating for their civil rights, was something she experienced intimately in a most wounding manner. To put it bluntly, there seemed to be no room in the American society of the 1960s for a mixed marriage, especially one mixing both races and classes. About this early experience, the difficult relationship with her husband and her divorce, Eakins concludes, "There was a time when I thought the ordeal of an out-of-caste marriage had catapulted me into a social realm beyond class, beyond gender, beyond historical conflict. I now see that the marriage and my subsequent claim to the culture of renunciation were but paradigms for the choice that I would struggle with again and again" ("Manifesto" 4). She still expresses the tension of this struggle for responsibility in her current writing, in what critic Frazier Russell praises as her ability to express "suppressed rage": "What is most striking about Pierre Baptiste is the way in which Eakins expresses the suppressed rage of her speaker and, by extension, his fellow slaves" (176).

Eakins revises her so-called skin color with her perception of a subsurface, mental, and moral "color"; to her, "whiteness" is "an absence of color, an absence of responsibility and self-awareness," whereas "to be a person of color means to acknowledge that we are hurt as well as blessed in our vulnerability. . . ." And she advocates a common goal for all responsible and, therefore, "colored" people: "Together we grow toward the bright light that contains all color, the light that is wisdom. Each of us reflects a luster that is part of the full spectrum of human possibility, pleasure, creativity, generosity, faith and beauty" ("Manifesto" 4). In visionary terms Eakins advocates and works for progress in her poetic innovations in her fiction, with open eyes and a sharp, incisive style, refusing the endless repetition of conformism and mainstream fiction.

Magazine Editing

Eakins's resistance to the censorship of convention takes the active form of her commitment as a magazine editor. In the early seventies Eakins was a member of the founding editorial board of *Box 749 Magazine* (The Printable Arts Society, Inc., New York City), which editor-in-chief David Ferguson sold on the streets of New York, along with poems for five cents apiece. Volume 1, number 1 came out in the fall of 1972 and cost $2.00; publication petered out after 1979. The writers published in *Box 749* included Miguel Algarin, John Yau, Konstantinos Lardas, Stephen Dixon, Per Olov Enquist, Lyn Lifshin, Sharon White, Richard Hoffman, Welch Everman, George Chambers, Edoardo Sanguinetti, Manuel Ramos Otero, and Chris Bursk. John Yau published his first poems in that magazine.

After the demise of *Box 749* and an interruption in magazine editing, in 1999 Eakins founded another literary magazine, on-line this time: *"Frigate: The Transverse Review of Books, Literature Uncompromised"* (www.frigatezine.com). The writers published included Elaine Terranova, Eric Darton, Kenneth Patchen, Jonathan Baumbach, Maxine Kumin, Marilyn Krysl, Dana Gioia, Michael Casey, and Robin Becker. The issues included essays, fiction, and book reviews. Eakins planned the issues, acquired review articles, essays, poetry, and fiction, supervised production, was in charge of promotion and publicity, all of which took up an enormous amount of her time. This is the main reason why in 2003 she discontinued active on-line publication: to preserve more time for her own fiction.

When asked why she dedicated so much time to magazine editing, Eakins explains how much it matters to her to belong to and to be active in her "literary citizenship" with all the people who write, edit, publish, and read literature that values singularity: "The community of those who care about complex, difficult writing is a small one . . ." ("Transverse Journey"). This is why Eakins is still involved, although as a contributing editor only, with the literary magazine *American Letters & Commentary* (www.amletters.org).

Throughout her editing career, and with the same concern for a common "literary citizenship," Eakins has also taught creative writing successively at New York University, in the Creative Writing Program at Trinity College in Harford, Connecticut, at the New School, and at the New York Institute of Technology, where she taught writing for architecture and the arts. She organizes summer workshops of creative writing, including one in Costa Rica in 2003.

Fiction

As for her writing, an early story published in the first issue of *Box 749* could be an introduction, although a modest one, to her style and purpose. "A Simple Plea for the Preservation of Eggs" is partly an autobiographical story in which a female writing persona engages in a dialogue of sorts with quotations from Norman Mailer and others, pondering on the issue of conception, be it a biological or, metaphorically, literary creation. This is a recurrent theme in her works, as she describes herself as a woman whose children are made of words (Pelleau, "Conversation" 81). The piece may be read as a fictional reflection on Eakins's first marriage, asking the question: "what other metamorphoses might they not have gone through had they known and believed in the pain and the joy of their growing?" (66). This question is what Eakins later explores throughout her fiction, in the collection of stories *The Hungry Girls* (1988) and in her novel *The Marvelous Adventures of Pierre Baptiste, Father and Mother, First and Last* (1999). Coming to terms with creation, with people's growth and inner metamorphoses, and understanding the mythologies people forge to give sense to their experience are what she sets out to explore in her metamorphic, mythology-forging language. Her animal-like metamorphic characters all seem to spring from her programmatic wish as expressed in "A Simple Plea": "Then we might come into a humanity as generously variegated, as fulsomely bawdy, as splendidly affectionate, as unabashedly artistic as the selves the dolphins have come into" (69). The dolphins' freedom sounds like a natural flower-power community with its utopian emphasis on harmony as necessary to foster musical and linguistic creation: "Leaping through the air, planing through the sea, disporting themselves like pagan gods. . . . They are proud to spend their days cavorting and talking and making love, playing and replaying symphonies of squeaking and whistling and clicking, warbled and woofed from ear to ear" (69–70). The rich phonic play of her language is clear here in an exuberant moment, and it is a constant quality of her prose, although she uses it differently in her later work. Her language sings out for our ears; she writes as for performance, calling forth the physical power of a live utterance, as I have argued elsewhere ("Patricia Eakins" 67–86).

Performance

Eakins is essentially a shy person whose generosity comes out by contrast in her performative readings of her work and her theatrical sense of how to captivate an audience with language. She is a master of rhythm, of the incantatory power of anaphora, as shown in her two performance pieces, "Dream of a Body" and "Returning the Bones," which are both from a three-part work called *Power in Opposite Parts.* It was part of an original performance by the multimedia artist Elizabeth Austin, who commissioned Eakins to write the text of *Trace Memories: The Cave Project,* a site-specific performance piece for a cave in Enfield, New Hampshire, in 1992.

All the art critics who reviewed the performance share a fascination for the shamanistic, incantatory magic of the piece, a deft blend of anaphoric poetry from Eakins's text and of Austin's performance piece, which Austin directed and produced, with her masks and recorded voices echoing in the cave. A reviewer described the performance with awe:

> An ancient sprite, face and frock painted with bold primary colors, sits cross-legged in a cave on a New Hampshire hillside. Flickering candles illuminate the walls and ceiling, painted the same bright yellow, deep red and brilliant blue as the visage. Several silhouettes of human forms seem to alternately emerge and recede from the rock while sounds seem to resonate from within the stone. The inclusive effect is of suddenly finding oneself in a primitive world, as though the mists of our collective memory had somehow dissipated. (Shane 70)

Or rather, I would say that our deepest reconstructed collective memory from ancient, geological times seems to come alive in the performance, reactivating our sense of kinship with cavemen, our lives stripped to the bare essentials; that is, not only coarse food to survive on physically but also poetic creation myths to live on metaphysically, answering our spiritual needs and our yearning for coherence between the past and the present so as to be able to step into the future. The reviewer describes the scene and repeats the words: "A voice intones: 'Drawn into the cave, drawn from the cave . . . a measure of time that marks the dance . . . moving into the future of the past'" (Shane 70). The reviewer describes the nighttime performance: "As the moon slides across the evening sky, a story is told. The storyteller introduces three characters: the 'She,' the one who wears the mask; the 'He,' a Native American woodland spirit; and the 'It,' which is the cave. The tale is told; it occurs all in the middle, rather than having the traditional beginning, middle and end. And when it is over we awaken to that other dream we call the present" (Shane 70). This echoes what Kathie Birat sees as an essential characteristic of Eakins's work in the novel *Pierre:*

> Pierre's world is one of shift, movement, change and endless transformation, a world that is all middle, without head or tail. In this sense his story must indeed begin, as he says, *in medias res,* since the search for beginnings and ends is doomed to failure. Pierre tells of his children examining a "serpent worm" at the bottom of the sea. He says they could see "neither head nor tail." "Nor did my offspring possess—even they!—the stamina and strength to paddle to the distant tails or heads of the beasts, but must extrapolate from the evidence of the middles . . ." (214). This is an apt description of Patricia Eakins's view of fiction, an endless extrapolation from the middle." (Birat 9–10)

Another reviewer of *Trace Memory* insists on the physical presence of the text as it comes from the performer's mouth and from loudspeakers, surrounding the listeners in the here and now insistently, with multilayered echoes from which one may not escape: "The stories . . . collected by Eakins under the title 'Power in Opposite Parts,' bombard the listener in fragments large and small. Some of the fragments come directly from Austin's lips. Others are pre-recorded, coming from speakers positioned about the cave" (Hakala 1). Reviewer William Craig captured the key mode of composition of such contrived language and art when he extolled the wonders of poetic (and dramatic) constraints to achieve true and seemingly artless art. This is contrived language so minutely honed that it sounds natural and effortlessly genuine and provides an essential moment of vision: "*Trace Memory* is an environment of sensation and language both found—like the cave itself—and contrived, where meaning is artfully discovered and revealed" (21). The result, according to him, is "a metafiction that is at once ghost story, Ice Age travelogue, domestic memoir and matter-of-fact seance. There are moments—deliberate and delicious collisions of language—when the overlapping voices of live and taped Austins deliver the kind of poetry that might be assembled from torn-up scraps of *The Egyptian Book of the Dead* and *The Kiwanis Camper's Guide to the Presidential Range.* The piece's dead-serious delivery doesn't suppress its authors' obvious delight in words and wordplay, the teasing power of narrative and the juxtapositional essence of poetic imagery" (21).

The piece was so striking that what remains of it today in a video recording, although certainly inferior to the actual performance, is very strong and retains the mesmerizing quality the reviewers witnessed. In addition, Eakins reprinted two of the three texts in *Reading Patricia Eakins* in 2002. "Dream of a Body" is based on the rhetorical figure of speech called the anadiplosis. One phrase, clause, or sentence ends on a word that is taken up again at the beginning of the following phrase or sentence, creating an echo within the lines and a sense of dispossession: something echoes the speaker's words as she speaks, laying the stress on the repeated word while suggesting shamanistic possession. Other voices seem to emerge from the speaker's utterance; the words resonate the past, or the future, or an unknown layering of time and tradition. At the same time a refrain or burden punctuates the narrative, as in ancient ballads, pondering on an experience that seems difficult to grasp. The following quotation begins and ends with the burdenlike echo around the word *phenomenologically:*

> ... Yet there persists the impression
> impression that a missing limb
> limb completes the dream, a body, tangible, intact, so
> so phenomenologically
> phenomenologically close, and in principle
> principle so alike as to make the restoration of a lost
> lost part drowned in the glacial
> glacial lake which drained from the river valley 9000
> 9000 years ago. .... Smaller lakes formed, leaving
> leaving high hilltops above water. The larger lake
> larger lake is still in a sense present
> present though not the same
> same in all respects. There persists
> persists the impression that a larger body of water
> water completes the dream of an older landscape, tangible, intact, so
> so phenomenologically
> phenomenologically close, though in texture
> texture very different from the rough, coarse outline. .... (101–02)

Abstract and philosophical notions ("phenomenologically close") come out concretely in these lines in the sonorities that call for the physical, articulatory aspects of language. The geographical elements are rendered in terms of so-called texture, but not precisely described as they might be in a realistic description, so that they come forward as abstractions rather than actual landscapes. In this tension between the concrete and the abstract, with the word *texture* drawing the attention to the *text* rather than to the world it depicts, the ancient landscape has the depth of a dream, geological times being re-created in the depth of the unconscious. This abstract and dreamy rendering of physical reality may have counterbalanced the concrete performance in the cave, giving meaning to the prosaic and keeping the delicate balance between the actual setting and an imaginary, fantasmatic cave of words for the audience to better penetrate the dream of a "Trace Memory."

In keeping with Eakins's writing for performance, six years after the cave performances, the story "The Hungry Girls" (from the collection *The Hungry Girls and Other Stories*) was adapted for "movement theater." The Collision Theory Ensemble recovers the tradition of carnivalesque performance involving music and at times clownesque acting. Stephanie Gilman and Kristin Tanzer of Collision Theory must have seen in Eakins's most Rabelaisian story something akin to their artistic concerns when they decided to adapt it for the theater. They and Eakins share a delight in disrupting the proprieties of conventions. The so-called hungry girls are enormous girly creatures who, instead of being properly submissive to their parents in keeping with the conservative values of nineteenth-century Normandy, prefer to devour everything up, including their mother and the villagers' belongings. Then where there is nothing left for them to eat, they will eat dirt. The story is told with a devouring sense of humor, which reviewer Jonathan Baumbach called "amorality on the rampage" (36) in his article for the *New York Times Book Review*. *The Hungry Girls — a Fairy Tale* was presented in 1997 at New York City Synchronicity Space and a year later at the New York International Fringe Festival. It was conceived and adapted by Stephanie Gilman and Kristin Tanzer. Their company advertised the play using quotes from Eakins that bring out a sense of delight in gruesome details:

> "In the mythical town of La Bouchoire, France in 1846 a girl is born. . . . [This girl has more daughters of her kind, reproducing exponentially.] With their gaping mouths and their jagged teeth, grabbing and stuffing their filthy cheeks . . . these girls are hardly human!" A ten-person ensemble creates this carnivalesque feral world filled with grotesque caricatures, mad chants, and crazy dances. An original movement-theater piece.

Eakins comments on her fruitful collaboration with Collision Theory: "When I was first approached by Kristin Tanzer of *Girl &*

Co., which has just changed its name to *Collision Theory Theater Ensemble,* I was intrigued by the company's wish to adapt the play for movement theater." She underlines what the company and her story have in common: "The notion of carnival is one aspect of the company's own aesthetic that is very resonant with mine—pleasure in naughtiness and horseplay and mischief, in table-turning and nose-thumbing. It might have been predicted that we would see eye to eye here. Less predictable was the degree to which I became committed to the physicality of the company's style . . ." (E-mail to the author). The adaptation brings out a fundamental aspect of her work, as her mode of composition is performance-oriented, and Eakins talks about "the position the words in my stories occupy, which is not, in my view, primarily on the page. Rather it is in the air, which carries spoken words to the ear. Since I have always written for the ear as much as for the eye, there are certain implications for character which makes my work well suited to an outward and physical theater such as *Collision's*" (E-mail to the author).

Very recently, Eakins has written the text and lyrics for a performance piece conceived by Collision Theory, entitled *Portrait (With Horse and Others).* The premiere was in New York City on 26 March 2003 on the Mainstage at HERE Arts Center in SoHo. The company presented the play as "an Orwellian fairytale set in a post-apocalyptic wasteland, *Portrait (With Horse and Others)* tells the story of a disparate group of people who are the lone survivors of a war-ravaged village" (web page of Collision Theory, <www.collisiontheory.org>). A small village somewhere in middle Europe, sometime at the beginning of the twentieth century, is the scene of postapocalyptic moments of derision, despair, and love. An old woman dances with the skeleton of her dead husband, her grandchild makes dolls of the bones, the bones speak to them, as does a horse, while books from the village library are burned for fuel and used for fodder, all in the continuous wartime noise of bombs and conflagrations. Parts of the play are set to the music of klezmer, the minor-key Jewish music of middle Europe. In her review of the play, Denise Mecionis stresses the dreamlike quality of the play, which seems to stem from "somewhere deep within the recesses of the human mind." She points out an essential characteristic of the play: "Reminiscent of Antonin Artaud, 'Portrait' has the peculiar quality of an improvised ritual or ceremony in which the central players are bound together without understanding the significance of his or her own or each other's roles."

The play may carry overtones of Kenneth Patchen's work in its fragmented lyrics and verse and in its wartime fear of total destruction. In the opening the librarian intones: "Blessed are the dead, for

their fingers never freeze/They curl inside their shadows warm.//
They don't need to eat and so they don't mind/Sausages of mud and
bread of straw//Blessed are the dead who live in fog among the
wolves./Forgotten is the sweet so nothing's bitter to them now."
This play underlines an important theme in Eakins's fiction, which
she shares with Kenneth Patchen (on whom she has written an essay for *Frigate*): the expression and denunciation of suffering, in
times of scarcity, of people who have to make do without the bare
essentials, people who have gone beyond certain limits of endur-
ance and who still put words between them and nothingness, people
whose expression and reactions prove they are still alive and
deeply, painfully human. The little girl in the play still chants
counting rhymes after she has lost even the bones she used for toys:
"Ten black berries in a blood-red hand;/Nine blazing gates around a
hill of bone,/Eight headless cats." And yet the play is not about despair, but about the magical moments of relief offered by what's left
of culture in the midst of devastation. People fight for life with inge-
nuity and craft, with humor in their bitterness. As Denise Mecionis
underlines, "Particularly memorable is a musical number in the
middle of the play which momentarily shatters the grim atmosphere of the scene and slips into an almost sinister cabaret song.
The entire show is studded with such gems and is a pleasure to
watch."

The Hungry Girls and Other Stories

Some of the stories in the collection *The Hungry Girls* explore the
limits of loss, isolation, and suffering and expose the hypocrisy of
social proprieties in front of destructive power. The story "The
Change" is set in a postnuclear area, where a scientist undergoes a
moral change in the midst of radioactive nature and mutant animals. In a metamorphic world in which even the species are no
longer separate and stable, in which what we take for granted is no
longer valid, something bare and essential emerges from the madness. Reduced to the bare minimum, something fragile and noble,
some glimpse of inexplicable truth surfaces, some utopia is granted
poetic reality. The mutant dogs, which consume radioactivity to
grow and might therefore save the earth and humanity after an
atomic blast, come to embody the scientist's most precious hope:

> At first I thought they were eating the blast, but now I think they are
> eating the sadness. And I would like to think they have always been
> here on earth. Wherever there has been an incredible destruction,
> there these dogs with the gay bright eyes and the little folded hands of
> insects, these dogs with bird crests, lion ruffs, and flowers beneath

their tails, have trotted sniffing and sucking. I would like to think that. The creatures may be an illusion, a dream I am vouchsafed or indulge myself because I know I will soon die. Yet they ignore me. They are absorbed with themselves, in flashing their glittering eyes. (46)

The rhythm alternates between long and rich metaphoric sentences and bare, minimal ones, showing stylistically the dispossession, the loss of illusion, from which a sharper vision may still emerge. The vision of the creatures "flashing their glittering eyes" is granted Blakean strength in the allusion to "The Tyger," in which the origin of the fantastic tiger is a source of wonder: "In what distant deeps or skies/Burnt the fire of thine eyes?" (55). Or perhaps the poetic vision is that of Coleridge's "Kubla Khan, or a Vision in a Dream," in which the prophetic poet is described as having "flashing eyes." The romantic belief in the power of words to change the world and spark a new (Shelleyan) fire in mankind may be found as a discreet profession of faith in some stories. The final words of "The Change" carry their belief in the performative function of language as an act of faith in which to write suggestively about an ontological "change" in the world, to inscribe it on the page is a way to enact it on the private stage that lies between the writer's and the reader's imaginations, letting us complete the mysterious ending: " 'I am here,' say the creatures. 'Here and listening. I am ready for what is to come. For the change' " (46).

And yet these fragile moments, open to our imagination and our sense of wonder, are not epiphanies of the kind we've had so much of lately, as writer Rosellen Brown puts it in her comment on *The Hungry Girls:* "That deadpan poise is what gives these stories their rare menacing wit: Aren't these things possible? These species sound so plausible, their behavior so—nearly—familiar. . . . Patricia Eakins writes beautifully: a fine ear and a sense of shape make uncommon music of her direct imaginings. If you've had enough fiction-as-usual—name brands, minor epiphanies, timid time-bound gestures—*The Hungry Girls* has some astounding things to tell." Several reviews also express their admiration for the "singular oddity" of the stories, which stand outside of the "currently fashionable" (Baumbach 36). Baumbach underlines that Eakins's stories "refuse explication, remain exotically opaque" (36). He justly argues that *The Hungry Girls* is "about the primordial universe unmediated by the civilized and the rational, but it is also implicitly about the imagining of self-sustained worlds, the making of convincing artifice," and he is confidant that "In time, *The Hungry Girls* will no doubt find its audience" (36).

Marc Chenetier was the first to write a scholarly article about *The Hungry Girls,* grouping Eakins's work with that of other fable writers, namely Wendy Walker and Don Webb. He extolls her capacity to bring out "the lyricism of the monstrous life": "In this half-entropic, half-proliferating universe, the songs of the species can be heard, the evolution of genes and the metamorphoses undergone by the work of a supreme artist-creator can be observed. One could describe this lyricism of the monstrous life and of the fantastic beauty of the unknowable as some sort of chromosomic oratorio. . . . The postapocalyptic landscapes of Denis Johnson's *Fiskadoro* bring identical tones to mind" (391). Chenetier presented Eakins's fiction to a group of French scholars studying contemporary American literature, and in turn a number of Eakins readers presented their critical work at a conference where she was invited to give a reading in Orleans, France, in October 1999. The five articles were published in *Reading Patricia Eakins: A Collective Volume of Essays on Patricia Eakins, with Excerpts from Her Fiction.* Four of the critical articles study her novel *Pierre* and one her collection of stories.

Robert Coover shares a similar concern for what Chenetier calls the "beauty of the unknowable" in his fairy-tale-like story "The Gingerbread House," in which the narrator asks unanswerable questions about the good fairy: "The good fairy, though a mystery of the night, effuses her surroundings with a lustrous radiance. Is it the natural glow of her small nimble body or perhaps the star at the tip of her wand? Who can tell?" (74). As in some of Coover's tales, Eakins's syncretic use of myths and fables also explores the truth of unconscious fears and questions about life in a form that offers recognizable and odd, displaced patterns at once. Her narrative patterns are uncannily recognizable and yet strangely foreign, in gems of sentences that resist easy projections and identifications from readers. She puts forward in her stories as well as in her novel the texture of language as a chiseled gem: carefully crafted, her sentences use the self-imposed constraints of a particular style or form of narration to shape experience. And the types of recognizable narrative conventions vary from one story to the next, with incredible variety: reconstructed Japanese tales of the long gone past in the story "Milady's Ploy"; nineteenth-century Normandy with Rabelaisian and many other winks to the French literary tradition in "The Hungry Girls"; the Persian world of *The Thousand and One Nights* in "Snakeskins"; the American west of the nineteenth century in "Daddy's Ibbit Wife"; the ice and snow of Inuit and Eskimo tales in "Oono"; Ancient Greek and Latin mythology in "Auravir"; a fairy-tale bear story in "Banda"; an African tale of initiation myth in "Meat Song"; a Tibetan tribe with unicornlike horses called "Yiqh-Yaqh" in the story by that name; a postnuclear blast atoll in the south Pacific in "The Change"; and a sugarcane plantation in the West Indies in the eighteenth century in "Murumoren, or Breach at the Casting," the story that was later developed into the novel *Pierre*. In only a few pages we are asked to travel imaginatively in time and place, changing culture as a snake sloughs off an old skin, with lightness and agility, slithering into a new set of literary conventions and mannerisms with delight. As Paul Violi comments in his afterword to the collection, "the myths span the entire cosmological-biological range of creation and destruction. They sometimes read like re-enactments of ancient myths applied to familiar genres: the western, the feral child, the nuke mutant, the courtly Japanese tale, the Persian parable . . ." (140).

And yet this is not just chameleonlike playfulness, as there is a distinct Eakinsian touch that runs throughout, a touch of oddity and respect for the borrowed mythology and culture and a capacity to create such distinct worlds in only a few sentences. The first sentence of the story "Forrago" is an example of the plunge into the form of the tale and the threat of a mysterious, unknown creature: "Now in the darkest and narrowest alleys of Porto Affraia, alleys too dark and narrow even for stand-up whores and small-time thieves, there thrive some small ratty creatures with greasy, ashen coats and greedy big eyes" (97). The conventions of the tale of wonder are clear in the syntax, with the suspense drawn from a long place-complement, which delays the predicate and induces a greater sense of expectation, as if a curtain was finally lifted from the stage with the final mention of the subject after the inversion, "there thrive some small ratty creatures . . ." and the following descriptions of the "creatures" with the forged name of "forrago." But then, instead of plunging us into a traditional type of storytelling, with possibly some event or adventure occasioned by the "creatures," we are given a humorous and anthropomorphic explanation of the forragos' reproductive habits and their viciousness. The young eat the mother's teats rather than suck them, the female forrago lures the male to mating and then eats him up with ferocious delight: "Full days after she has eaten him tail and ear, his shrunken member falls from her./And she snaps it up" (98). In this irreverent and gruesome tale, construed like a revenge of the shrews of unimpeded bacchanal ferocity, the hilarious humor comes from the friendly tone of the teller who is seeking the audience's benevolence. Right after the female forrago has gobbled down her lover's shrunken penis, the teller of the tale addresses the audience in a friendly, conciliatory manner: "You shake your heads; you allow she is evil." Then she goes on to have us gobble down the most improbable justifications in a doctorial tone, "And indeed she is remorseless wicked, yet even she enlarges the stock of blessing in this world" (98), and launches off into a paragraph-long explanation of the greatness of forragos when dead and rightly used: "And when the musk is squeezed from the vicious rumps, an exquisite perfume is refined" (98). The teller then displays a traditional poetic image to extoll the greatness of the forrago smell in synesthetic celebration ("the look of the moonlight"), only to destabilize the traditional romantic image of moonlight immediately: "It smells like the look of the moonlight falling across the water, a deceptive path a man might drown in were he the fool to yield to its beckoning. I do not recommend it myself" (98). The friendly tone of the narrator is humorously misleading, since it does not take us by the hand in a stable narrative journey, but plays with our disgust, our hilarity, our complicity in handling the taboos of propriety with matter-of-fact sternness and tongue-in-cheek irreverence. The narrator then goes on to turn coats and obscure the right and wrong polarities in the end of the story: "Yet 'tis said a seaman mounting a frail whose earlobes have been daubed with this essence will die consumed by the teeth of bliss, and never once think of his home. And 'tis said that a convicted murderer in Porto Affraia was put to death at his own request by a whore wearing forrago musk. Who would not prefer it to the rope or knife?" (98).

The final rhetorical question annuls the reservations we might have had about the greatness of the female forrago, whose siren enticements are forgotten in the gratitude we should feel for the oxymoronic, masochistic pleasure provided in the expression "the teeth of bliss." The wonderful creatures perversely turn a small death metaphor into an actual death that feels like a small, pleasurable one: "die consumed by the teeth of bliss." As Paul Violi explains in his afterword to the collection of stories, "The momentous is never purely one effect but an awesome mix of feelings, often contradictory, that overwhelms one simultaneously. We're surprised to find, speechless as we are, that we can contain them all. Isn't that what the good writing does?" (139). He captures the essence of the stories when he explains: "One never gets the feeling, as in some bestiaries, that the author of *The Hungry Girls* is a person-of-letters and the stories are an amusement. The many humorous notes Eakins hits do not lighten her stories' seriousness but accentuate it, perhaps because, in a world in which life is an omnivorous blind force, the blessings and rewards are bound to be accidental and ironic, e.g., the beauty of life is redeeming; in this she reverses Rilke, as if to say that beauty is not the beginning of terror but survives it" (139). I could go on to quote the complete afterword, as it is certainly the best criticism on the stories so far. His analysis of the narrative voice in particular captures an essential Eakins feature: "the contrast of subtle, bemused, distanced narrator describing momentous events is a wonderful effect, as is the sense of deep rapids when the speed of the narration belies the depth of the story" (139). The stories are "narratives that rely not so much on 'plot' as on more realistic progression, cumulative and revelatory, the tension sustained by the brilliant description, the growth and effects unfolding as the author eyes them" (140–41). The stories are so dense and rife with many possible threads to unravel that, as Eakins once playfully put it, there is a potential novel in each story. There was a potential play in the story "The Hungry Girls" as Collision Theory later put it up for the stage. And Eakins developed the story "Murumoren, or Breach at the Casting" into her novel *The Marvelous Adventures of Pierre Baptiste,* which was published ten years after the story.

The Marvelous Adventures of Pierre Baptiste, Father and Mother, First and Last

The introduction to the story summarizes the plot of the novel, since the story is the end of what became the full novel: "In 1754 an exceedingly valuable slave named Pierre, trained as a bookkeeper, escaped by sea in a rum cask from a sugar plantation in the French Anduves. He floated away from the shipping lanes to wash up on the shore of the island we know as Big Cayana, then uninhabited and bearing no name" (*Hungry Girls* 101). Those two short sentences are developed into 175 pages in the novel, from part 1 to 6, explaining Pierre's upbringing and life on the plantation, how he acquired his learning, his marriage, his occupations, why he had to escape the plantation, and his perilous sea journey until he was marooned on a desert island. Then the story, which tells about his life on the island and his pregnancies and bearing metamorphic children to a female fish, runs until the end of his life and of the novel, covering parts 7 and 8, from page 176 to 249.

In a paper given at the University of Montpellier for a conference on recent interpretations of the slave-narrative tradition, Kathie Birat argues that Eakins has reinvested the slave narrative in her novel in a "wildly inventive pastiche": "It is based on a clever use of the conventions of the slave narrative and a clear perception of the ways in which the original authors used these conventions both to inscribe and to transcend their condition as bondsmen." Her reading seems to agree with Thomas Pughe's analysis that "If as a slave Pierre represents otherized, exploited nature, he stands, once he has been metamorphosed into father-mother, for nature as an all-encompassing process. He is Eakins's enabling metaphor, the source of wonder and thus the source of post-pastoral writing" (95).

Birat explains: "The pyrotechnics of Eakins's verbal energy, the very inventiveness which she displays are a clear sign of her relation to postmodernism, with its fascination for the ways in which language invents the world. But it is the intertext, which includes not only the slave narrative but the entire eighteenth-century project of an orderly representation of human knowledge, which gives this verbal inventiveness its power by placing it in a meaningful tension with the very idea of rationality." Birat adds that

> while seeking to justify their credibility in the crystal-clear objectivity of a purely mimetic representation, the slave narrators knew that their ultimate liberation could only lie in a shaking of the unreasonable assumptions underlying a presumably rational world. By using Buffon and the eighteenth-century project of describing the natural world as the epistemic underpinnings of her fictional world, Eakins is able to study the ways in which language eludes the grasp of reason, revealing its affinity with the unruly and chaotic nature of life itself.

The playful language of Pierre is a way to refuse the paralyzing stillness of the master's scientific classification: "language finds itself once again capable of following the endless permutations of life; language itself undergoes permutations which do not obey the laws of logic and reason. Hence, Pierre defines his children as 'PHILOSO-FISH SAVANTS.' " Here Birat agrees with Antoine Caze's thorough analysis of the Oulipian playfulness at work in Eakins's language and what is at stake in the narrator's playful verbal craft. Caze argues that "From the outset, indeed, his stable identity as narrator—and perhaps his reliability as well, although we would probably prefer to ignore that—appears to be split into so many tiny pieces by the splitting power of the written sign" (13–14).

Several critics have also underlined Eakins's distrust for any system that imposes scientific order upon life in an attempt to contain it and master it. Shortly after the publication of *The Hungry Girls,* Greg Boyd wrote, "Borrowing from any number of conventions both sacred and profane, from contes fantastiques to creation myths to traditional Japanese courtier tales, these stories seek to provide, like the myths and fables they often emulate, explanations for mysteries beyond the kinds of knowing fostered by scientific thought" (39). This is a topic Eakins also explores in her novel, in which she deals with cultural myths and mysteries before the separation that occurred around or after the Enlightenment, the separation between facts and fiction, between literature and science: "I kept reading about how science in the past hadn't been careful to distinguish between fact and fancy. And I began to wonder—perhaps science had taken a route that took it away from poetic truth" (qtd. in

Pelleau, "Conversation" 73). The critical reception of her novel often lays the stress on what escapes the scientific urge to classify the world, taking it away from "the vivid." In this respect Claire Fabre analyzes Pierre's fascination for the orchid, precisely because that flower escapes the rigid categories of Buffon's natural-history classification: "Thus, the orchid, a plant which naturally grows with very little soil and can feed on putrefied material, belongs to a category which the natural historian refuses even to name, in other terms it has no place in the systematic catalogue of the real. The periphrastic expression Dufay uses to allude to it only recalls its hybrid nature—'the devil-take-the-stinking-fish-hole crumbs'—and its relegation to the realm of the unnamable" (Fabre 33). Fabre explains that "through the character of Dufay, Pierre's narrative exposes two (faulty) sets of order which coexist: the order of the plantation and that of the eighteenth century's encyclopedists" (34). She concludes that Pierre's "eventual wreckage on the new island puts into practice an aesthetics of proliferation opposed to a vertical colonization of the real by the encyclopedic taxonomy and, incidentally, to any form of verticality" (40). She stresses the symbolic import of the orchid in this effective form of resistance: "As it condenses all of these attributes, the orchid could well serve as an emblem for the poetical (and political) force of Eakins's novel" (40).

In the novel the three-page "overture" is possibly one of the densest and most poetically intricate moments in the book, in which an aged Pierre explains why he has written his "testament" or, rather, the story of his life and of how he came to start a new genealogy with the marvelous "offspring" he conceived with his beloved "sea shade" (2). The moment has the awesome nobility of an anamnesis, as well as that of a loving praise of his descendants, gilled homonculus fishy infants for whom his love comes forth in his poetic descriptions. Some of his "offspring" have died and have turned into sirens luring him to join them now that his life is ending: "On calm, cloudless nights, when the dome of heaven is bright with stars, they lie in the breaking moonlit waves, combing them to ribbons, silver rushing through their teeth. Yet, while they live, they are never truly in repose. Their gold-and-pink-flecked bodies quiver in foam, their green-white tresses writhe like eels among strands of sea-weed, while fishes fin in the shifting tangles" (2). Such rich alliterative and densely metaphoric writing sets up the opening of the novel in what Pierre calls "a swift-stopping lyric mode," as this is a demanding "overture" whose lyricism may not be sustained for long, so that he humorously begs us to bear with his highly poetical opening by promising it to be "swift-stopping." Pierre's narration can also be matter-of-fact, cutting, ironic, as well as tender, but in high eighteenth-century diction. His language is noble, verging on the precious mode, always imparting power and weight to the story of his life. He is an autodidact, with an autodidact's fondness for big words and fancy style. Language is precious to him in a way that is not to a person who takes education for granted.

The eighteenth-century imitation, with its "encyclopedic dream of itemizing and naming the whole world" (Fabre 35), is conveyed through the use of the ampersand (&), which, according to Fabre, "acts somewhat like the period dress of his narrative: this minimal sign, used throughout the novel in all passages involving an enumeration or a list, is like a prop helping Eakins to forge her illusion" (35). Pierre's narrative is realistic in its re-creation of the eighteenth-century idiosyncrasies and proves the slave's capacity to learn the language of his masters to perfection, the better to express his plea and to surpass his masters in expression, as Phyllis Wheatley or Frederick Douglass did in their own times. For Eakins, working within a formal constraint is a means to find a voice as an interpreter of the past tradition in letters and to give her own shape and edge to the re-creation, influencing the tradition as she uses it. As Michael Perkins writes about the novel, "Fiction is not only about stories, it is about language. Eakins's language is eloquent and vivid. . . . Like John Barth in *The Sot-Weed Factor,* Eakins writes in the high style of the eighteenth century. It is thus credible that Pierre Baptiste might well correspond with his hero, the writer Buffon, a member of the French nobility and the greatest naturalist of his time" (1). And yet, while making this correspondence plausible in the pastiche of eighteenth-century language and conventions, Eakins explores the mystery of life that Buffon contained and categorized. She explores a world of metamorphosis and change, a world rich in uncertainty and wonder (Birat). In her work Marc Chenetier reads "a fascination for the profound equivalence between thematized metamorphosis and the use of words" ("Introducing" 302). He defines Pierre Baptiste's world as "a temporally vague but graphically precise universe, an uncertain world of mutations under the wand of her language," which presents "a kind of fluctuating new genetic sphere, a world where life knows how to be only mystery and uncertain becoming" (302). The more uncertain and marvelous the world Pierre describes, the more "graphically precise" he is to make this world real through word forging and to inscribe his identity and his lineage in it.

Brigitte Felix, in her study, argues that Pierre's obsession with leaving an inscription or a written word is the only way for him to truly exist, and she puts her study under the epigraph of Claude Richard's *American Letters:* "The program is clear: to improve lived time by a scriptural practice, by an inscription of the letter. From the first letter, the notch on the stick, the inscription of the rune on the wood, there is renewed pleasure of the founding gesture of writing with each stroke of the knife-pen (in *Gordon Pym,* you write with a *pen-knife*). . . . Become a writer, become a sculptor of letters, to restore the subject's being-in-time" (Felix 43). Felix sees Pierre's obsession with inscription as "re-inventing the politics of metafiction": "whereas the more conventional aspects of the metafictional practice seem to be taken for granted—the narrative as a comment on its own writing—, Pierre Baptiste shows an obsession with writing as the production of a material trace, like a return to the A, the B, and the C of the writer's activity" (53). She argues that Eakins's playing with typefaces and capitalization as well as with puns "presents the dance of words, the *choreography* of signs on the page," and this bears on our reading: "we become engaged in an activity that is closer to the decoding, if not conjuring, of hieroglyphics" (58).

One example of decoding is the use Eakins makes of pronouns to designate Pierre. To render his alienation as a slave, she uses a split in the pronouns, changing the narration from a first-person narrative to a third-person narrative from one paragraph to another and sometimes within the same sentence. Caze analyzes the process at work when Pierre discovers a new creature, "the mutant bee (described 21 sq.). . . . Just as he mentions this hybrid creature, this *changeling,* Pierre himself switches from first to third person in his account: his own person(a) splits up, his identity contaminated as it were by the hybrid nature of the bee" (19). Caze explains in a footnote that the switch is a "constant feature. But here, it is quite remarkable: Pierre recedes from the first-person discoverer to the third-person slave, even as he secretly keeps the initiative" (19). Caze concludes that as "Pierre describes himself as a changeling only a few pages later. . . . [S]uch disorder of the world will be expressed in the disorder of the words which Pierre will finally master by becoming the writer of his own account" (19).

The shift from first- to third-person narrative shows a fight within a split identity and an attempt to recover a sense of self. The search is fulfilled only when Pierre uses the double pronoun "I-and-I" of Rastafari wholeness later on in his narrative. In the first part of the novel Pierre is split in a schizophrenic perspective, before he brings the strands of his selfhood together in his writing. At one point, we are told in the third person that "he had no commonplace book" (33), while on the following page, he finds a way to get pieces of paper on which he can articulate his experience: "Soon, then, I inveigled the kitchen help to steam tea packets over the stew pots so I could have the labels" (34). He finds a voice when he writes in the first person, yet the slips to the third-person narrative show that he is still partly alienated. Significantly, he uses his own voice when he explains that he puts the tea labels with his writings on it in his pouch with what remains of his family history: "a talisman pouch I carried in my bosom, with relicts of my lineage" (34). As Morgan Blair explains, Pierre's utterance is alienated until he creates life on his own terms:

> Pierre undergoes a series of captivities in his three passages toward becoming both mother and father to his new species progeny. That his mouth is their womb, his tongue their food is logical outcome for him because the language trapped in his mind has not nourished his life except as wishful dreams, has, except in excised fashion, not past his lips. It has entered him through his ears and eyes and has had no exit until, on his desert island, it finally becomes an act of his hand. (178)

The first identity-defining gesture of Pierre once he sets foot on his island is to name it after himself, in a telling moment when he automatically uses the double pronoun of Rastafarian speech, which he had never used for himself up to then, but only for his wife Pélérine Verite (70). Here he finds a new form of expression, and his feet find a new form of dance unconsciously inscribed in his body memory:

> Then I found my feet moving, my body swaying. Yet who chanted, who drummed? My bare feet marked the time with a resonant slap, but a greater heart than mine beat "Uncle! Uncle!" in my breast. I and I turned and swayed in a pattern I did not know I knew, twisting my and my body to shape the letters of an airy alphabet, and in that alphabet, to spell *Uncle God*. Then the world hissed and turned blue, as if swallowed by the sea: I and I picked up the pebbles with which I had not long previous formed in mortal language the words "Pierre Baptiste de l'Isle de L'Oncle"; I placed them in my and my mouth, and the sea spit back the world. I and I made a broom of silver-thatch, and swept-wrote His name in the letters of enigma in the garden of sand, and knew then and then my place. (185)

Naming is done in concert with nature, in an exchange and mythical re-creation of the world, by which the sea agrees to his naming when it "spits back the world" he has created in naming it. In an intricate poetical gesture—the metaphor clearly establishes that the creation is made of words—Pierre has now been made poet by the sea, etymological creator. He no longer is his master's amanuensis. He is a free poet, a free writer, a creator of new worlds through language.

The repetition of the adverb "then and then" also echoes double pronoun identity, as he could come to a sense of self only once rooted and settled on a land he can call his, inscribing his mark on it, as he later inscribes his story on homemade paper, and significantly, the word "alphabet" is also repeated twice when he writes letters of the alphabet in the air with his dance. Every thing is doubled, every gesture becomes an inscription, as "I and I" exists for himself only when he sees himself mirrored in his own writing. Eakins here explores poetically the meaning of the double pronoun in Rastafarian speech to found Pierre's identity as a narrator of his own life, therefore having power over his destiny in the sense that he can record it and interpret it to draw meaning from his experience. Adrian Anthony McFarlane explains the meaning of the Rastafarian usage: "the I-an-I locution creates a linguistic device that provides a new sense of self-liberation for a people of the African diaspora. . . . The power of the I lies in its ability to command the self; its reflexiveness is its strength, and its purpose is to create a new identity and meaning for the speaker. . . . In addition, whereas the singular ('I') denotes the empirical I, which one sees and feels, the plural ('I-an-I') denotes a harmonious synthesis of the empirical and the metaphysical: I am one with Jah Ras Tafari" (107–08). The use of Rastafarian pronouns shows that Pierre's search for identity is also a spiritual quest.

Frazier Russell's review of the novel insists on the final "image of grace," which invites the reader's involvement: "In the end, Pierre's tale is offered to us as an act of redemption that will only be complete when we partake of it like a sacrament. The final tableau of this novel—an extraordinary vision of Pierre's rescue of his fellow slaves in a "ship of sugar threads . . . manned by hundreds of spiders" in which "all the sufferers" will be brought home to paradise— presents us with a unique and unforgettable image of grace" (176– 77). The spiritual dimension is also present in the stories in *The Hungry Girls;* as Paul Violi stresses, "their spiritual range is that of an encompassing vision" (140).

In an interview conducted in 1998, Eakins explains critical comments on an uncollected story ("R'ha-l'a R'a-H'oum"), saying, "There's a meanness to these people's lives, their physical lives, but a certain grandeur in their religious conceptions. I don't know if I would call this any kind of emblem for my own mentality, but one thing really surprises me. That is the metaphysical element. When I read through these stories as a body of work, I see that there is a rather fierce metaphysical curiosity, an appetite, really, that has no place in my conscious life. I'm not a believer, but I am hungry to believe" (qtd. in Pelleau, "Conversation" 84). After 11 September

2001, Eakins said that she felt she had "entered history." I would argue that she had entered it much earlier, but 11 September was a catalyst. Her reflection took a spiritual form, and she was confirmed in the Episcopal Church, in an open-minded, socially committed, and active community in her neighborhood in New York City.

Throughout her writing, Eakins has found a language to capture in her stories and her novel the mystic moment of vision, which she often calls the "gleaming." Elsewhere, I have listed the recurrence of "gleaming" as a sign of spirituality in her fiction:

> In "Milady's Ploy," dead bodies mysteriously "gleam" and take on a form of enigmatic transcendence, as "The dead, stripped of their clothing, had gleamed in the moonlight" (36). This recalls the "Rapturous Gleaming" of the "cult of Fatima's Redemption" in the story "Snakeskins," a cult that dramatizes the access of dead bodies to glory, associating the words "gleaming" and "glory" . . . : "And the sun will shine a gleaming path across the salt lagoon of his body, and he will travel it to glory, Forever" (27). ("Patricia Eakins" 83).

This echoes the part in *Pierre* when the slaves honor the dead: "And the solemn dance with which we honored the sacrificial gleaming on the water—the very path to the beyond—was received with shrieks and titters of merriment in the great house, as the cap to the evening's entertainment" (69).

The notion of spirituality, of the giving and receiving of spiritual guidance, and of communion with others through storytelling is at work in the link Eakins establishes between her storyteller and the audience. The opening sentence of the story "Salt" begins in a direct address to the audience sitting around the teller of the tale: "You sit before me your heart a cup, and who am I to gainsay you drink?" (*Hungry Girls* 57). When asked to comment on the sentence, Eakins said,

> If the heart is a cup, then it is open, ready, to be filled; the "drink" is the sustenance the seeker—the one who has come with the cup—thirsts for. The "drink" is the story that follows, or the story the speaker supposes the seeker wishes to be told. . . . The first sentence suggests a seeker with an urgent question, a difficult question, perhaps an unanswerable one. The speaker cannot refuse to speak to a seeker whose heart is so radically receptive, but she questions her fitness to be called on. At the same time, the speaker is humbled by a spiritual responsibility (who am I) to provide "drink" for the heart that thirsts. (E-mail to author)

The second sentence sets the limits of what the speaker may give: "Not that I recall the days of living under the waves, before the slukie drove us into the fire of air" (57). Eakins explains: "In the second sentence, the speaker says what she can and cannot offer. She doesn't remember the oldest days, and she was not an eyewitness to certain events that she is about to recall but she is connected to the oral tradition. After her disclaimer, she leaps right into the story and tells it as if she had been present" (E-mail to author).This is the gift of the imagination, which the teller can offer to her listeners or readers. She can impart a reconstructed vision and poetically forge a creation myth in an effort to make sense of the present.

Significantly, *Kirkus Reviews* described *Pierre Baptiste* as "Bizarre, marvelous, and horrifying at once: a refreshing escape from the mundane" (394). The mundane, or the things of this world, becomes the wordly, as opposed to the heavenly, spiritual. The other-than-mundane here is seen as both "marvelous" and "horrifying." It is what we not only cannot explain, but also may not control, and therefore it is potentially frightening. The novel moves into unchartered territory as it escapes the recognizable pastiche of eighteenth-century slave narrative and natural history, the encyclopedic worldview. The unexpected loss of recognizable patterns may be what makes the novel difficult to pin down, in particular toward the end of the narrative. I have argued elsewhere (in "La Derive du recit dans *The Marvelous Adventures of Pierre Baptiste* de Patricia Eakins") that once Pierre sets out to sea in his barrel and suffers from thirst and prolonged exposure to the scorching sun, realistically, his narration unravels in a looser manner, with more embedded stories from African folklore. One passage revises the Western myth of the creation of the world (166 ff.). In another, the whites are observed as if by an African, in all their cultural strangeness (152 ff.). In yet another, Pierre recalls a story the overseer of the plantation once told the slaves (about the "Jitseys" (160 ff.)). Or he recalls a story Rose told him when he was a child, the story "The Children of Two Doors" (171 ff.). Pierre's own vision becomes more and more fragmented, and several voices are orchestrated in the possessed theater of his mind. He then seems to be making up the tools of his new fragmented world-vision as he moves to uncharted narrative territory. Story time is dilated into mythical time, as the past he summons to life in his barrel is dilated into an amorphous, continuous present. The access to mythical time allows for many embedded tales, as Pierre had pointed out in an earlier passage: "He could not and cannot separate the strand of Kwafesi's tale from the stand of his own in the unraveling yarn" (127). The present of the narration and that of the writing seem to coincide as story time leaps out of historical time, into a time of fantasy and dream or nightmare or a utopian moment mixing the strands of several narratives. Mimicking the delirious consciousness of the narrator, the tale moves away from the conventions of a realistic novel, and it is precisely then that Pierre encounters a ship of escaped slaves, bound in fetters and famished, sailing to their death in a spectral passage that calls forth Coleridge's *Rime of the Ancient Mariner* in a fantastic moment: "Then he saw the brightnesses were indeed, their ribs, that did seem to protrude from dark flesh, giving them the appearance of skeletons, who rowed their boat to the other world" (143).

Pierre reaches literary liberation once he abolishes the dream of reaching the other side of the ocean, when he leaves the trappings of other tales, be they African or French, and other literary borrowings to set up his own conventions and expression. Pierre lets go of logical links and delves in the delight of purely gratuitous poetical associations, opening narration to the language of fantasy and erotic dreams, gathering the previous images of the novel in a hieratic moment of bliss: "At the close of day, the sun-gilt twigs finer than threads of the thinnest-spun sugar; the tree hung with gold-illuminated sugar leaves that looked to that shepherd-man sailor like fleeces of golden perfect wool, golden fleece between a golden woman's legs, the legs of the Sea-One, stretched gold and purple at close of day, Her labia opening, closing, opening, closing" (216). And at the very end of the novel, when Pierre nears the end of his narration and therefore the end of his life, he recalls the ship of sugar his fellow slave and martyred wife had spun out of sugar threads, and his escape by sea to the other world takes the form of rich poetical and proliferating images, setting him loose: "Through the clouds reflected in the cistern, I see my Pélérine, who comes in her ship of sugar threads, gossamer on the light. It is manned by hundreds of spiders, golden-bellied, crimson-legged, opal-eyed, amethyst-tongued. Yes . . . through gold and purple light glides the *PÉLÉRINE*, a ship that needs but one great sail, that spreads so high the top is lost in clouds" (248). This is the image of grace Frazier Russells finds, as I do, unforgettable. It works as an anamnesis, a remembrance of things past bringing together previous images from his life on the plantation and other moments from the narrative, recovering and condensing them in a poetical set of associations for the sheer delight of their improbable, irrepresentable madness; this final image is a clear invitation to enjoy the word-forging rather than to actually picture the wealth of baroque fantasy at work in the hyphenated concatenations.

Novel in Progress

Eakins is now working on a novel set in the Catskill Mountains, the place where she and her husband have renovated a house. There she usually takes part in organizing the Outloud Festival in Claryville, New York, every summer (from 1986 to the present), and invites writers and poets to read their work. She says that the new novel is "closer to home" than her previous fiction: it is both closer in time, as the narrative seems to be set in the nineteenth or early twentieth century, and closer in place, no longer on a Caribbean island. Yet the sheer poetry of the excerpts she has published and the capacity of her writing to render the most humble growing and murmuring in nature gives the writing a sense of wonder. It echoes the strangeness and vivid strength of Edith Wharton's most uncharacteristic novels, *Summer* and *Ethan Frome*. It carries the same love for life in front of the sternness of custom and prejudice in a prose that celebrates the love between two sisters in the midst of tension, exhausting daily chores on a farm, and a family's harsh disowning of their fallen daughter, a prose of magnificent beauty, not so much in spite of the harshness or rising above it, but together with it, expressing one's regret and passion.

The story is seen from the viewpoint of the remaining daughter, who has otherwise no liberty. Her passivity gives greater intensity to her bearing witness to her sister's escape and downfall. She is fascinated and paralyzed by envy, dread, and pain in her elegy to the absent sister. From within the prison of her conventional vision, a crying voice emerges, tense and calm at the same time, envious and resigned and yet loving, as it is expressed through their prosaic occupations in a dense prose which reflects their conflict: "Bushels and bushels of beans I could snap no faster in the cream-colored basin with the blood-red rim chipped out like shale, layers of dark blue under-enamel rimming rust" ("Bounty" 306). There is a castrating violence in the repetitive steadiness of the work, and the sweat shows the disproportionate strenuousness of the gesture burdened with anger: "With the smallest knife I snipped the pointed ends of the beans, then pulled the spine strings, trying to pull all across each bean in one draw, then snap the beans in three, not fast but steady in my work, not once wiping from my forehead drops of sweat falling in my eyes while Alice, stretching, walked down the stairs of the porch to the pump, doused her head" ("Bounty" 306). This is an excerpt from the end of the novel, ironically entitled "Bounty," when instead of marveling at her sister's baby taken for "bounty," the narrator tells about the loss of her sister, ravished from her world by contemporary buccaneers (most likely in prostitution) because she has had an illegitimate child. And all this is said without explanation, avoiding dialogue between the characters and taking refuge in the material occupations of rural life, which in turn cry out over people's silence. To emphasize the loss, the narrator depicts her world before the loss, a world of tension and plenty at once, shown through the filter of an uneasy yet elegiac vision whose lyricism is quelled by the pain of the loss.

Another published excerpt from an earlier part of the novel is entitled "Stopping in Snow." It shows the character Amy as she goes into the hills, which are deep in snow in the winter, to take photographs of birds. This triggers a reflection on the limitations of art in front of nature, as Amy wonders, after taking the picture of a blue jay: "That was her shot. She wondered if the camera would record the intimacy of it" (164). The sense of intimacy has been established in the text by Eakins's use of the phonic quality of language to render the silence and the sharpness of muffled sounds in a snowed-in landscape as if we were there in Amy's snowshoes: "The soft crunch of her snowshoes signaled in the stillness" (164). Amy goes on to imagine what the photograph record would miss, telling in a nutshell the story of the bird in the winter: "The image wouldn't capture the menacing cruise, the insolent peck, the elegant gangster's daintiness of this solitary thief, scratcher, survivor, making the best he could in the bare-bones winter world" (165). Then Amy underlines her own unworthiness in front of the story she has imagined, triggered by the brief sight she has been granted: "Bold fellow, she didn't deserve him, she didn't have to . . ." (165), and the second reservation is not only about her unworthiness, but about her not "having to" go out and be there to take a picture when the bird came; there was no necessity for her to go out of her way to record, no matter in what limited fashion, the image of the blue jay eating seeds. So the final sentence is twofold: just as Amy was granted the gift of the blue jay, we too, out of no necessity, are given "a bright blue gift" in the story: "But for now she was present in the snow, and the jay before her was a bright blue gift" (165). Eakins's prose is made of such "bright blue gifts" for us who are "present in the snow."

If Eakins is, as she figuratively puts it, putting "together a soup from shattered stones," picking up the strands of variously wounded cultures and their representative characters in her stories and novels, she does not do so as a literary tourist with an eye for exoticism, but to sustain our vital aspiration for meaning. She does not beautify the world in her beautiful command of language, but unsettles our expectations in her shifts in style and narration. She does not explore literature or the world as a detective encoding or decoding clues in a postmodern puzzle, but as a quilt sewer and a sower of dreams, putting pieces together that echo our most inchoate visions. She seems to be putting the pieces of our unconscious together, starting with her cave performance pieces, not controlling the fragile processes of our imaginings, as the scattered lyrics of her recent play, *Portrait (With Horse and Others)*, show, but orchestrating the chaos into something to hold on to. In that, the precision of her language conveys a sense of power to her most experimental rendering of the psyche. And most important, a sense of wonder, the wonder dreams are made of, emanates from her texts, as if her narration had the power to penetrate our dreams and to give a language to our hidden fears and desires. This may well be why her fiction works toward images of grace, not in epiphanic revelations but forging images that are poetically vivid and memorable, expressing the wonder of life and of dreams in a renewed confidence in the power of words not to transcend life, but, simply, to praise it.

Works Cited

Baumbach, Jonathan. "Amorality on the Rampage." Rev. of *The Hungry Girls and Other Stories*, by Patricia Eakins. *New York Times Book Review* 5 February 1989: 36.

Birat, Kathie. " 'Weaving Sails and Plots': Patricia Eakins's Recreation of the Slave Narrative in *The Marvelous Adventures of Pierre Baptiste*." Revisiting Slave Narratives Conference. University of Montpellier, April 4–5, 2003.

Blair, Morgan. Rev. of *The Marvelous Adventures of Pierre Baptiste*, by Patricia Eakins. *Marvels & Tales: Journal of Fairy-Tale Studies* 14.1 (2000): 178–80.

Blake, William. "The Tyger." *The Norton Anthology of English Literature.* 3rd ed. Ed. M. H. Abrams, et al. New York: Norton, 1974. 2: 55–56.

Boyd, Greg. Rev. of *The Hungry Girls and Other Stories*, by Patricia Eakins. *Asylum* 4.4 (1989): 39.

Brown, Rosellen. Advance Comments on *The Hungry Girls*.

Caze, Antoine. "Reduplication and Multiplication: Split Identities in Eakins's Writing." *Reading Patricia Eakins: A Collective Volume of Essays on Patricia Eakins, with Excerpts from Her Fiction.* Orleans: UP of Orleans, 2002. 13–26.

Chenetier, Marc. "Introducing Particia Eakins." *Cahiers de Charles V* 29 (2000): 301–03.

—. "Metamorphoses of the Metamorphoses: Patricia Eakins, Wendy Walker, Don Webb." *New Literary History* 23 (1992): 383–400.

Coover, Robert. "The Gingerbread House." *Pricksongs & Descants.* 1969. New York: Plume, 1970. 61–75.

Craig, William. "Cave Art." *Valley News* (West Lebanon, NH) 29 Oct. 1992: 21.

Eakins, Patricia. *Cahiers de Charles V* 29 (2000): 305-10.
—. "Dream of a Body." *Poetry in Performance* 28 (May 2000): 148–49; *Reading Patricia Eakins: A Collective Volume of Essays on Patricia Eakins, with Excerpts from Her Fiction*. Orleans: UP of Orleans, 2002. 101–06.
—. *The Hungry Girls and Other Stories*. San Francisco: Cadmus, 1988.
—. "Manifesto of a Dead Daughter." *Race Traitor: The Journal of the New Abolitionism* 4 (Winter 1995): 1–5.
—. *The Marvelous Adventures of Pierre Baptiste, Father and Mother, First and Last*. New York: New York UP, 1999.
—. *Portrait (With Horse and Others)*. A Play Conceived and Created by Collision Theory, Text and Lyrics by Patricia Eakins, Original Music by Jon Madof. Unpublished Script, 2002.
—. "The Shade Man." *Iowa Review* 24.2 (1994): 96–105.
—. "A Simple Plea for the Preservation of Eggs." *Box 749* 1.1 (1972): 61–71.
—. "Stopping in Snow." *Reading Patricia Eakins: A Collective Volume of Essays on Patricia Eakins, with Excerpts from Her Fiction*. Orleans: UP of Orleans, 2002. 163–65.
—. "A Transverse Journey to the *Transverse Review*." Publishing Opportunities for Writers of Poetry, Fiction, and Creative Nonfiction. Geneva, New York. April 2002.
Fabre, Claire. "The Orchid: A Hybrid Flower for an Imaginary Eighteenth Century in *The Marvelous Adventures of Pierre Baptiste* by Patricia Eakins." *Reading Patricia Eakins: A Collective Volume of Essays on Patricia Eakins, with Excerpts from Her Fiction*. Orleans: UP of Orleans, 2002. 27–41.
Felix, Brigitte. "The Performance of 'Delicate Duties' in *The Marvelous Adventures of Pierre Baptiste*, or, Living by Letters." *Reading Patricia Eakins: A Collective Volume of Essays on Patricia Eakins, with Excerpts from Her Fiction*. Orleans: UP of Orleans, 2002. 43–66.
Hakala, Sonja. "*Trace Memory*: Touchstones & Performance Art in Enfield." *River* Sept.–Oct. 1992: 1.
McFarlane, Adrian Anthony. "The Epistological Significance of 'I-an-I' as a Response to Quashie and Anancyism in Jamaican Culture." *Chanting Down Babylon: The Rastafari Reader*. Ed. Nathaniel Samuel Murrell, William David Spencer, and Adrian Anthony McFarlane. Philadelphia: Temple UP, 1998. 107–21.
Mecionis, Denise. Rev. of *Portrait (With Horse and Others)*. Show Guide, 11 June 2003. <www.backstage.com>.
Millard, Elizabeth. Rev. of *The Marvelous Adventures of Pierre Baptiste*, by Patricia Eakins. *Rain Taxi* Summer 1999: 18.

Palleau-Papin, Françoise. "La Comparaison en mue dans les nouvelles de Patricia Eakins." *Revue Francaise d'Etudes Americaines* 73 (June 1997): 14–21.

—. "A Conversation with Patricia Eakins." *Sources* (Orleans, France) 5 (Fall 1998): 71–93.

—. "La Derive du recit dans *The Marvelous Adventures of Pierre Baptiste* de Patricia Eakins." *Cahiers de Charles V* 29 Dec (2000): 311–27.

—. "Patricia Eakins, Linguae Regeneratrix, or Hybrid Onomatopoeias." *Reading Patricia Eakins: A Collective Volume of Essays on Patricia Eakins, with Excerpts from Her Fiction*. Orleans: UP of Orleans, 2002. 67–86.

Perkins, Michael "Poetic Achievement of Haunting Beauty." *Woodstock Times* 17 June 1999: Sec. 2.1.

Pughe, Thomas. "Post-Colonialism and Anti-Pastoralism in Patricia Eakins's *The Marvelous Adventures of Pierre Baptiste* and Caryl Phillips's *Cambridge*." *Reading Patricia Eakins: A Collective Volume of Essays on Patricia Eakins, with Excerpts from Her Fiction*. Orleans: UP of Orleans, 2002. 87–98.

Rev. of *The Marvelous Adventures of Pierre Baptiste, Father and Mother, First and Last,* by Patricia Eakins. *Kirkus Reviews* 15 March 1999: 394.

Russell, Frazier. Rev. of *The Marvelous Adventures of Pierre Baptiste,* by Patricia Eakins. *American Letters & Commentary* 12 (2000): 176–77.

Shane, Douglas R. "Elizabeth Austin: Creating Memory." *Upper Valley Magazine Preview of the Arts* Sept.–Oct. 1992: 70.

Violi, Paul. Afterword. *The Hungry Girls and Other Stories*. By Patricia Eakins. San Francisco: Cadmus, 1988. 139–41.

A Patricia Eakins Checklist

Novels and Stories

Oono. Chapel Hill: I-74 Press, 1982.
The Hungry Girls and Other Stories. San Francisco: Cadmus, 1988.
The Marvelous Adventures of Pierre Baptiste, Father and Mother, First and Last. New York: New York UP, 1999.

Uncollected Fiction and Essays

"A Simple Plea for the Preservation of Eggs." *Box 749* 1.1 (1972): 61-71.
"Death in My Country." *Fiction International: Central American Writing* 16.2 (1986): 105-07; *Reading Patricia Eakins: A Collective Volume of Essays on Patricia Eakins, with Excerpts from Her Fiction*. Orleans: UP of Orleans, 2002. 113-16.
"Fertility Zone." *Minnesota Review* 29 (Fall-Winter 1987): 46-50; *Reading Patricia Eakins: A Collective Volume of Essays on Patricia Eakins, with Excerpts from Her Fiction*. Orleans: UP of Orleans, 2002. 127-35.
"Serial Connection." *Other Voices* 8 (Spring 1988): 29-33.
"Love Worms." *Unscheduled Departures: The Asylum Anthology of Short Fiction*. Ed. Greg Boyd. Santa Maria: Asylum Arts, 1991. 57-62.
"R'ha-l'a R'a-H'oum." *Conjunctions* 18 (1992): 339-44.
"The Shade Man." *Iowa Review* 24.2 (1994): 96-105.
"Manifesto of a Dead Daughter." *Race Traitor: The Journal of the New Abolitionism* 4 (Winter 1995): 1-5.
"Bounty." 1996. *Cahiers de Charles V* 29 (2000): 305-10.
"Dream of a Body." *Poetry in Performance* 28 (May 2000): 148-49; *Reading Patricia Eakins: A Collective Volume of Essays on Patricia Eakins, with Excerpts from Her Fiction*. Orleans: UP of Orleans, 2002. 101-06.
"Sleeping through the World's End: An Essay on Kenneth Patchen's *Sleeper's Awake*." *Frigate: The Transverse Review of Books*. July-October 2000 <www.frigatezine.com>.
"The Other Side." *Third Bed* 5 (2001): 67-82; *Reading Patricia Eakins: A Collective Volume of Essays on Patricia Eakins, with Excerpts from Her Fiction*. Orleans: UP of Orleans, 2002. 143-56.
"Black Food." *Reading Patricia Eakins: A Collective Volume of Essays on Patricia Eakins, with Excerpts from Her Fiction*. Orleans: UP of Orleans, 2002. 117-26

"The Widow's Handiwork." *American Letters & Commentary* 13 (2001) 46-50; *Reading Patricia Eakins: A Collective Volume of Essays on Patricia Eakins, with Excerpts from Her Fiction.* Orleans: UP of Orleans, 2002. 137-41.

"Call from Home." *Reading Patricia Eakins: A Collective Volume of Essays on Patricia Eakins, with Excerpts from Her Fiction.* Orleans: UP of Orleans, 2002. 157-58.

"Returning the Bones." *Reading Patricia Eakins: A Collective Volume of Essays on Patricia Eakins, with Excerpts from Her Fiction.* Orleans: UP of Orleans, 2002. 107-11.

"Stopping in Snow." *Reading Patricia Eakins: A Collective Volume of Essays on Patricia Eakins, with Excerpts from Her Fiction.* Orleans: UP of Orleans, 2002. 163-65.

Patricia Eakins
Photograph by Michal Heron

Book Reviews

Thomas Bernhard. *Three Novellas: Amras, Playing Watten, Walking.* Trans. Peter Jansen and Kenneth J. Northcott. Foreword Brian Evanson. Univ. of Chicago Press, 2003. 174 pp. $25.00.

This volume is a welcome addition to the translated oeuvre of one of this century's most important and celebrated (outside the U.S.) writers. As Brian Evanson argues in his intelligent and perceptive forward, we can see many of Bernhard's topics and techniques developed in miniature in these novellas, from the themes of madness, suicide, and philosophical speculation to the stylistic techniques of unparagraphed prose, obsessive repetition, and an emphasis on the musicality of language. For readers already familiar with Bernhard's work, these new translations are a valuable complement to the novels and plays, for here one may more easily trace the movement from the more expansive experimentation of *Amras,* through a sort of "middle passage" of *Playing Watten,* to the stylistic breakthrough into the crystallized obsession of *Walking* (published a mere two years after *Playing Watten*). For new readers of Bernhard, however, I'm not sure that this volume would be the best of introductions. *Amras,* which details the confinement of two brothers who survive a suicide pact in which their parents have died, is narrated by one of the brothers and is composed of letters, journal entries, his sibling's scribblings, and other fragments. The prose remains disjointed, uneven, and ultimately perplexing. The novella lacks the distillation and purity of the later works and even seems to be missing the humor and lyrical music of the novel *Gargoyles* (1967); it finally seems more of a Gothic grotesque than a major or important work. In *Playing Watten*—the story of a morphine-abusing doctor who refuses to play his weekly game of cards after the suicide of one of the players—we see a transition from disjointed fractions or unfinished fragments to unbroken, unparagraphed prose, with longer, somewhat repetitive sentences. It is finally with *Walking,* however, that Bernhard's writing comes into its own. We have the familiar acerbic meditations on art, madness, philosophy, and suicide, here in the context of two friends taking a walk. This novella, a fine introduction to Wittgenstein, contains one of the best encapsulations of Bernhard's aesthetics and ontology: "The art of existing against the facts, says Oehler, is the most difficult. . . . If we do not constantly exist *against,* but only constantly *with* the facts, says Oehler, we shall go under in the shortest possible space of time." It is with *Walking,* worth the price of admission, that we understand how Bernhard's writing, a writing constantly struggling *against,* is a consistent, desperate, humorous, bitter, and all-too-human attempt to keep from going under. [Jeffrey DeShell]

Janice Galloway. *Clara.* Simon & Schuster, 2003. 425 pp. $25.00.

This extensively researched biographical novel about concert pianist Clara Schumann requires a supple mind. Accept this as a viable version of Clara's life, and the piano lid of doubt will cease its incessant slamming across your bruised knuckles. Galloway, intent on faithful, empathetic renderings, spent six years writing the book, studying letters, diaries, and biographies, along with detailed histories of the era, to create a swirling demonstration of the Schumanns' daily life. Galloway choreographs a visceral sleight-of-hand, tugging the reader within variable degrees of proximity to Clara's voice and those of both her overcontrolling father and Robert Schumann, composer slash addled husband. Stripped of heroic veneer, a demivulgar fecundity hangs in the air—seams of gloved hands seep, a bandage is the color of cheese, cigar smoke fills florid rooms. Enmeshed with Robert—to whom she feeds "jellied wine from her own fingers" while he suffers "pains and fears he could not describe"—Clara tours Europe and performs brilliantly. Ever dutiful, Clara copes with whatever comes up. After a miscarriage, blood clots slithering through her body, she calculates stain-potential and opts for a maroon dress for the evening's performance. Robert is a guy who is evidently irritated by everything, including the color of the walls. Aggravated by his wife's success and his inability to support his large family, Robert comes across as a bit of a weenie. Clara, equal parts breadwinner and Stepford wife, alters her behaviors to accommodate everyone around her. Her own diary was, for a time, dictated to her by her father, who felt compelled to manipulate how the family would be perceived by future historians and biographers. Show me a two-artist-eight-baby household, in any era, where at least one parent isn't on the brink of insanity; that the female partner endures the burden of responsibility better is perhaps simply an underdocumented occurrence. [Jean Smith]

A. B. West. *Wakenight Emporium.* FC2, 2002. 128 pp. Paper: $10.95.

Like David Markson's *Wittgenstein's Mistress,* this book is charming first for its syntax, drawing its effect more from the narrator's voice, her mental stutters and turns of phrase, than from the various items she discusses. Not that these items lack charm. In thirty-one vignettes—which the narrator calls "quarrels"—that voice (and so the book) describes a universe of humans, Martians, and extraordinary animals, governed by physical laws slightly more elaborate than the ones most of us are familiar with. In place of plot, the details of this universe come to us through a progression of thoughts and second-thoughts: "I can't recall what I was going to say about the future. . . ." she tells us halfway through a chapter called "The Thing about the Future"; then, a few lines later: "Oh yes. This was it: a fragment of prose." In this meandering way we learn about "quick time," the penises of flying ants, how birds see the world, the curious patterning of the palindrome moth, and the direction of the future, which is "up." The narrator's voice is in turns scientific and maternal, not just storylike but *storybook*like, which means that at times her quips can feel cute or corny (depending, I guess, on the predisposition of the reader); however, she doesn't seem overly concerned with how her words are taken, which is another aspect of her charm. Instead, she works through her series of meditations as if with a greater purpose in mind, ostensibly seeking a kind of truth, even if, as she says, "the very suggestion that the promotion of a few truths could avert our now-unavoidable annihilation crowns wishful thing with . . . is mere wishful thinking" (*sic*). Failure to avert annihilation notwithstanding, West's book is a beautiful attempt to move the reader outside of mundane human experience—hence the focus on external perspectives: physics, Martians, birds, and insects with their own "raspy little affairs"—in order to arrive at a broader sense of humanity and the big scheme of things. [Martin Riker]

Nicole Brossard. *The Blue Books*. Trans. Larry Shouldice and Patricia Claxton. Coach House, 2003. 352 pp. Paper: $19.95.

"She rides eager astride the delible ink." This volume reprints translations of the first three "novels" by a major experimental Quebecois writer, originally published in the early 1970s. In her preface Brossard recalls the excitement of this period when young writers saw the text as the site for social and personal transformation, which in her case focused on emerging new identities as Quebecois, female, and lesbian. In these works Brossard develops her transgressive writing procedures, in which the novel is evoked only as a set of presuppositions to be written against and exploded. Linearity, indeed any form of formal predictability, is rejected as representative of patriarchal power, against which this writing deploys all means possible. The works insistently point to themselves as texts and elicit the active participation of the reader. Fiction for Brossard is precisely the consciousness of possibilities denied by the powers that be as unrealistic. These three works evidence a clear trajectory as Brossard rapidly complicates and broadens the scope of her writing so that each serves as preparation for the demands of its succeeding text. *A Book* is relatively abstract and homogeneous in style, characters and settings are sketchy, and at least half the text is directly critical and self-reflective in manner. The text consists of ninety-nine short segments printed one per page, leaving ample blank space intended to activate the reader in generating the book. *Turn of Pang* is formally similar but incorporates a much broader range of linguistic registers and visual effects, as well as being more overtly political. A natural extension of these textual complexities, *French Kiss, or, A Pang's Progress* is the real dazzler of the collection. The text is ostensibly organized around a drive by Marielle along Sherbrooke Street, which transverses Montreal. As always for Brossard, the city itself is the text, with its labyrinthine possibilities and diverse voices, haphazard and simultaneous goings-on, its apparent thereness and incessant imaginative remaking. Marielle too, or alternatively her car, named Violet, becomes an expanding and unpredictable text. Separately are various other characters, two of whom perform the French kiss in the heart of the Latin Quarter. Actually, of course, the kiss is a stretch of text, very effectively translated by Patricia Claxton, in which Brossard pulls out all the stops of linguistic play and association to enact the full erotic and exploratory possibilities of the text as kiss. *French Kiss* is a wonderful achievement, linguistically exuberant and politically sophisticated. [Jeffrey Twitchell-Waas]

Steve Tomasula. *VAS: An Opera in Flatland*. Art and design Stephen Farrell. Barrytown/Station Hill, 2003. 367 pp. $34.00.

Square is looking for an end to the story he is writing. His mother-in-law wants Square and his wife, Circle, to have a second child and go to the opera (but in reverse order). Circle, who besides a daughter has had a miscarriage and an abortion, wants Square to have a vasectomy. Square's indecision regarding all of this forms the plot of *VAS*, a beautifully vibrant collaboration between writer Steve Tomasula and artist Stephen Farrell. The story is told in fits and starts, separated by and interwoven with meditations on 100+ years of eugenics, pieces of dismembered comic books, and medical illustrations both antiquated and cutting-edge. The prose, which balances terrifying facts and a desperate humor with an ease worthy of David Markson, worries over what we are making of ourselves and our fictions about ourselves. These concerns, as implied by Square's name, are borne from wanting to not be hip to the times, a desire voiced by the novel's Johann Wolfgang von Goethe epigraph: "Men are to be viewed as the organs of their century, which operate mainly unconsciously." In these days of hyper-Cartesian obsession with accessorizing and rewriting bodies, how can anyone regard a vasectomy—with its ancestry of forced sterilization programs (of the Nazis and the U.S. and nearly every other industrialized nation)—as an innocent procedure? In the desire to *have* bodies and not *be* bodies, how ideologically resonant is Square (and the reader) to—picking one example from the novel's many—the U.S. Public Health Service's Tuskegee untreated-syphilis experiment? If that sounds preposterous, then it is to Tomasula's credit that the novel makes it seem much less so. Reading *VAS*, I felt pushed a bit higher above our own cultural Flatland, an experience both disturbing and enlightening, and one for which I am grateful. [Adam Jones]

Yaakov Shabtai. *Past Continuous*. Trans. Dalya Bilu. Overlook, 2003. 389 pp. Paper: $16.95.

Zikhron Devarim (Remembrance of Things) was first published in 1977, four years before Yaakov Shabtai died at age forty-seven. *Past Continuous*, its English translation, was published in 1983. A new edition of that translation reclaims for English readers one of the supreme achievements in Israeli fiction. The novel, Shabtai's first, begins by announcing: "Goldman's father died on the first of April, whereas Goldman himself committed suicide on the first of January." Set in Tel Aviv, *Past Continuous* focuses on the nine months between April Fool's Day and New Year's Day, which are bracketed by the death of a father and his son. It concentrates on the activities and affiliations of Goldman, Caesar, and Israel, three friends in their forties whose names are suggestive of the three varieties of Jewish experience—ghetto, assimilationist, and Zionist. After revealing the novel's most dramatic event, Goldman's suicide, in his first sentence, Shabtai implicates his reader in a network of shifting relationships among hundreds of characters, disdaining mere plot but generating a dense, dynamic colloid of human lives. *Past Continuous* is constructed according to the principle of association: one name leads to another, and the reader's attention often hops in midsentence, sentences whose verbs lack allegiance to any single tense. A compulsive philanderer, Caesar believes that life is "fluid and formless and aimless, and everything was possible in it to an infinite degree, and it could be played backward and forward like a roll of film." The style that Shabtai forges for a mutable world, in which Goldman's sister Naomi can fall out the door of a moving car and pass away forever, is one fluid, restless paragraph for the entire length of the novel. It could and should be played backward and forward. However, though her translation from Hebrew is otherwise supple and fluent, Dalya Bilu chose to divide the quick, dense mass of Shabtai's original into discrete paragraphs and to introduce punctuation not present in *Zikhron Devarim*. The novel becomes more accessible, though at the cost of compromising Shabtai's Heraclitean vision. Even so, *Past Continuous* is not an easy book to get into, though it is nearly impossible to get out of. Moving testimony to the fleetingness of all we encounter, it has earned an enduring place in contemporary Hebrew fiction. [Steven G. Kellman]

Douglas Glover. *Elle*. Goose Lane, 2003. 205 pp. Paper: $17.95.

Based on the true story of a Frenchwoman abandoned on the Isle of Demons during one of Jacques Cartier's colonization trips to Canada in the mid-sixteenth century, Douglas Glover's new novel and its eponymous narrator are trapped between the Old World and the New. Left for dead on an island populated by shit-covered rocks and seabirds, Elle, a headstrong girl fond of reading, fucking, and public executions, survives by stumbling through a mad terrain of ice, reminiscence, and intense solitude. As she recounts this ordeal/adventure, languages, landscapes, religions, and cultures mix in a dreamlike mélange in what she calls an unofficial nonhistory or antiquest. And like many a dispossessed antiheroine, Elle's reality is that she has always been alone. "My mind screams, I want to go home. But then I have a depressing thought—all my life, even in France, I have struggled to learn new customs, found myself on the outside looking in, always spoken of in words I could not fathom." Elle's understanding of European society's treatment of women, if not unique, is certainly evolved, but during her time on the island she becomes almost clairvoyant in her expectation of what a modern world will require from the Western mind; in exile she is transformed into a woman aware that she belongs nowhere and to no one and that she is not alone in this. Simultaneously, she goes through a somewhat more remarkable transformation: she becomes a bear. While it remains unclear to both Elle and the reader whether or not this transformation occurs only in her mind, Elle knows that what she has certainly become is "more like a garbled translation than a self." As she loses touch with her original sense of self/reality, the reality of the narrative also becomes less clear and perhaps less important. We pass through a period of disorder in Elle's hallucinatory brilliance; Greek myth, medieval theology, and Native American creation stories come together in a patchwork of observation until finally Elle is left with a splintered new image of humanity, outside the collective story-making machines of her time. A surprisingly likable character in all her degenerate in/coherence, Elle's tale is not only smart and strange, but funny too, and really rather touching. [Danielle Dutton]

Prakash Kona. *Streets that Smell of Dying Roses*. Fugue State, 2003. 246 pp. Paper: $14.00

"Joy is finite, but grief infinite." So goes the unofficial premise of this hauntingly beautiful and meditative treatise on the aura of the streets, in particular those of Hyderabad, India, not only the birthplace of the author but a place where tradition, modernity, fear, loathing, joy, and oppression live simultaneously. But while Kona's eye seems never to waver from the deprivations and animal instincts inherent in the underbelly of street life, joy and exaltation are found here, too, often in unexpected places. Kona's style is at times hallucinatory, ethereal, gritty, and poetic. It is a meandering narrative, a rough guide of sorts to living in one's surroundings, wherever that may be, with eyes and heart wide open. Kona's narrative is sensory in the extreme sense: one can feel the oppressive heat, smell the rotting and decay, and at once feel empathy for the lacking and be moved by the innocence of their situation. Preoccupation for social equality is paramount here, and poverty is both feared and despised, though recognized with a steely determination to present things as they truly are. With clarity and vision, though begging more questions than providing answers, Kona stimulates the social and moral conscience. When Kona writes, "I never thought a street could be more real than the streets of Hyderabad," we believe him because by the end of the narrative, satisfyingly, we feel exactly the same way. [Michelle Reale]

Andrzej Stasiuk. *Tales of Galicia*. Trans. Margarita Nafpaktitis. Twisted Spoon, 2003. 140 pp. Paper: $14.00.

Tales of Galicia begins with what appear to be separate incidents occurring in the southern Polish hinterland that gradually become interwoven as episodes multiply and unspoken or unnoticed connections emerge. They depict the working poor, obscure denizens of small towns and rural residents of nearby collective farms, or what has become of them in their decline, a meltdown apparently as rapid as that of the Soviet Union. These touching, opinionated, rugged characters, reveling in their plague of miseries and occasional epiphany, reveal an unquenchable thirst for life, for more of what life affords, for what they believe is their due. Stasiuk's terse soundings resonate hauntingly among these nearly destitute, desperately unhappy, joyfully exuberant ne'er-do-wells, whose cries of heartache and drunken cheer echo back and forth as the tales cohere into a novel, their forms of hunger felt as akin to one's own, like their thwarted ambitions, prostrate beneath ineluctable destiny. We also should enjoy the author's marvel of impressionistic economy: entire careers and personalities nailed by a single event, a matter of significant choice, a wry twist of fate. While some magical touches in defiance of realism are to be expected, here their sudden mystery works, casting a subtle spell over the events they enchant, setting the stage for the emergence of the novel's unexpected hero, one returned from the dead, uncomfortably in search of the peace of mind that eluded him in life. The understated nature of Stasiuk's art, his familiarity with the multitudes of ways in which desperation may dog people's lives, as well as his unobtrusive display of intimacy with their several flights to doom, prompts one to long for speedy translation of his other works, for by this slim volume alone Stasiuk warrants recognition as a man of letters of a very high order indeed. [Michael Pinker]

Raymond Queneau. *We Always Treat Women Too Well*. Trans. Barbara Wright. Intro. John Updike. Foreword Valerie Caton. New York Review Books, 2003. 169 pp. Paper: $12.95; *Witch Grass*. Trans. and intro. Barbara Wright. New York Review Books, 2003. 313 pp. Paper: $14.00.

If you'd like fries with your philosophy, then *Witch Grass* is an excellent place to go. The delight Queneau (1903-1976) took in transposing Descartes into spoken French leaps off the page, and the result of his efforts is a hilarious novel of ideas and social manners, with metafiction present as well. *Witch Grass* is packed with acute observances of domestic situations, crackling and believable dialogue, intrigues concocted in a chip shop, a mystery surrounding a blue door, evidence of how a caricature can metamorphose into an entity, and discussions about being and nonbeing. A blurb on the back cover of this edition suggests that Queneau's world could be menacing, but this pays insufficient attention to a saving humor, which was always genial, though never toothless. It is displayed in intricate wordplay, flat or sharp one-liners, repetition of lines and situations, and the formal effects he is perhaps best known for (see *Exercises in Style*, one of his most popular books). Pierre declares that he is observing a man. Asked whether he's a novelist, Pierre replies, "No. Character." In the Queneau world this appears unremarkable. Philosophical concerns are presented on a variety of planes, but with a light touch that neatly transforms them into good-humored fiction that provokes thought. The weight of the work is never too much on one side or another, and the apparent digressions always lead back to the main body of the novel.

We Always Treat Women Too Well, an altogether different work, employs some of the same devices: repetition, wordplay, offbeat humor. Set in Dublin during the 1916 uprising, this cartoon of Irish rebels—their names lifted freely from Joyce's *Ulysses*—was published in 1947 under a pseudonym, "Sally Mara." It may now find more admirers of its sensibility than it did on its first appearance. Written in protest at the enthusiasm present in France for black humor and gangster novels, the novel is filled with graphic violence and sexual scenes that never attempt to be cathartic or prurient. Because of its content, the status of *We Always Treat Women Too Well* in Queneau's oeuvre has been disputed. Inadvertently, such an argument is continued in this edition by the inclusion of two introductory essays aimed at establishing the novel's importance. Updike is subtly patronizing; Caton gives away the plot completely. A full enjoyment of the novel's antics and purposes is best achieved by reading the text without benefit of these commentators. Wright's notes here, as in *Witch Grass,* prove sufficient introduction, and she is as respectful in these as she is in her excellent translations. [Jeff Bursey]

Sandra Newman. *The Only Good Thing Anyone Has Ever Done.* Harper-Collins, 2003. 389 pp. $24.95.

In a debut novel full of deft twists and unexpected intersections, Sandra Newman's narrative spans a world's worth of exotic locations and manages to weave together plotlines as diverse as germ warfare, professional blackjack, and New Age quackery. The novel's depressed yet genial narrator, Chrysalis Moffat, already frail from her work on a deconstructive treatment of *Dr. Faustus* and further traumatized by her mother's death, retreats beneath her bed, only to be coaxed out by her drug-addled, emotionally stunted brother Eddie. Together they open the Tibetan School of Miracles in their mother's mansion with Eddie's acquaintance Ralph, a charismatic former potter, designated as the venture's sham guru. The farcical sequence of events that follows, relayed in Chrysalis's wry, self-deprecating voice, is entertaining, but not nearly as engaging as the back story that gets filled in along the way. Switching to a terse, outline-driven report format at times, Chrysalis conveys bare-bones summaries of key events out of chronological sequence without robbing the reader of the pleasure of watching as the pieces finally fall into place. The back-story's seemingly unrelated threads—Chrysalis's search for answers about her scientist father and her own origins as a Peruvian orphan, Eddie's quest for his long-lost first love Denise, Ralph's past relationship with his gypsy/prostitute mother—dovetail in surprising ways as the three principal characters begin to implode within the confines of their thriving spiritual center. While Newman was a student of the late W. G. Sebald, the audacious sprawl of the plot brings to mind the pyrotechnics of Kurt Vonnegut or T. C. Boyle; that said, this is a highly original, readable novel that's somehow deeply cynical and yet ultimately sympathetic to the fates of its damaged characters. [Chris McCreary]

Karl Iagnemma. *On the Nature of Human Romantic Interaction*. Dial, 2003. 212 pp. $22.95.

Iagnemma, who works as a research scientist at MIT, is clearly aware of various scientific investigations into the nature of atomic particles; ethnological surveys of "primitive" societies; the workings of digestive systems; the nineteenth-century explorations of the brain. He recognizes that although science and pseudoscience try to chart underlying forces that govern existence, they cannot really achieve knowledge of human interaction. He is an heir of Hawthorne, another American writer fascinated by the failure of experiments (see "Rappaccini's Daughter"). Poe, Melville, James—well versed in biology, psychology, and ichthyology—are also romance writers obsessed with the curious inabilities of science to marry humanism. And of course Iagnemma joins such distinguished contemporaries as Pynchon, DeLillo, and McElroy in their extravagant romances involving entropy, fractal shapes, and information multiplicities. In every story in Iagnemma's collection there are references to mathematical theorems or "kingdom, order, species" or theory. Thus in the wonderful "Children of Hunger" the physician claims that his wounded patient allows him to "observe, not simply hypothesize, the stomach's actions." "The Phrenologist's Dream" has a description of a head "crisscrossed with thin black lines that divided her skull into thirty-five organs, combativeness and wonder and acquisitiveness and wit sectioned into neat parcels." The narrator of the title story tries to complete his thesis, entitled "Nonlinear Control of Biometric Systems." Iagnemma's scientists are usually astonished by the cruel, ironic, horrifying others—lovers, friends, and partners—who rebel against abstract equations, plotted surveys, cold abstractions. And, therefore, the stories play with reversals, insanities, "common sense." And the collection becomes, in many ways, a cabinet of curiosities. It asserts that we don't know what is coming; that there "are events in nature . . . that cannot be explained or reproduced, that simply are." And finally we bow to shock and awe and incomprehensible faith. [Irving Malin]

Louis-Ferdinand Céline. *Fable for Another Time*. Trans. and intro. Mary Hudson. Notes and preface Henri Godard. Univ. of Nebraska Press, 2003. $55.00; paper: $25.00.

Reading Céline can be an odd experience: one is simultaneously drawn to his masterful and original style and, at times, particularly with some of his later work, disturbed by his reactionary politics. In *Fable for Another Time* Céline offers a story that cuts very close to his own life. The narrator, like Céline, is a man in prison, accused of collaboration with the Germans. *Fable* is his attempt to reveal the hypocrisy of his accusers, to justify himself, and finally, to move past the accusations and back into the literary world. Mary Hudson offers a nimble English version of *Fable*'s original French, conveying Céline in all his thorny and questionable glory. Nevertheless, despite *Fable*'s deft linguistic turns, despite its many strengths from a stylistic perspective, it is much harder to set the question of Céline's politics to one side here than it is with Céline's other works, largely because Céline is continually thrusting the question into the reader's face, suggesting that the reader too isn't blameless. The novel is at once admirable and unsettling, yet at the same time, because of Céline's obsessive circling around his imprisonment, oddly static. Though *Fable* is well worth the attention of those who have already read Céline's other work, those coming to him for the first time might be better advised to begin with *Journey to the End of Night* or *From Castle to Castle* instead. [Brian Evenson]

Ira Sher. *Gentlemen of Space*. Free Press, 2003. 291 pp. $23.00.

Ira Sher's excellent first novel, *Gentlemen of Space,* inscribes itself in the tradition of those works—e.g., Kazuo Ishiguro's *When We Were Orphans*—in which, according to the narrative designs of its sufferer, the weight of personal loss is borne by many. Florida high-school science teacher Jerry Finch wins an essay competition that allows him to join NASA's last mission to the moon. He blasts off with Neil Armstrong and Buzz Aldrin, hops around and collects rocks, is made a national hero, then goes missing. Jerry's housing complex, already besieged by well-wishers and hangers-on, becomes the site of a round-the-clock vigil. After a desperate search, the astronauts return empty-handed. However, like the citizens camping out near Jerry's apartment (whom they join), they keep the faith that Jerry is still alive and, in solidarity, vow not to take off their spacesuits until he is found . . . or so our narrator, Georgie Finch, Jerry's son, nine at the time of these events, would have us believe. It may be the case that in the fictional world so handsomely sculpted by Sher, NASA sent astronauts to the moon in 1976 and that one of them, Jerry Finch, went missing, but as things get stranger and stranger—with astronauts going crazy, Georgie getting phone calls from his father in space, so many people believing someone could stay alive for weeks on the moon, Neil Armstrong courting Georgie's mother—it becomes clear that something else, something ultimately more devastating, is going on. This book-length projection of Georgie's grief, anger, and uncertainty onto a national screen is beautifully handled, carefully paced, and freighted with mystery. *Gentlemen of Space* is one of those books you wish the author had found a way not to end. [Laird Hunt]

Edmund White. *Fanny: A Fiction*. Ecco, 2003. 369 pp. $24.95.

Fanny is an extraordinary break from Edmund White's previous work. It purports to be the final book by the prolific Victorian writer Francis Trollope, the uncompleted biography of her friend Francis Wright, a free-thinking feminist who attempted to create a utopian community in the antebellum South. We follow these two extraordinary women from the beginning of their friendship in early-nineteenth-century London, through their visits with Lafayette, to their ill-fated journeys up the Mississippi and Ohio Rivers—with a long stopover in Cincinnati, White's birthplace—and side trips to Haiti and Italy. Yet despite being a comic, historical novel with a female narrator, *Fanny* maintains a clear connection to White's long-standing preoccupations. White has always played with a campy humor, even when it was difficult to distinguish from his lyricism. But it is Wright, and especially Trollope, who are most familiar. They emerge as rebels against a social order that would constrain them, survivors in a world that would destroy them, and lovers—but not of each other—in a world that would keep them from sexual fulfillment. They succeed because of their wit, their intelligence, their "gumption," as well as their well-developed ability to ignore whatever truths get in their way. Thus the two Fannys are much like the characters of White's trilogy of autobiographical novels. Indeed, the book harkens back to White's earliest work, his play *Blue Boy in Black,* which told the tale of an indomitable black maid in the home of a successful writer who, after breaking up her employer's marriage, seducing him, and becoming his second wife, launches her own literary career. *Fanny,* like *Blue Boy in Black,* is a darkly comic work about race in America and about the kind of ruthless willpower necessary to prevail against the forces arrayed against those who are black, female, or gay. [David Bergman]

Nine of Russia's Foremost Women Writers. Glas New Russian Writing 30. Trans. Joanne Turnbull, et al. Glas, 2003. 286 pp. Paper: $17.95.

Nine is a delightful collection of familiar and unfamiliar names whose considerable range and striking individuality highlight the richness of contemporary Russian fiction by women. Three early stories illustrate variations on the abuse that pregnant women endure from the state medical establishment. Svetlana Alexiyevich's lonely "voices" recount a series of childbirth horrors. Maria Arbatova's mother-to-be cannot be granted proper care, let alone a name. Nina Gorlanova satirizes the bleak comedy of incompetence that expectant mothers face. Each protagonist delivers herself of more than she might have imagined, including withering contempt for what ails the new Russia. Anastasia Gosteva, the most experimental of this company, uses her blasé heroine's inner monologue to suggest the fashionable frenzy of a new intelligentsia's cultural sophistication and myopic human relations. Ludmila Petrushevskaya's two stories unfold delicate explorations of characters on the edge: an old woman so taken by Robert Taylor in *Waterloo Bridge* that she believes she has glimpsed him fleetingly reincarnated; a father desperately trying to revive his dear dead child in yet another nightmare hospital. Margarita Sharapova follows two circus athletes left in the lurch on a tour of Siberia as they pursue a comic railway-journey to rejoin their elusive troupe. Olga Slavnikova offers the first chapter of a novel about a certain Krylov's early life, zany and perverse amid the spiritual expansiveness of the Urals. Natalia Smirnova's two tales are parables, one of a family of women finally dispatching a plague of conniving shoemakers, the other of clever "Nina" turning a fortunate rendezvous with an attractive man into a relationship. Finally, Ludmila Ulitskaya unravels the figure of a modern Penelope, deftly capturing the pathos of one repeatedly inveigled by the convincing designs of other women's lies, perhaps standing for all of us subject to the enchantment of a well-told tale. [Michael Pinker]

Paul West. *Cheops: A Cupboard for the Sun*. New Directions, 2002. 262 pp. $25.95.

Cheops is Paul West's twenty-second novel, and as with W. B. Yeats before him, West's muse gets younger and more vibrant with each new book. Once again West wanders into a corner of history, in this case ancient history, to imagine an unlikely meeting of titans who joust and inspire one another. The novel features multiple narrators, the most important of which are the Egyptian god Osiris, the pharaoh Cheops, and the Greek historian Herodotus. Cheops's dream of astral travel is fulfilled when Osiris allows Herodotus to visit Egypt two thousand years before his birth and interview the pharaoh whom he disparaged in the tenth book of his history. This Herodotus is a sensationalist hack who somehow wins the pharaoh's favor, and presiding over the verbal and intellectual competition is a god who reaches up into the twentieth century to bring the music of Frederick Delius to Cheops to soothe him on his passage into eternity. Since the early 1980s West has written one fascinating historical novel after another, but *Cheops* stands as perhaps his most audacious. The anachronisms that appear in early works here become a central motif as West suggests that all human events, wherever they occur in time, impinge upon one another and define what it means to be human. The Delius sections, a narrative within the narrative, are delightful, not only a paean to but an argument for the centrality of music in human experience as perhaps the most refined of the arts. West's historical fictions remind one of Foucault's phrase about "reverse discourse," in this case a narrative that interrogates and problematizes other narratives. Herodotus's Cheops becomes one version among many, but not one born of malice or ill will. Instead, West illustrates the often-overlooked notion that history is as much a narrative as fiction and often just as impressionistic and individual. *Cheops* is further evidence that West remains one of our most challenging and invigorating novelists. [David W. Madden]

Michael Schulze. *Love Song*. White Light (www.whitelightpress.com), 2003. 999 pp. $49.95.

Consider the villagers who first encounter that mutant creature conjured in the lightning-struck laboratory of Victor Frankenstein, who stand suddenly in the presence of massive, brutal novelty, a beautiful sort of beast, spliced from familiar bits but a strikingly new commodity, thunder-stepping about their village, demanding notice, terrifying and yet darkly intriguing. To read *Love Song,* a work twenty years in the creation, an audacious and uncompromising descent into the American fascination with violence and the contemporary pornography of horror, is to be abruptly within the terrifying/intriguing sphere of brutal novelty, something "deep, formless, and profoundly dangerous." It plays with genres—the horror story, the play-within-a-play, the psychosexual mystery-thriller—in streams of language that test the weight-bearing capacity of the printed page. Imagine splicing Poe and Pynchon and Burroughs. What begins as a campy homage to an eccentric producer of fifties horror flicks transmutes into a mutant-story that defies summary: a crackpot behavioral scientist conducts horrific experiments in genetic splicing; a rampaging serial rapist-murderer terrorizes a quiet Midwestern town and becomes a cult hero deemed good for local businesses; an experimental garage band, fronted by a genetic mishap with a second head and an eerie gift for atonal jazz, pursues experimental performance pieces—each part of the American fascination with the darkest elements of sexuality, violence, excess, mayhem, drugs, and celebrity, summarized by the horror-film genre itself (the book moves in and out of an ongoing horror-film project; the text here ends with a massively inventive—and at times impenetrable—working script of the film). And we read, compelled like those stunned villagers by the magnitude of our repulsion and confusion (the book is not for the squeamish: Schulze details sadomasochistic sexuality and brutal killings); we become voyeurs, ultimately participants in the very horror we find so repellent. It is an unsettling, provocative reading experience. [Joseph Dewey]

Ray Gonzalez. *Circling the Tortilla Dragon.* Creative Arts, 2002. 156 pp. Paper: $15.00.

Known primarily as a poet (seven books) and an editor (the *Bloomsbury Review,* twelve anthologies, *LUNA*), Ray Gonzalez here offers a mélange of short-shorts and prose poems that never fail to mystify. "The poets dance to a full moon because they don't know what else to do with themselves," one piece begins. In another a spider takes up residence in a dead baby's shoes and a moth brings a message from the baby itself. Trash men casually toss into their compactor the Komodo dragon that has just eaten the narrator's cat. "I raised him on too many nopales," a mother laments when a cactus begins growing from her son's head. Elsewhere a man returns from the dead to haunt the boys who shot him, and a devil wearing a Tupac Shakur T-shirt tells a son to shoot his wife-beating father. Few of the stories extend past two pages; most are about a page and a half. Gonzalez's mix of the banal and the extraordinary is in every sense marvelous. His stories speak from chinks in the world's bright surfaces. Old myths are torn down even as new ones are tentatively offered then just as quickly withdrawn; laughter gathers; the sidereal logic of dreams bleeds into the waking world—all in, say, 560 words. Gonzalez's stories often remind me of Tomaso Landolfi, while recalling Boris Vian's explanation of method: the projection of reality onto an irregularly tilting and consequently distorting plane of reference. Call them what you will—flash fiction, stories, sketches, illuminations—the texts of *Circling the Tortilla Dragon* desire and embrace us. [James Sallis]

T. C. Boyle. *Drop City*. Viking, 2003. 444 pp. $25.95.

In this, his ninth novel, T. C. Boyle turns his snarky eye on post-*peace, man,* pre-Prankster hippiedom. The denizens of Drop City, CA, are, on the surface, what one might expect: high-school dropouts who've decided to tune out and turn on, draft dodgers, children born into the antitrade of communal living; confused, naive, and eager, the lot of them. Their big-bearded leader is a middle-aged "visionary" whose philosophy of LATWIDNO (Land Access To Which Is Denied No One) eventually brings the Law down on Drop City and propels those inhabitants with the spirit for it to journey to Alaska for a fresh start. Enter Sess Harder and his city-turned-mountain-wife Pamela and their ongoing feud with fellow mountaineer Joe Bosky, airplane-flyin' lush and trap poacher. While at first these characters skate on the dangerously thin ice of caricature as they watch their disparate yet collective desire for love become a raw struggle for survival against the at-times-ruthless landscape, Boyle's slippery method of making each flawed individual capable of his or her own form of transcendence (though none quite capture it), while avoiding the purplish, overmetaphored writing that drowned his last effort, *A Friend of the Earth,* reveals in even the smallest roles a lazy (but mostly genuine) fascination with the world and its extremes of beauty and ugliness. *Drop City* offers neither an ending of joyful liberation nor sadness and pain, though there is plenty of both running throughout the novel, in competing measures, to go around. The members of Drop City and their adoptive brethren are left, instead, with a kind of potential—a starry hope that could either snuff itself out like a wet match or burn indefinitely. The soul of this novel is so full and earnest, so realistically fragile, so accepting of its own stumbling youthfulness, you might gladly go down either road and never look back. [Brian Budzynski]

Millicent Dillon. *A Version of Love*. Norton, 2003. 261 pp. $23.95.

Marx and Freud may be the two great toppled idols of our age, but what happened to Marx is clearer than what happened to Freud. Dillon's risky and gripping tale takes us back to the 1950s, when Freudian psychoanalysis was king. The divorced Edmond begins an affair with his perplexed, vulnerable psychiatric patient Lorle (= "Lorelei") while patronizing Vern Gosling, a rustic figure living in the remote Sierra foothills of California, a virile paragon who can teach Edmond the ropes of male bonding. Both men served in World War II, and the book is, tacitly, the story of what happened during "the explosion of the paradigm," when the wheels of the postwar boom, and its certainties, began to come off. Dillon shreds our normative outlook. Revelations—some shocking—about sex, drugs, manipulation, violence, and death make Lorle realize that Edmond's power games, in trying to extend his psychoanalytic authority to all of life, shake the confines of his personal integrity. *A Version of Love* is like *Light in August* or *Far from the Madding Crowd* as a woman leaving one man, ending up (tentatively) with another, frames a plot that nonetheless defers to atmosphere and ideas. Taut, lyrical, rife with a sense of the catalyzing tension of every act of being alive, Dillon's sinewy, sensual (literally so, engaging all the senses) prose grapples equally with the "risk in repetition, in a foreshortened history of desire," the landscapes of the Sierras, Big Sur, and Mexico, and the feel of eating moldy cheese in a rundown urban apartment. Dillon records an era of transition, with one eye always on our own present moment, also one of transition, perhaps to the "rough beast" that Yeats feared, perhaps not. [Nicholas Birns]

Alvin Greenberg. *Time Lapse.* Tupelo, 2003. 308 pp. $22.95.

For Walter Job, the protagonist of Alvin Greenberg's darkly comic novel *Time Lapse,* "death is an easy thing to manage. Life is another matter." Walter, an accomplished professor of modern literature, leads a double life as a hired killer. This makes for some hectic academic conferences, to say the least: "And when he has let the dead man slump back into the swivel chair, he will roll the wire up and put it back in his pocket and, touching nothing else, gather up his papers and briefcase and depart. He will drive the easy hour and a half on the freeway back to Cincinnati, where the Society for the Study of Modernist Aesthetics will have completed the first day of its annual July meetings, and he will be aware, once again, how, just like that, a death will have been managed, so very easily." While Walter's dual employment is the source of some of the novel's funniest and most unsettling moments, it is more than just a clever gimmick. Instead, it can be seen as just one example of a killer instinct that is disturbingly ubiquitous. Significantly, Walter's initiation into the murder business stems from a husband's drunken threat against his wife in a bar rather than the high-stakes underworld of the cinematic thriller. The novel shrewdly dissects not only the lurking presence of violence but also its naive simplification in popular media. The easy escape of a woman from the hands of a killer on television prompts wry and morbid reflection: "Only by such a vision of the incompetence of death, thinks Walter, is humanity shielded from reality." Greenberg, on the other hand, refuses to indulge such a vision. Beginning as an academic farce, *Time Lapse* develops into a provocative novel of ideas. [Pedro Ponce]

Albert Goldbarth. *Pieces of Payne.* Graywolf, 2003. 214 pp. Paper: $15.00.

Reading Albert Goldbarth is like watching the valedictory address at a university created by a merger between Clown College and MIT. His poetry is aggressively intelligent, full of pratfalls and rimshots, and, embracing low culture as readily as high, science as readily as literature, encyclopedic in a manner far more common to novelists such as Pynchon and McElroy. In this, Goldbarth's first novel, readers of his poetry will recognize some familiar roof-jumping. Here's the story: Eliza Phillips meets former teacher Albert Goldbarth for drinks, during which she speaks of her divorce and recent lesbian marriage, of celestial order and beauty, and of growing up in the home of her philandering, surgical-superstar father. But the hanger gives no notion of the clothing hung thereon. The meeting comprises eighty-seven pages. Remaining pages consist of footnotes and commentary. Everything gets thrown into the hopper—news items, verse, appointment books, quotations, lists, mini-essays—as the novel's long legs stride as Yeats's fly over subjects as disparate as Columbus, werewolves, Fanny Burney's nineteenth-century mastectomy, *Moby-Dick,* ancient Japan, a man with fiberglass tiger-whiskers implanted in his upper lip, quantum physics, supermarket tabloids, the Legion of Super-Heroes. The title commemorates astronomer Cecilia Payne, a role model for Eliza. "I wanted big theories that unified," Eliza says of her parents' divorce and her early fascination with astronomy. One cannot read *Pieces of Payne* without thinking of *Hopscotch* or of Nabokov's poem-and-exegesis *Pale Fire,* but Goldbarth is, as always, much his own man. Impossible to mistake the author here: the play of this man's mind over the landmarks and detritus of our time. Eliza's conversation sets off and fans to flame sparks in Goldbarth's mind that cannot fail to ignite the reader's. [James Sallis]

Jean Frémon. *Island of the Dead.* Trans. Cole Swenson. Green Integer, 2003. 281 pp. Paper: $12.95.

This book is about resemblances and differences, modeling, imitating, shadows, and doubles. It is about lines between one species or genus and another. In particular it is about interactions and distinctions between humans and animals. It is about the process of giving form to the inchoate, seeing patterns in seemingly shapeless phenomena. "What is resemblance?" the narrator asks at one point. "What is imitation?" Like a rebus, this novel invites the reader to see and create connections between the numerous short, apparently disjointed sections that comprise it. We overhear conversations and meditations about bats' and elephants' penises, Chinese ghosts, the Balinese cockfight, the extent to which Darwin's theories of evolution were prefigured in the work of his grandfather, the relationship between Goncharov's *Oblomov* and Samuel Beckett, Glenn Gould's performance technique, mating habits of octopi, the practice of using Latin to denote things in nature, the evolution of Mickey Mouse, Shostakovich's legendary process of composing (pastiche), parrots speaking, birds imitating other birds' songs, Poussin's paintings, the narrator's experience reading a "real" character from his past into a Seurat sketch, the Shakers (who choose not to reproduce themselves), Beethoven's plagiarisms, genetic projects to create miniature vegetables, the ellipsis . . . etc. There are also named characters who make appearances (Sam, Soskine, Emilie, Pilotier, Wilson, Melanie, Pinchard, Milner, Van Gulick), as well as some who never "appear" yet who are referred to (Roman, Gertrude, Thomas, Dawkins, Sidis, Mahdi). What is a character, after all, we might ask, but the creation of a resemblance? Can a character exist? If so, where? "Books, paintings are real ghosts," the narrator posits. This book is unlike any ghost I have encountered. It is the difference that is so striking. [Allen Hibbard]

Toby Olson. *The Blond Box*. FC2, 2003. 285 pp. Paper: $14.95; *Utah*. Green Integer, 2003. 493 pp. Paper: $12.95.

Toby Olson has always been compelled by the mystery of mystery. Whether investigating the mystery of redemption, the alluring pull of the aesthetic impulse, the taking-in of a sweeping natural landscape, or the promise of salvation premised by love and the sweet friction of sex, Olson—like D. H. Lawrence—has long accepted the writer's responsibility to endow the unsuspected immediate with the weight of enchantment without possessing the vocabulary (or, frankly, the interest) to thin that response into the explicable. *The Blond Box* shimmers in a rich sheen of mystery—it begins campily within the genre (a double murder unsolved for twenty years that involves a treasure map, a traveling sex show, and a legendary jazz pianist and juggler) but quickly involves as well the pulling mystery of art (characters are, in turn, mesmerized by the audacious experimental canvases and implicit terrorism of Marcel Duchamp); the intriguing mystery of history (characters wrestle with imperfect recollections, mine newspaper archives and inhabit libraries and dissertations, manage awkwardly the heft of nostalgia and regret, reel within the play of coincidence and chance); and ultimately the luminous mystery of narrative itself (Olson braids three narrative threads that spin a mesmerizing symbol-system of resonance and that foreground ultimately the intricate intensity of plot itself: the account of the 1949 murders themselves outside a dusty Arizona town; the account of a pulp sci-fi writer in 1969 Philadelphia, interested in using the mystery as the subject of the latest installment in his soft-porn detective series, who sends his grad assistant on a fact-finding mission to Arizona; and a draft of that wildly original sci-fi/political futuristic thriller, complete with emendations to the writer for revisions). At every turn Olson reminds his reader how information inevitably recovers ambiguity, how the tidiest sense of remembered history and constructed plot are more journeys into accident and chance, how everyday lives must play out against and amid the luminous, albeit clumsy, mystery of attraction and want. The language, as always with Olson, is broad, adamant, and stunning, this text a conjured place fit for extended habitation.

Utah, reissued as part of the Green Integer Masterworks of Fiction series, testifies to Olson's enduring place in contemporary fiction. David, a masseur whose powerful touch can ease pain and coax revelation, finds himself in crisis: the haunting love of his life has abandoned him to pursue her aesthetic inclinations out west, and his closest friend has wasted away into a death-too-soon. David undertakes a journey west to jumpstart his own dead heart and along the way to clarify his own place at midlife and to settle his past, an ambitious (and potentially clichéd) agenda that Olson manages with originality, dignity, and richness. That David's reclamation ultimately occurs at a mysterious Utah artist colony, that it involves lost children, shattered marriages, compelling adultery, and a creepy vengeance-with-angry-bees scenario, reminds readers of Olson's legitimate position not only as a Lawrencean advocate of the redemptive power of art but also his legacy as a pure, engrossing storyteller. [Joseph Dewey]

Thomas Berger. *Best Friends*. Simon & Schuster, 2003. 209 pp. $24.00.

Best Friends is Thomas Berger's twenty-second novel and evidence that his ironic, inventive muse remains as vibrant as ever. Without the fanfare that should accompany his brilliant accomplishments, Berger has created a fictional oeuvre as rich and varied as any in contemporary American letters. The novel centers on a pair of friends in midlife—Sam Grandy, a feckless though happily married man with no determinable career, and Roy Courtright, heir to a substantial inheritance, who deals in classic cars for upscale clients. The two have been boon companions since youth, know one another thoroughly, and are devoted to each other. When Grandy suffers a heart attack, Courtright is forced to examine a relationship he has long taken for granted. Suddenly involved in family intrigue, deception, financial impropriety, and sex, Courtright comes to despise his friend. Berger has often explored a psychological hinterland where characters suddenly find that the cherished, predictable certainties of their lives have morphed or disappeared altogether. These figures—whether a staid, middle-class businessman, the idle rich on their island retreat, citizens of a small burg, or a white man who shuttles between two ethnic worlds—suddenly discover that the Other is themselves. In *Best Friends* that Other is one's most intimate companion, and the sense of personal and emotional dislocation is overwhelming. Berger has always been fascinated with the disjunction between appearance and essence, and Courtright finds himself contemplating such discrepancies, with no clear resolution to the dilemma. Berger writes in an immaculate prose that is extraordinarily precise and exacting and at the same time delightfully ironic. He excels at abrupt shifts between high and low language that perfectly register the wild emotional shifts of his characters. Every sentence is a foray into new, unexplored emotional territory. As is also the case in many of Berger's novels, the conclusion is a subtle cliffhanger that sends the reader scurrying back through the text to disentangle the narrative's tight coils. *Best Friends* is simply a gem. [David W. Madden]

Robert Buckeye. *The Munch Case*. Amandla (Box 431, East Middlebury, VT 05740), 2003. 165 pp. Paper: $18.00.

Awaiting electroshock therapy, Edvard Munch, painter of *The Scream,* begins to narrate a series of broken fragments. These fragments juxtapose memory and presence, art and life, bourgeoisie and bohemia. They serve as a prelude to the ensuing novel, encapsulating the form, themes, and images of Robert Buckeye's *The Munch Case,* a novelization of Edvard Munch's early career. But *The Munch Case* is no stale historical novel. It is a translation of Munch's work across media: from painting to the novel, from the canvas to the text block. It is the novel Munch would have written about himself were he to have written instead of painted. Descriptions are composed like Munch's paintings, "shaft[s] of moonlight on water." Details reappear with obsessive frequency: the Seine, face-as-mask, the color blue, large eyes, aesthetics, and alcohol. In a beautiful metafictional gesture, Munch develops, in conversations and reflections, the aesthetics that govern the composition of the novel. The book becomes a piece of the fin de siècle decadence it depicts, down to the tropes: tuberculosis, red lips and rogue, the judgmental psychoanalyst and the suffering artist's obsession with sex, alcohol, and the night, obsessions that fuel the artist even as they threaten to destroy him. "Some days I felt I had lived more life than life could bear . . . Until I had had too much. . . . By now I knew the price." The powerful juxtaposition of fragments drives us deep into Munch's anxiety, into the painter's extreme sensitivity: Buckeye's Munch is no Caspar David Friedrich, staring at the edge of nature. Instead, he is a man at the edge of his sanity, staring at himself. [Matthew L. McAlpin]

Gerard Donovan. *Schopenhauer's Telescope.* Counterpoint, 2003. 306 pp. $25.00.

Gerard Donovan's debut novel intertwines dense philosophical ruminations with simple conversational dialogue in a story that reveals humankind's potential for love as well as our potential for evil. Through debates, allegories, fairy tales, moral anecdotes, intellectual jousts, and even a short "screenplay," Donovan's narrative depicts a self-conscious and often morose examination of the human condition. He explores the horrific actions of various historical figures as well as the potential insidiousness hidden within the neighbor next door. The title of the book springs from an odd suggestion by Arthur Schopenhauer, stated here by one of the characters in the novel: "to gain perspective on any problem, we should travel fifty odd years into the future and invert a telescope, look through the wrong end . . . at ourselves as we are, and make decisions with the benefit of hindsight." This peculiar obsession with perception, time, human behavior, and, ultimately, ethics and morality is what colors Donovan's novel. The story involves mostly dialogue between two characters—a history teacher and a baker—in a small, unnamed northern European village during a civil war. The two characters discuss a long history of human cruelty throughout the world, from the horrible mass slaughters of Genghis Khan's army to King Leopold's sponsoring of African genocide in the 1890s to the fires of Dresden. While conversing, the baker digs a hole that is clearly a grave intended for one of the men and possibly many more. This view from Donovan's "telescope" is bleak and sparse. As readers we are forced to imagine the vast horrors humankind has inflicted from antiquity to the twentieth century. However, it is the almost intimate exchange between the two main characters that ultimately becomes the most striking and often startling part of the book. [Mark Tursi]

William Owen Roberts. *Pestilence*. Trans. Elisabeth Roberts. Four Walls Eight Windows, 2003. 214 pp. $19.95.

Pestilence is a novel of debauchery and religious excess set in the fourteenth century during the onset of the Black Plague. Religion is the common thread between two vying storylines as Salah Ibn al Khatib, a young Arab brought up in the cool hallways of Muslim academe, sets out across the Christian "infidel" countries of Europe to kill the king of France. Roberts alternates Salah's clashes with the corrupt and superstitious peoples of Europe with the narrative of a Welsh township called Dolbenmaen, where the end of the world has been presaged by omens but can't be prevented by any amount of penance. Roberts has done his research on the time period, but the book speaks to the present—as one god (of religion) is replaced by another (money), we see a familiar world emerge from Roberts's mélange. However, he is not here to preach—like a kid playing gross-out, Roberts delights in shocking the reader, and his portrayal of medieval Europe abounds with uncomfortable (for both characters and reader) situations. There's Salah, who finds himself wandering through stinking sewers and locked in a tomb with the rotting corpse of a cardinal; add to that the slices of life from Dolbenmaen—a leper's bestiality, a serf's pedophilia—and you have a book not meant for the squeamish. Roberts's language is unaffected and straightforward, countering the epic scope of the novel; the elaborate plot is rendered in short vignettes that convey much in few words. *Pestilence*'s jacket offers comparisons to Salman Rushdie and Umberto Eco, but the book's playfulness lies not in its symbolism, puzzles, or semiotics, but rather in its indulgence in the nuances of the period. Roberts revels in the particulars, creating small triumphs: well-wrought scenes like the one in which Salah emerges from the tomb wearing the cardinal's robes, and the monks who witness his "resurrection" variously wet themselves, run into walls, and lick his feet. These small successes don't necessarily add up to a fulfilling whole; *Pestilence* isn't exhaustive or sweeping, and there are holes in the plot and questions unanswered, things that don't happen in Rushdie's or Eco's writing. Roberts often sets up minor suspenses that end up falling flat, and Salah's story ends abruptly and unsatisfactorily. However, Roberts is a young writer, and *Pestilence* is his second novel (his first translated from Welsh to English). If later books exhibit the exuberance and enthusiasm of this one, readers will have much to look forward to. [Megan McDowell]

Norman Rush. *Mortals*. Knopf, 2003. 715 pp. $26.95.

Norman Rush's first book since *Mating* (1991), *Mortals* is a rich novel of sexual politics set in Botswana during the early days of the post-Cold War era. Rush's protagonist, Ray Finch, is a contract agent for the CIA masquerading as an English professor in Botswana's capitol of Gaborone. Ray and his wife, Iris, whom he obsessively adores after seventeen years of matrimony, argue over Ray's continued involvement with the agency, with their relationship suffering the results. While a sketch of the plot resembles that of a paperback thriller, the high level of word craft, outstanding wit, and Rush's mature intellectual probing raises *Mortals* to the forefront of contemporary literature. Ray's romantic idea that one of the worthiest goals a man can pursue is to find an woman and worship her for the rest of his existence is neither a new nor liberating notion, but Rush's insights betray an unusually keen intellect on the topic of romantic love. If the book has a flaw, it is the length, but even the most exhausting passages are oddly likeable, like a beloved mate whose faults you dote on, as Ray does Iris's. Although Rush's novelistic form and approach is straightforward, his ambition and genius are amply evident in the realms of sexual and political intrigue, where his careful building of ideas and complications simmers into full-fledged outbreaks in both areas. Rush's indictments of the U.S.'s post-Cold War foreign policy charge that the U.S. is guilty of instigating otherwise dormant or harmless elements into violent actions, a serious and immediate subject that the author is nevertheless able to color with humor and levity. In a book of many investigations, the preeminent one is suggested by the title—as well as *Mortals*'s musings on *Paradise Lost*—given absolute free will, what is the best life a man can choose for himself? With great diligence and difficulty, Rush answers the question in a meditative and satisfying manner. [Jason Picone]

A. L. Kennedy. *Indelible Acts.* Knopf, 2003. 191 pp. $23.00.

This collection's twelve stories wonderfully capture the motivation, the tangled mechanics of love. It must be read slowly—as slowly as we read the great loves in *Swann's Way* or *The Wings of the Dove.* (I do not claim that this book is as profound as those novels, but I want to define their dense rendering of love's affections and afflictions.) The first story, "Spared," conveys the slippery words of a man and woman waiting in line at a grocery. Greg, who is married, tries to seduce Amanda by joking. They amuse themselves by playing with words. Greg "had dipped his head and spoken close, close as a kiss beside her ear, because this was appropriate under the circumstance and because he'd hoped that she might like it." Amanda and he are, it seems, actors who speak lines to caress their minds. And it is precisely this complicated dance of rhetoric that leads to bodily desire. There is an intricate design in these stories. The lovers—whether in Venice or London—use language to deny their solipsistic yearnings; at the same time they know that "conversation" really contains private monologues. There are two levels of meaning, and often the levels are somehow not in harmony. Thus Kennedy's style is a kind of arc. Look, for example, at the opening of "A Wrong Thing"—an example of her ambiguous titles: "I would prefer not to open my eyes, not this morning. In the end I know I have to, but I'll do it against my will." The narrator, like many of Kennedy's lovers, is unbalanced—longing not to act, not to face the other—but his very unwillingness hints at his desire. Yes and no! Possess and dispossess! Such binaries come together if only briefly, causing satisfaction and guilt. Kennedy demonstrates that love, like art, mysteriously turns at unexpected times. It is difficult to find one's way in the woods (words) of desire. It makes us wonder, finally, whether love deserves or creates an adverse reaction. [Irving Malin]

Anthony Powell. *Venusberg*. Green Integer, 2003. 253 pp. Paper: $10.95; *O, How the Wheel Becomes It!* Green Integer, 2002. 188 pp. Paper: $10.95.

Anthony Powell is best known for *A Dance to the Music of Time,* a series of twelve interlinked novels that serves as Great Britain's answer to Proust. Green Integer has chosen to reissue several of Powell's novels outside of the *Dance* series, in this case one novel written near the beginning of his career (*Venusberg*, 1932) and the first novella written after the *Dance* series was finished (*O, How the Wheel Becomes It!,* 1983). In *Venusberg* Lushington goes as a special correspondent to a Baltic State, has a long affair, and eventually goes back home. Its characters include an extremely opinionated valet and a count who sells cosmetic products. It reads like Evelyn Waugh's satiric novels and, at its best, is exceptionally funny, the dialogue extremely snappy. Yet somehow, out of such figures of fun, Powell manages to construct a dark, moving, and convincing ending. In *O, How the Wheel Becomes It!* Powell trains his eye upon Shadbold, a minor literary figure whose life becomes complicated when a dead friend's work begins to receive attention and by his discovery in this friend's diary of events that bring him to question his reading of the past. Slightly darker than *Venusberg,* it still possesses Powell's keen wit, departing slightly from the realism of *Dance* to satiric effect. Indeed, these two books show that Powell's range goes far beyond the admittedly brilliant *Dance*—that he, like Waugh, has strengths as a satirist as well as a realist. They suggest that Powell's early work, having fallen under the shadow of *Dance,* has been underestimated. *Venusberg* in particular proves that Powell is worthy of a second look. [Brian Evenson]

M. John Harrison. *Things that Never Happen*. Intro. China Miéville. Night Shade, 2003. 443 pp. Paper: $15.00.

Desire and sickness permeate the stories of M. John Harrison. These dreamy visions explore the uncertainty of self, the fragility of the body, and the inevitable spoiling of desire upon fruition. *Things That Never Happen* offers a panorama of haunted worlds that Harrison has forged from a curious mix of science fiction and realism. He began writing at the end of the 1960s for *New Worlds,* the British hotbed of speculative fiction, and his first stories possess the postapocalyptic mood, neurotic charge, and despairing worldview of British New Wave writers Ballard, Aldiss, and Moorcock. Like Ballard, Harrison paints ordinary worlds riddled with debris and entropy, in which a first-person narrator has a transformative encounter with another, more volatile character. Rather than simply create other worlds, Harrison uses fantasy to examine why people desire fantasy, desire life to be other than it appears to be. For instance, in "Egnaro," "A Young Man's Journey to London," and "The East," the reader follows characters who seek a secret world that may exist in the hidden spaces of this world. All of Harrison's stories balance the mystery of the mundane with the monotony of the magical. Throughout the great diversity of material offered in this collection, Harrison displays a masterful control of character, language, and landscape and an ability to expose the unnerving sense of the inexplicable that runs beneath the surfaces of life. *Things that Never Happen* provides a generous introduction to a woefully underrecognized author. Pieces like "Running Down," "Isobel Avens Returns to Stepney in the Spring," "Seven Guesses of the Heart," and "Science & the Arts" are exceptional stories of vision that live in the mind for days. Although Harrison's world may appear dark, you find yourself wanting to book the next trip that will let you move there. [David Ian Paddy]

Roberto Pazzi. *Conclave*. Trans. Oonagh Stransky. Steerforth, 2003. 231 pp. Paper: $14.95.

A pope who seems larger than life has died. Who will replace him? Although this novel starts out as though it were revisiting *The Shoes of the Fisherman,* it slowly takes on a magic-realist style. The cardinals realize that their conclave will take more than a few days, and as the days turn into weeks and months, the pressure of making a choice plays on the psyches of these mostly elderly men. There is much illness, several deaths, and behavior that seems to lack any secular explanation. One cardinal disappears, two try to escape out a window, and nearly all of them engage in a St. Vitus dance that can be stopped only by an incantation from an African archbishop. Evil seems to be embodied in a number of infestations—of rats, scorpions, and bats—which are visiting the Vatican like the plagues of Egypt. They leave teeth marks in the paintings of the saints, consume pictures of previous cardinals, and in general lay waste to the great works of art that the Church owns. Only images of Jesus and the Madonna are spared. In desperation the chief engineer arranges for cats, then chickens, then owls, to be brought in to fight the various plagues. The cardinals are left to ponder where God is and whether He has decided to appear "not among the ranks of the wealthy Catholics, but among the poor Muslims." A last gasp of evil, in the form of a great storm, engulfs the Vatican and a choice for a new pope is finally made by acclamation, with the help, apparently, of some angels. Pazzi's novel is a serious examination of some of the problems facing the Catholic Church, yet in a style that is beguiling and mystical. [Sally E. Parry]

Matt Ruff. *Set This House in Order.* HarperCollins, 2003. 479 pp. $25.95.

Subtitled "A Romance of Souls," Matt Ruff's third novel *(Fool on the Hill;
Sewer, Gas & Electric)* is essentially a love story of sorts between two people
suffering from multiple personality disorder. This novel is narrated entirely by Andy Gage, a twenty-six-year-old who through therapy was able to
create a workable system for living with her twenty-plus personalities.
Currently living in Seattle, Andy lives an orderly and restrained life until
Penny—another girl suffering from multiple-personality disorder—comes
to work at the virtual-reality company where Andy is employed. Penny
doesn't know that she's a multiple when she first meets Andy, but one of her
other personalities enlists Andy's help in getting Penny to acknowledge and
deal with her chaotic life situation. A series of traumatic occurrences ensue—including an encounter with a man who murdered his family, which
causes a relapse on Andy's part in which her body is taken over by one of
her "bad" personalities—before Penny is finally able to come to terms with
her mental landscape and order is restored to Andy's life. Putting aside the
highly unlikely scenario of these two people meeting one another, there is
something compelling about the plot development of this novel. Ruff is a
decent writer, although his earlier books (especially *Sewer, Gas & Electric*)
were much funnier, riskier, and more interesting. There is a certain voyeuristic element to this book, which really hurts it; a sort of "what would it
be like if?" quality that is intriguing like bad Lifetime movies. More inter-
play between the content of the story and the form of the novel could have
resulted in a much better book. [Chad W. Post]

Lidia Yuknavitch. *Real to Reel.* FC2, 2003. 175 pp. Paper: $13.95.

Yuknavitch's third collection continues her exploration, in the grand spirit
of Acker and Atwood, of feminist and postfeminist issues—with the delight
of language, the sensuality of the sentence and various body parts, and a
fascination with the movies; how film and the narrative tropes of popular
cinema affect, infect, and become important, if not intrepid, pieces of our
lives. Each story is a gem that could not have been written by anybody but
Lidia Yuknavitch; i.e., there is a powerful, singular voice at work. The first,
"Scripted," is broken into three columns composed in the first, second, and
third person—the same person, but variations of the theme, the life, and
the resolution, telling us "don't bother thinking or being. . . . get real."
Yuknavitch gets reel in the second piece, "Male Lead," in the speech patterns of Keanu Reeves as he's being interviewed on *Inside the Actors Studio*—possibly the version that was hosted by the ever-pompous and
long-winded James Lipton. Then comes a short screenplay, or a work of fiction in screenplay format, "Outtakes." We're shown streetwise, smart-
mouthed kids who hang out in a 7-Eleven, reminiscent of Kevin Smith's
Clerks or Eric Bogosian's *Suburbia,* as well as a prison drug-smuggling plot
worthy of a *Law & Order* episode. Yuknavitch could have a novel in that
plot alone, and it's obvious that in the longest text herein, "Siberia: Still

Life of the Moving Image," the author is ready to take on the full-volume form. "Siberia" is the perfect companion-piece to Mary Wollstonecraft's banned and nearly forgotten short novel of Gothic incest, *Matilda*. At the core of the pieces in *Real to Reel* is the timeless exploration of the father, or father-figure, and how these men shape the lives and art of women—hell, the end of Yuknavitch's "Chair" says it all. [Michael Hemmingson]

Uwe Timm. *Morenga*. Trans. Jennifer Lyons. New Directions, 2003. 340 pp. $25.95.

In 1923 Joyce said, in praise of Hemingway, "He has reduced the veil between literature and life, which is what every writer strives to do." Uwe Timm is to be similarly commended for achieving that end with *Morenga*, a novel first published in Germany in 1978. Set in German West South Africa in the first decade of the twentieth century, the novel presents colonial life by way of a narrative symphony that includes historical documents alongside imagined sketches. As Timm faithfully recounts historical events, he penetrates the structures endemic to the colonial experience. When exposing Colonel Deimling's plan to "smash the Witboois," for instance, the narrative delves into the nuances of the Colonel's language: "Deimling's typical vocabulary for skirmishes and battles: crush, shatter, smash." Yet a *Cape Times* interview with Jakob Morenga makes clear that there is also a new developing language: "Yes, I'm perfectly aware [of Germany's power], but the Germans don't know how to fight in our land. They don't know where to get water, and they know nothing about guerilla warfare." It is this attention to the nuances and shifts of language and place that makes Timm's novel so successful and compelling. By examining the past, we are more fully exposed to ourselves and to our lives, including political expression. After Morenga is killed, Captain von Hagen, General Staff of the Colonial Guard, writes his account, including the following remark that falls under the category of the importance of German and English cooperation: "The natives of South Africa will now realize they're not fighting the Germans, or the English, or the Dutch, but that *now the entire white race stands united against the black*." It is through language that we conduct our lives, and it is through narrative that we examine them. Uwe Timm never drops into the mucky realm of didacticism; he simply writes literature that has removed the veil. [Alan Tinkler]

Antoine Bello. *The Missing Piece*. Trans. Helen Stevenson. Harcourt, 2003. 248 pp. Paper: $14.00.

The professional speed-puzzle circuit, having been established by an American billionaire/jigsaw-puzzle enthusiast and promoted to World Series-levels of international popularity, is shaken when star players are targeted by a killer who doses his victims with Pentothal, hacks off one of their limbs, and replaces it with a Polaroid showing the corresponding limb of a different victim. Bello's inventiveness throughout is impressive, satirizing professional sports and contemporary literary criticism, and he offers readers a lot to play with in the process: color-commentators' breathless (and culturally tactless) descriptions of puzzle assembly, the controversy surrounding the world's most difficult puzzle (the suspiciously French "Pantone 138," a square tray housing a thousand identical half-inch-square pieces that can produce billions of indistinguishable combinations, "But only one of them is correct"), the political machinations of the academic Puzzology Society, exploits of the savant Spillsbury and the ragingly libidinous Olof Niels, academic treatises on the "universal equilibrium configuration for the puzzle" (discovering what happens when workmen simultaneously build and demolish a wall), and on and on, all of it related via newspaper clippings, minutes of meetings, e-mail, magazine articles, television transcriptions, and the like. Most of it is very funny, and the satire fires in all directions. This novel is ostensibly a mystery, though, and the last chapter of the book gamely presents a solution, but it's doubtful that readers will care who the culprit is—the book's originality is far more interesting than the whodunit aspects, and the narrative lags a little toward the end, when narrative ennui sets in and Bello's treatment of the puzzle conceit begins to lack the ironic humor of the rest of the novel. It's a first-novel flaw, but it's overlookable: *The Missing Piece* is ultimately very good. Add Bello to the long list of folks you should be keeping an eye on. [Tim Feeney]

Sergio Troncoso. *The Nature of Truth*. Northwestern Univ. Press, 2003. 259 pp. $22.95.

Sergio Troncoso must have had Paul de Man in mind when he wrote his first novel, *The Nature of Truth*, as he takes up a similar story—that of a German professor whose connection to the Nazis is discovered by a researcher—and a set of themes that are at the heart of the controversy and confusion over a theorist such as de Man, namely, the consequences involved in insisting on the relativity of truth and the connection between theory—what one espouses—and practice—how one lives. In Troncoso's novel the professor who conceals his Nazi past, the researcher—Helmut Sanchez—who decides to take justice into his own hands (by murdering the professor), the detective who blames the crime on the professor's gay lover but, because he does not have the evidence, finds his own way of punishing the man, and Sanchez's girlfriend, Ariane, who does not turn him in after finding out about the murder, all make their own determinations about what constitutes the truth. And like the professor, they seem to get over their guilt rather quickly and with little suffering. Even Sanchez, who is the most conflicted, manages to justify the murder and by the end seems content with himself as he sets up house with Ariane in New Mexico, where his mother lives. Some of the issues of identity, the connection between Helmut's own identity and his sense of guilt concerning the professor's sympathies, and the political and philosophical issues that make the story itself so rich, get short shrift in Troncoso's novel, and he sometimes resolves internal conflicts too quickly and easily. Nonetheless, *The Nature of Truth* is an interesting and provocative read. [Valerie Ellis]

Nina Berberova. *The Accompanist*. Trans. Marian Schwartz. New Directions, 2003. 94 pp. Paper: $11.95.

The title character of this slim, spare novel is our narrator, Sonechka Antonovskaya, a young woman of modest means who comes to work for a glamorous opera soprano, Maria Nikolaevna Travina, at the height of postrevolutionary Russia's hard times. Written in 1936 and published to much acclaim in Europe, *The Accompanist*'s central narrative is propelled by a brand of envy and longing at once eerie and sublime. This wanting sits largely with Sonechka's dueling desires: the desire to *be* Maria and the desire to accept the lesser gift of her love—an option problematic only partly because it's never actually offered. This emotional seesaw also characterizes Sonechka's feelings toward Pavel Fyodorovich, Maria's dubiously employed bourgeois husband. Rather predictably, Pavel's presence heightens tensions that were already high, particularly once Sonechka learns of Maria's ongoing extramarital affair. Still, Berberova is clearly playing with more here than initially meets the eye, because while the tricky triad of emotions include jealousy as well as rage, what makes *The Accompanist* such a captivating read is that the passion play isn't necessarily the "real" story at all. Take, for example, the framing device Berberova employs at the story's very start. This first narrative voice soberly explains that the pages before us were acquired for him "by a Mr. L. R., who bought them from a junk dealer," who in turn had bought them off a landlady from "a cheap hotel where a Russian woman had lived and died." We're also told that her various personal effects were up for sale as well, referring to these items as "all that is left after a woman vanishes." Like Berberova's short, elegant tale, such a provocative turn of phrase seems ripe for mulling over, even after the writer is gone. [Stacey Gottlieb]

Marshall Boswell. *Trouble with Girls*. Algonquin, 2003. 306 pp. $22.95.

Boswell, already well known as the author of one of the most incisive books on the *Rabbit* tetralogy, here tackles growing up in the late 1970s and eighties. This ground, already well furrowed fictionally, has rarely been assayed by someone who knows as much about the art of fiction as does Boswell, and this really helps. Despite misdating that crucial artifact *Flashdance,* Boswell's sense of the period's pop culture is sure and almost painfully exhilarating. The scene is surveyed with amiable irony and a tolerance for different life-choices (Boswell writes well about a strip club in "Stir Crazy," a difficult challenge). In "Born Again" we see a tribute to the deployment of the Krugerrand in *Rabbit Is Rich,* a meditation on Bob Dylan's Christian conversion, and an elegiac notice of the transition from the funky seventies to Reaganite winter. *Trouble* is not a conventional bildungsroman. The need to "be a whole person at last, fully integrated, all problems solved" is teased, not mimicked, by the book's loose structure, which implies that the self is always a work in progress. The plot ending is happy, as the titular issues of our protagonist, Parker Hayes, with the opposite sex are resolved in marriage to Rachel, one of whose most appealing traits is having owned a cat named Margery Kempe. Yet a honeymoon rental-car catastrophe lets us know that the anarchy of life will not thereby be stilled. Boswell renders the mentors, friends, ex-friends, and girlfriends in these stories as an ensemble cast, not an undifferentiated backdrop against which Hayes's journey to maturation is staged. This forestalls any "narrative governed by symbols and carefully orchestrated leitmotifs." *Trouble with Girls* has a poise that makes it brainy as well as fun. [Nicholas Birns]

J. Robert Lennon. *Mailman*. Norton, 2003. 483 pp. $24.95.

Although I have not read his earlier novels, I am so impressed by this audacious work that I will immediately order—by mail!—Lennon's three other novels. He has captured not only the tortured mind of mailman Albert Lippincott, but the American dream that turns swiftly from comedy to terror (comic terror). The novel fuses the thriller and the philosophical inquisition. Mailman is not sure that he is a man; that he exists; that he is more than the common carrier of news. He is, of course, paranoid, wondering who pursues him and why: "You never know when they're in there; you never see them. Sometimes you hear their slow footsteps, if you happen to be under the catwalk when they pass overhead. Like a goose on your grave." And he is, of course, afraid that they will discover his crimes—his thefts of personal mail, his creation of false responses to people waiting in fear or hope for their messages. As we learn more about delivery, we recognize that Lennon is exploring the meaning of communication. Once Mailman was a thoughtful student who made a theory about the nature of things: "everything *small* was a mirror of something *large* and everything *large* a mirror of something *small.* . . . The future stretched infinitely *forward* and the past infinitely *back,* and Mailman . . . was at the *very center,* he was *point zero,* the very thing that would *divide the age of comprehension from the age of understanding . . . he* was the *vessel.*" Mailman may have an ordinary job—not a profession—but he has divine power and intelligence. (Or does he?) Lennon moves from the onrushing insanity of Mailman to the redemption of his existence. Mail becomes a wonderful symbol of the principle: *"Nothing sent is worth anything unless it gets where it's going."* The novel becomes, in effect, a road novel, or better yet, a pilgrim's progress, in which we learn to appreciate the courage to exchange letters, to express truths about ourselves living in close proximity (family, nation, planet). Thus the secret of this extraordinary work is that letters—written words—are our salvation. *Mailman* is, finally, a radiant mirror of the days of our lives—a triumphant work of art. [Irving Malin]

Nelly Reifler. *See Through*. Simon & Schuster, 2003. 148 pp. $21.00.

The fourteen stories that make up Nelly Reifler's terrific first collection form a kind of cabinet of fear and wonder in the mind. They achieve this by skillfully fusing aspects of realism, surrealism, and dark fairy-tale, with results that echo the sharply dreamed, impeccably crafted and arranged work of an Angela Carter, a Rebecca Brown, or even a Lydia Davis: individual stories shine, but it is in the marvel of their juxtaposition, their accumulation that their power comes fully into relief. Contextualizing echoes aside, whether dealing with the survival strategies of a misspecied squirrel, exploring the psyche of a little girl whose first job goes horribly, willfully wrong, examining identity theft, casual murder, plague, or prostitution, the stories form a fascinating topos all their own. "The baby was smart. Too smart. He was also sickly," begins a particular favorite of mine. "Baby," a wise and wicked little treatise on postpartum malaise, works as well as it does because Reifler uses the tools of Flaubertian realism to ground what could simply have been presented as a very, very bad dream. Another standout, "The River and Una," examines the particularities of waxing and waning sexuality with a Rohmeresque eye for obsessive, energy-packed detail (think *Claire's Knee*): "My sister opened one eye and looked at me. A corner of her mouth curled: almost a smile. The tip of her tongue came out and licked the center point of her top lip. I looked into her opened, unfocused eye. The surface looked greasy." There is much on offer here, but part of the pleasure of *See Through* is Reifler's clear understanding of the art of concision: the stories manage to say a great deal (very clearly) while at the same time providing enough space for the reader to be haunted by their implications. [Laird Hunt]

Arno Schmidt. *Radio Dialogs II*. Trans. and intro. John E. Woods. Green Integer, 2003. 405 pp. Paper: $13.95.

This pocket-sized volume is the second of three collecting Schmidt's musings on writers and their works. As one might expect from this most ludic author, one of the more undeservedly unknown masters of twentieth-century prose, these essays are hardly traditional academic exercises. Rather, they appear in the form of two- or three-part conversations between nameless speakers, playlets about such figures as Herder, Frenssen, Bulwer-Lytton, and Joyce, and were originally broadcast on German radio mainly in the 1950s and sixties. As most of the names under discussion are relatively unrecognizable to readers of English—raise your hand if you've never heard before of Johann Schnabel's 2,300-page utopia, *Felsenburg Island*—the central appeal of this translation of *Radio Dialogs* lies not in what Schmidt says about other writers, but in what his comments suggest about his own work. The Joyce chapter is most telling in this regard. In it, two of Schmidt's somewhat Beckettian characters attempt to make sense of the many connotations of the coinages in *Finnegans Wake*: "A: . . . What *does* an Englishman . . . think about when he hears the syllable <*vail*>?" "B.

(reserved): Well, a poetical <valley>: . . . and <gauze> or <haze>. — (experi-menting): <vale, veil—: wail?> . . ." "A.: Hmyes. There are, of course, still more . . . but that's enough. . . . We had best invent a new technical term for use on this compelling evening of Ours. . . . What shall We call this basic structure of the linguistic fabric that ties so many things together? What might be available? – *(feigns enlightenment)*: <Etymology>: the system of genuine meaning : let Us simply baptize this polyvalenced fellow an <*etym*>—agreed?" "B. Presuming there's not some other new trick hidden in it." Many of Schmidt's books, of course, are rich in meaning precisely because they are built of such etyms. These are strung together by a system of punctuation far more difficult to parse than in the above example; *Radio Dialogs* would have benefited from a more comprehensive introduction to Schmidt's methods and perhaps an explanation of how this kind of typo-graphical holy-foolery came across in an aural medium. Such supporting material isn't essential, however, and the book is unquestionably an in-triguing puzzle that provides an infinite number of launching points for study and imagination. [James Crossley]

Saúl Yurkievich. *In the Image and Likeness*. Trans. Cola Franzen. Catbird, 2003. 109 pp. Paper: $11.00.

In his poem "Why I Am Not a Painter" Frank O'Hara wonders at a painter friend's matter-of-fact talk about composition: "Yes, it needed something there." Argentinian Saúl Yurkievich, like O'Hara, is a poet who also writes essays about art. The creative prose of *In the Image and Likeness* goes fur-ther, imagining the interior lives of Velázquez, Goya, and Kurt Schwitters. These portraits are followed by shorter prose experiments. In "Trunkiness" Yurkievich embraces and literally tries to become one with an oak trunk. It could be Apollo's fantasy of union with Daphne after she has turned into the laurel tree. Yurkievich explains: "A certain zone of cognition is established between the trunk and me. And within this field there is an interchange between my humanness and its trunkiness . . . ness for ness." Throughout the collection he pushes his brain onto things, smothering things with stacked adjectives and verbs in Franzen's mimetic translation. His objects are almost lost beneath the lacquerlike play, and his verbal economy might be read as irony. But the long piece on Schwitters, a rare third-person piece for Yurkievich, reheats an old trope—the urban alienated—and serves us a man we already know. Collage artist Schwitters, like Yurkievich, loves the pathetic fallacy. "For every object that he recuperates, he knows that he saves, awakens, a latent past." This dadaist loves life. In his nostalgia for the detritus of industry and infrastructure, this Schwitters is akin to a Ben Katchor or Chris Ware. These comic artists, along with Schwitters, O'Hara, and Yurkievich himself, are obsessed by the imposition of the verbal mind onto visual space. Here is Schwitters in the studio: "He folds over the edge of the solar circle to avoid the tangency with the lilac. . . . A geometric orga-nization orders the impulse." [Benjamin Lytal]

Knut Hamsun. *Knut Hamsun Remembers America: Essays and Stories, 1885-1949.* Trans. and ed. Richard Nelson Current. Univ. of Missouri Press, 2003. 155 pp. $29.95.

Knut Hamsun (1859-1952) lived and worked in the United States on two occasions in the 1880s and recorded his impressions in a series of newspaper articles, reminiscences, and stories. Hungry for experience but handicapped by his limited knowledge of English, he eked out a precarious living in a succession of menial jobs: farm hand, road builder, Chicago streetcar conductor, etc. Gathered into one volume for the first time, the resulting material offers a fascinating, humorous glimpse into immigrant experience in the age of the bonanza farm and breakneck industrialization. Violent Anglophobia marks the early writings. Even stronger than Hamsun's disapprobation of American and English society is his dislike of the Irish, a naked prejudice that surely had its roots in Hamsun's own experience as a member of a cultural minority, the crucial difference being that Irish Americans spoke the dominant language and thus enjoyed an advantage that the young Norwegian writer envied. By tracing the roots of his frustration we begin to see how this candid social observer, who won the Nobel Prize for Literature in 1920, later came to make the misjudgments that led him to support fascism in the Second World War. Students of literary modernism, cultural marginalization, and American power will also find much of interest here. "No more than any other country on the planet can America stand alone," Hamsun reflects in 1928 in an article that puts resentment aside and praises America for its flowering arts, its generosity, and its industriousness. "America is not the world. America is a part of the world and must live its life together with all the other parts." [Philip Landon]

Books Received

Abani, Chris. *Daphne's Lot*. Red Hen, 2003. Paper: $13.95. (F)

Alcalá, Kathleen. *Treasures in Heaven*. Northwestern Univ. Press, 2003. Paper: $15.95. (F)

Amado, Jorge. *Tent of Miracles*. Trans. Barbara Shelby Merello. Intro. Ilan Stavans. Univ. of Wisconsin Press, 2003. Paper: $16.95. (F)

——. *Tieta*. Trans. Barbara Shelby Merello. Intro. Moacyr Scliar. Univ. of Wisconsin Press, 2003. Paper: $18.95. (F)

Ball, Pamela. *The Floating City*. Penguin, 2003. Paper: $14.00. (F)

Bannan, Jennifer. *Inventing Victor*. Carnegie Mellon Univ. Press, 2003. Paper: $15.95. (F)

Barthelme, Frederick. *Elroy Nights*. Counterpoint, 2003. $24.00. (F)

Begley, Louis. *Shipwreck*. Knopf, 2003. $23.00. (F)

Belfer, Lauren. *City of Light*. Delta, 2003. Paper: $12.95. (F)

Birkets, Sven. *My Sky Blue Trades*. Penguin, 2003. Paper: $14.00. (NF)

Brennan, Jonathan, ed. *When Brer Rabbit Meets Coyote: African–Native American Literature*. Univ. of Illinois Press, 2003. $39.95. (NF)

Brodeur, Adrienne, and Samantha Schnee, eds. *Francis Ford Coppola's Zoetrope All-Story 2*. Intro. Francis Ford Coppola. Harvest, 2003. Paper: $14.00. (F, NF)

Carey, Peter. *My Life as a Fake*. Knopf, 2003. $24.00. (F)

Carter, Marie, ed. *Word Jig: New Fiction from Scotland*. Intro. Joy Hendry. Hanging Loose Press, 2003. Paper: $16.00. (F)

Chandraratna, Bandula. *Mirage*. Black Sparrow, 2003. $24.95. (F)

Cicero, Noah. *The Human War*. Fugue State, 2003. Paper: $12.00. (F)

Ciresi, Rita. *Remind Me Again Why I Married You*. Delacorte, 2003. $23.95. (F)

Cleage, Pearl. *Some Things I Thought I'd Never Do*. One World/Ballantine, 2003. $23.95. (F)

Conn, Andrew Lewis. *P*. Soft Skull, 2003. Paper: $15.00. (F)

Courtmanche, Gil. *A Sunday at the Pool in Kigali*. Trans. Patricia Claxton. Knopf, 2003. $23.00. (F)

Daniel, A. B. *Incas, Book 3: The Light of Machu Picchu*. Trans. Alex Gilly. Touchstone, 2003. Paper: $14.00. (F)

David, Stuart. *Nalda Said*. Turtle Point, 2003. Paper: $14.95. (F)

Davidson, Lynn. *Ghost Net*. Univ. of Otago Press, 2003. Paper: AU$29.95. (F)

Dawes, Kwame. *A Place to Hide and Other Stories*. Peepal Tree, 2003. Paper: $14.95. (F)

Dayton, Tim. *Muriel Rukeyser's "The Book of the Dead."* Univ. of Missouri Press, 2003. $24.95. (NF)

Despentes, Virginie. *Baise-Moi*. Trans. Bruce Benderson. Grove, 2003. Paper: $12.00. (F)

Didion, Joan. *Where I Was From*. Knopf, 2003. $23.00. (NF)

Di Robilant, Andrea. *A Venetian Affair*. Knopf, 2003. $24.00. (F)

Domini, John. *Talking Heads: 77*. Red Hen, 2003. Paper: $17.95. (F)

Dorfman, Ariel. *The Nanny and the Iceberg*. Seven Stories, 2003. Paper: $14.95. (F)

Druzhnikov, Yuri. *Angels on the Head of a Pin*. Trans. Thomas Moore. Peter Owen/Dufour, 2003. $34.95. (F)

Dumas, Henry. *Echo Tree*. Foreword Eugene Redmond. Intro. John S. Wright. Coffee House, 2003. Paper: $15.95. (F)

Duve, Karen. *Rain*. Trans. Anthea Bell. Bloomsbury, 2003. Paper: $14.95. (F)

Dyja, Thomas. *Meet John Trow*. Penguin, 2003. Paper: $14.00. (F)

Eberstadt, Fernanda. *The Furies*. Knopf, 2003. $26.00. (F)

Embiricos, Andreas. *Amour Amour*. Trans. Nikos Stangos and Alan Ross. Green Integer, 2003. Paper: $11.95. (F)

Evenson, Brian. *The Brotherhood of Mutilation*. Earthling Publications, 2003. Paper: $10.00 (F)

Ewing, Barbara. *The Trespass*. St. Martin's, 2003. $24.95. (F)

Fesperman, Dan. *The Small Boat of Great Sorrows*. Knopf, 2003. $24.00. (F)

Files, Gemma. *Kissing Carrion*. Intro. Caitlin R. Kiernan. Prime, 2003. Paper: $17.95. (F)

Foley, Mick. *Tietam Brown*. Knopf, 2003. $23.95. (F)

Franklin, Robert J. *The Adventures of Eric Hamilton*. Ariel, 2003. Paper: $16.95. (F)

Garcia, Cristina, ed. and intro. *¡Cubanismo! The Vintage Book of Contemporary Cuban Literature*. Vintage, 2003. Paper: $14.00. (F, NF)

Garrett, Greg. *Cycling*. Kensington, 2003. $23.00. (F)

Gass, William H. *Tests of Time*. Univ. of Chicago Press, 2003. Paper: $18.00. (NF)

George, Margaret. *Mary, Called Magdalene*. Penguin, 2003. Paper: $16.00. (F)

Gerdes, Eckhard, ed. *A-Way with It! Contemporary Innovative Fiction*. Journal of Experimental Fiction 24. Writers Club, 2003. $34.95. (F, NF)

Ghazy, Randa. *Dreaming of Palestine*. Trans. Marguerite Shore. Braziller, 2003. $19.95. (F)

Gilbert, Elizabeth. *The Last American Man*. Penguin, 2003. Paper: $14.00. (F)

Gillespie, Michael Patrick. *The Aesthetics of Chaos: Nonlinear Thinking and Contemporary Literary Criticism*. Univ. Press of Florida, 2003. $55.00. (NF)

Glock, Allison. *Beauty before Comfort*. Knopf, 2003. $20.00. (NF)

Gordon, Neil. *Sacrifice of Isaac*. Penguin, 2003. Paper: $14.00. (F)

Gorodischer, Angélica. *Kalpa Imperial: The Greatest Empire that Never Was*. Trans. Ursula K. Le Guin. Small Beer, 2003. Paper: $16.00. (F)

Green, Roger. *Hydra and the Leonard Cohen Bananas: A Midlife Crisis in the Sun*. Basic, 2003. $25.00. (NF)

Greenfield, Elana. *At the Damascus Gate: Short Hallucinations*. Green Integer, 2003. Paper: $10.95. (F)

Griffith, Michael. *Bibliophilia*. Arcade, 2003. $24.95. (F)

Guterson, David. *Our Lady of the Forest*. Knopf, 2003. $25.95. (F)

Han, Shaogong. *A Dictionary of Maqiao*. Trans. Julia Lovell. Columbia Univ. Press, 2003. $27.95. (F)

Harrison, Nicholas. *Postcolonial Criticism: History, Theory, and the Work of Fiction*. Polity, 2003. Paper: £14.99. (NF)

Hay, Elizabeth. *Garbo Laughs*. Counterpoint, 2003. Paper: $25.00. (F)

Hayden, Tom. *Rebel: A Personal History of the 1960s*. Red Hen, 2003. Paper: $19.95. (NF)

Hecht, Anthony. *Collected Later Poems*. Knopf, 2003. $25.00. (P)

Holthe, Tess Uriza. *When the Elephants Dance*. Penguin, 2003. Paper: $14.00. (F)

Honigmann, Barbara. *"A Love Made Out of Nothing" and "Zohara's Journey."* Trans. John Barrett. Verba Mundi/Godine, 2003. Paper: $16.95. (F)

Hotz, Ron. *The Animal Sciences*. Coach House, 2003. Paper: $15.95. (F)

Huby, Peter. *Carthage*. Dewi Lewis Publishing, 2003. Paper: $13.95. (F)

Huneven, Michelle. *Jamesland*. Knopf, 2003. $24.00. (F)

Hwang Suk-Young, et al. *The Voice of the Governor-General and Other Stories of Modern Korea*. Trans. Chun Kyung-Ja. Intro. Kim Uchang. EastBridge, 2002. Paper: $14.95. (F)

Ioannides, Sylvia. *Mediterranean: Tales Told to a Bird Woman*. Livingston, 2003. Paper: $14.95. (F)

James, P. D. *The Murder Room*. Knopf, 2003. $25.95. (F)

Jones, Stephen Graham. *The Bird Is Gone: A Manifesto*. FC2, 2003. Paper: $13.95. (F)

Joseph, Diana. *Happy or Otherwise*. Carnegie Mellon Univ. Press, 2003. Paper: $15.95. (F)

Joyce, Graham. *The Stormwatcher.* Night Shade, 2003. $40.00. (F)

Kenaz, Yehoshua. *Infiltration.* Trans. Dayla Bilu. Steerforth, 2003. Paper: $19.95. (F)

Kingston, Maxine Hong. *The Fifth Book of Peace*. Knopf, 2003. $26.00. (F)

Kohler, Sheila. *Stories from Another World*. Ontario Review Press, 2003. $22.95. (F)

Lancelotta, Victoria. *Far.* Counterpoint, 2003. $24.00. (F)

Latham, Aaron. *The Cowboy with the Tiffany Gun.* Simon & Schuster, 2003. $25.00. (F)

Lawrence, Pat. *Bedford.* Six Gallery, 2003. Paper: $12.00. (F)

Lentricchia, Frank. *Lucchesi and the Whale.* Duke Univ. Press, 2003. Paper: $15.95. (F)

Lewis, Jim. *The King Is Dead.* Knopf, 2003. $24.00. (F)

Lewis, Trudy. *The Bones of Garbo.* Ohio State Univ. Press, 2003. Paper: $22.95. (F)

Lightman, Alan. *Reunion.* Pantheon, 2003. $22.00. (F)

Link, Kelly, ed. *Trampoline: An Anthology.* Small Beer, 2003. Paper: $17.00. (F)

Littell, Robert. *The Sisters.* Overlook, 2003. $24.95. (F)

LoBosco, Rocco. *Buddha Wept.* GreyCore, 2003. $21.95. (F)

Lowell, Robert. *Collected Poems*. Ed. Frank Bidart and David Gewanter with DeSales Harrison. Farrar, Straus & Giroux, 2003. $45.00. (P)

Mader, William. *The Hunted Moon: A Novel of Amazonia.* Cold Hill, 2003. Paper: $21.95. (F)

Makine, Andreï. *A Hero's Daughter.* Trans. Geoffrey Strachan. Arcade, 2003. $23.95.

Malin, Jo, and Victoria Boynton, eds. *Herspace: Women, Writing, and Solitude.* Haworth, 2003. Paper: $29.95. (NF)

Manning, Kate. *Whitegirl.* Delta, 2003. Paper: $13.95. (F)

Masilela, Johnny. *We Shall Not Weep.* Kwela, 2003. Paper: $9.95. (F)

McCulloh, Mark R. *Understanding W. G. Sebald.* Univ. of South Carolina Press, 2003. $34.95. (NF)

McMurtry, Larry. *By Sorrow's River.* Simon & Schuster, 2003. $26.00. (F)

Meirose, Jim. *Breakfast, Meat, and Other Stories.* Neshui, 2003. Paper: $15.00. (F)

Mesler, Corey. *Talk.* Livingston, 2002. Paper: $14.00. (F)

Meyer, Steven. *Irresistible Dictation: Gertrude Stein and the Correlations of Writing and Science.* Stanford Univ. Press, 2003. $55.00. (NF)

Michelsen, G. F. *The Art and Practice of Explosion*. Univ. Press of New England, 2003. $24.95. (F)

Mitchell, Ed. *Gold Raid*. California Coast Publishing, 2003. Paper: $15.95. (F)

Montero, Mayra. *Deep Purple*. Trans. Edith Grossman. Ecco, 2003. $22.95. (F)

Moore, Susanna. *One Last Look*. Knopf, 2003. $23.00. (F)

Morrison, Toni. *Love*. Knopf, 2003. $23.95. (F)

Morrow, Bradford. *Ariel's Crossing*. Penguin, 2003. Paper: $14.00. (F)

Moses, Kate. *Wintering: A Novel of Sylvia Plath*. St. Martin's, 2003. $23.95. (F)

Murnane, Gerald. *The Plains*. Foreword Andrew Zawacki. New Issues, 2003. Paper: $14.00. (F)

Naficy, Majid. *Father & Son*. Red Hen, 2003. Paper: $8.95. (P)

Naipaul, V. S. *Literary Occasions: Essays*. Ed. and intro. Pankaj Mishra. Knopf, 2003. $24.00. (NF)

Nash, Susan Smith. *I Never Did Tell You Did I? (Unsent Letters)*. Avec, 2003. Paper: $14.00. (F)

Niffenegger, Audrey. *The Time-Traveler's Wife*. MacAdam/Cage, 2003. $25.00. (F)

Nkosi, Lewis. *Underground People*. Kwela, 2003. Paper: $12.95. (F)

Novak, Barbara. *The Margaret-Ghost*. Braziller, 2003. $19.95. (F)

Olsen, Lance. *Hideous Beauties*. Images Andi Olsen. Eraserhead, 2003. Paper: $13.95. (F)

Olster, Stacey. *The Trash Phenomenon: Contemporary Literature, Popular Culture, and the Making of the American Century*. Univ. of Georgia Press, 2003. Paper: $19.95. (NF)

Orringer, Julie. *How to Breathe Underwater*. Knopf, 2003. $21.00. (F)

Page, Jake. *The Lethal Partner*. Univ. of New Mexico Press, 2003. Paper: $13.95. (F)

Page, Ra, ed. *Comma*. Comma/Carcanet, 2003. Paper: $19.95. (F)

Penna, Richard. *Yielding Ice about to Melt*. Dufour, 2003. Paper: $14.95. (F)

Phillips, Caryl. *A Distant Shore*. Knopf, 2003. $23.00. (F)

Read, Kirk. *How I Learned to Snap*. Penguin, 2003. Paper: $13.00. (NF)

Reid, Van. *Peter Loon*. Penguin, 2003. Paper: $14.00. (F)

Rice, Anne. *Blood Canticle: The Vampire Chronicles*. Knopf, 2003. $25.95. (F)

Rice, Stan. *False Prophet*. Knopf, 2003. $23.00. (P)

Roberson, Matthew, ed. *Musing the Mosaic: Approaches to Ronald Sukenick*. State Univ. of New York Press, 2003. Paper: $23.95. (NF)

Roseman, Janet Lynn, PhD. *The Way of the Woman Writer.* 2nd ed. Haworth, 2003. Paper: $17.95. (NF)

Sallis, James. *Cypress Grove.* Walker & Company, 2003. $24.00. (F)

Salmon, Elon. *When There Were Heroes.* Dewi Lewis, 2003. Paper: $13.95. (F)

Salzman, Mark. *True Notebooks.* Knopf, 2003. $24.00. (NF)

Sanford, Annette. *Eleanor & Abel.* Counterpoint, 2003. $22.00. (F)

Scalapino, Leslie. *Zither & Autobiography.* Wesleyan Univ. Press, 2003. Paper: $14.95. (NF, P)

Schilling, Vivian. *Quietus.* Penguin, 2003. Paper: $14.00. (F)

Schmidt, Mirko F., ed. *Entre parentheses: Beiträge zum Werk von Jean-Philippe Toussaint.* Edition Vigilia, 2003. Paper: €12.90. (NF)

Schmitter, Elke. *Mrs. Sartoris.* Trans. Carol Brown Janeway. Knopf, 2003. $19.95. (F)

Schoemperlen, Diane. *Red Plaid Shirt.* Penguin, 2003. Paper: $14.00. (F)

Schutt, Christine. *Florida.* Northwestern Univ. Press, 2003. $22.95. (F)

Scliar, Moacyr. *The Centaur in the Garden.* Trans. Margaret A. Neves. Intro. Ilan Stavans. Univ. of Wisconsin Press, 2003. Paper: $15.95. (F)

Scott, Manda. *Dreaming the Eagle.* Delacorte, 2003. $23.95. (F)

Sedaris, Amy, Paul Dinello, and Stephen Colbert. *Wigfield: The Can-Do Town that Just May Not.* Photos. Todd Oldham. Hyperion, 2003. $22.95. (F)

Selin, Alexander. *The New Romantic.* Trans. Richard Cook. Glas, 2003. Paper: $17.95. (F)

Sergeev, Andrei. *Stamp Album: A Collection of Things, Relationships and Words.* Trans. Joanne Turnbull. Glas, 2002. Paper: $17.95. (NF)

Shan, Sa. *The Girl Who Played Go.* Trans. Adriana Hunter. Knopf, 2003. $22.95. (F)

Shem, Samuel. *The House of God.* Delta, 2003. Paper: $11.95. (F)

Sheppard, Stuart. *Spindrift.* Creative Arts, 2003. Paper: $15.95. (F)

Sheridan, Peter. *47 Roses: A Love Story.* Penguin, 2003. Paper: $14.00. (NF)

Sigo, Cedar. *Selected Writings.* Ugly Duckling Presse, 2003. Paper: $7.00. (P)

Snow, Randolph. *Tourmaline.* Univ. of Queensland Press, 2003. Paper: $16.95. (F)

Solwitz, Sharon. *Bloody Mary.* Sarabande, 2003. Paper: $13.95. (F)

Soto, Gary. *One Kind of Faith.* Chronicle, 2003. Paper: $14.95. (P)

Spiegelman, Peter. *Black Maps.* Knopf, 2003. $22.95. (F)

Stefans, Brian Kim. *Fashionable Noise: On Digital Poetics.* Atelos, 2003. Paper: $12.95. (NF)

Stoltzfus, Ben. *Valley of Roses.* Cypress, 2003. Paper: $14.95. (F)

Synopsis, Q. *Johnny Werd: The Fire Continues.* Spineless, 2003. Paper: $10.00. (F)

Tel, Jonathan. *Freud's Alphabet.* Counterpoint, 2003. $24.00. (F)

Thesen, Sharon, ed. *The Griffin Poetry Prize Anthology: A Selection of the 2003 Shortlist.* Anansi, 2003. Paper: $14.95. (P)

Timberg, Scott, and Dana Gioia, eds. *The Misread City: New Literary Los Angeles.* Red Hen, 2003. Paper: $16.95. (NF)

Tomasula, Steve. *In & Oz.* Night Shade, 2003. $25.00. (F)

Toufic, Jalal. *Distracted.* 2nd ed. Tuumba, 2003. Paper: No price given. (NF)

Trouillot, Lyonel. *Streets of Lost Footsteps.* Trans. and intro. Linda Coverdale. Univ. of Nebraska Press, 2003. Paper: $16.95. (F)

Tucker, Holly. *Pregnant Fictions: Childbirth and the Fairy Tale in Early-Modern France.* Wayne State Univ. Press, 2003. $34.95. (NF)

Ullmann, Linn. *Stella Descending.* Trans. Barbara Haveland. Knopf, 2003. $23.00. (F)

Updike, John. *The Early Stories: 1953-1975.* Knopf, 2003. $35.00. (F)

Upward, Edward. *A Renegade in Springtime.* Ed. and intro. Alan Walker. Enitharmon/Dufour, 2003. $33.95. (F)

Valentine, Katherine. *A Miracle for St. Cecilia's.* Penguin, 2003. Paper: $13.00. (F)

Vanderbes, Jennifer. *Easter Island.* Dial, 2003. $22.95. (F)

Vandermeer, Jeff, and Mark Roberts, eds. *The Thackery T. Lambshead Pocket Guide to Eccentric & Discredited Diseases, 83rd Edition.* Night Shade, 2003. $24.00. (F)

Van Loon, Karel. *A Father's Affair.* Canongate, 2003. $23.00. (F)

Vargas Llosa, Mario. *The Language of Passion: Selected Commentary.* Trans. Natasha Wimmer. Farrar, Straus & Giroux, 2003. $24.00. (NF)

Vega Yunqué, Edgardo. *No Matter How Much You Promise to Cook or Pay the Rent You Blew It Cauze Bill Bailey Ain't Never Coming Home Again.* Farrar, Straus & Giroux, 2003. $25.00. (F)

Verhelst, Peter. *Tonguecat.* Trans. Sherry Marx. Farrar, Straus & Giroux, 2003. $25.00. (F)

Vida, Vendela. *And Now You Can Go.* Knopf, 2003. $19.95. (F)

Virtue, Noel. *The Redemption of Elsdon Bird.* Peter Owen/Dufour, 2003. Paper: $19.95. (F)

Vizenor, Gerald. *Hiroshima Bugi: Atomu 57.* Univ. of Nebraska Press, 2003. $26.95. (F)

Vvedensky, Alexander. *The Gray Notebook*. Trans. Matvei Yankelevich. Ugly Duckling Presse, 2003. Paper: $7.00. (P)

Wiebe, Dallas. *Vibini in the Underworld*. Obscure Publications, 2003. Paper: No price given. (F)

Wilson, Jonathan. *A Palestine Affair*. Pantheon, 2003. $23.00. (F)

Wineapple, Brenda. *Hawthorne: A Life*. Knopf, 2003. $30.00. (NF)

Wolff, Geoffrey. *The Art of Burning Bridges: A Life of John O'Hara*. Knopf, 2003. $30.00. (NF)

Wright, Franz. *Walking to Martha's Vineyard*. Knopf, 2003. $23.00. (P)

Yachnik, Mike. *Five Mil*. Illus. Andy Clarkson. Xlibris, 2003. Paper: $21.99. (F)

Yoshikawa, Mako. *Once Removed*. Bantam, 2003. $22.95. (F)

Zimler, Richard. *Hunting Midnight*. Delacorte, 2003. $24.95. (F)

Zimmerman, Aaron. *By the Time You Finish Reading This Book You Might Be Dead*. Spuyten Duyvil, 2003. Paper: $13.00. (F)

Contributors

NEIL MURPHY has published articles, reviews, fiction, and interviews in the *Irish Review,* the *Irish University Review, Graph, Asylum Arts Review,* the *Irish Literary Supplement,* the *Literary Review,* and *Force 10.* His book, *Irish Fiction and Postmodern Doubt,* will be published by Edwin Mellen Press in January 2004. He is currently working on a comprehensive study of contemporary fiction and teaches twentieth-century literature at Nanyang Tech. University, Singapore.

FRANÇOISE PALLEAU teaches American literature at the University of the Sorbonne Nouvelle (Paris 3). Since completing her Ph. D. on Willa Cather, she has edited a book on Patricia Eakins and published articles on contemporary American writers, including Jeffery Renard Allen, Russell Banks, Mary Caponegro, Jayne Anne Phillips, and John Edgar Wideman. Her current work focuses on David Markson.

LAURA SIMS lives in Madison, Wisconsin. She has written book reviews for *Boston Review* and *Rain Taxi,* and her poetry has appeared or is forthcoming in *Fence, Boston Review,* the *Hat, jubilat, LIT, Northwest Review, 3ʳᵈ Bed, Nedge,* and *Antennae.* She was chosen as a finalist for the 2002-2003 Fence Books Alberta Prize and was a semifinalist for the 2002-2003 Alice James Books New York/ New England Prize for her first poetry manuscript, *Practice, Restraint.* She would like to find a publisher for her manuscript very soon.

Annual Index

References are to issue number and pages, respectively

Contributors

Books Reviewed

Reviewers' names follow in parentheses. Regular reviewers are abbreviated: JD=Joseph Dewey; BE=Brian Evenson; TF=Tim Feeney; IM=Irving Malin; MP=Michael Pinker; CP=Chad Post; JS=James Sallis

Robert Creeley • Gertrude Stein
dous Huxley • Robert Coover • Jo
rth • David Markson • Flann O'Bri

www.dalkeyarchive.com

uis-Ferdinand Céli e • Marguer
ung • Ishmael Reed • Camilo José C
Gilbert Sorrentino • Ann Quin
icholas Mosley • Douglas Woolf
aymond Queneau • Harry Mathews
kki Ducornet • José Lezama Lima
dan Higgins • Ben Marcus • Colem
owell • Jacques Roubaud • Dju
rnes • Felipe Alfau • Osman Lins
avid Antin • Susan Daitch • Vikt
klovsky • Henry Green • Curtis Wh
Anne Carson • John Hawkes • Fo
adox Ford • Janice Galloway • Mich

Your connection to literature.
DALKEY ARCHIVE PRESS

CONJUNCTIONS:40

40 x 40

Forty Works by Forty Writers

Our celebratory 40th issue features a new
novella by Robert Coover, a previously unpublished interview with Angela Carter, a
new play by Joyce Carol Oates, and a 16-
page full-color portfolio by the enigmatic
"Charles Rosenthal." The issue also includes new work by William T. Vollmann,
Han Ong, Susan Steinberg, Christopher
Sorrentino, Lois-Ann Yamanaka, Can Xue,
Joy Williams, Rick Moody, Paul West,
Mary Caponegro, Maureen Howard, Eliot
Weinberger, William H. Gass, and many
others. 408 pages, $15.

CONJUNCTIONS

Edited by Bradford Morrow
Published by Bard College
Annandale-on-Hudson, NY 12504
(845) 758-1539

Visit www.conjunctions.com

PAST PURRFECT CONTRIBUTORS HAVE INCLUDED:

André Aciman
John Ashbery
J. M. Coetzee
Robert Coover
Annie Dillard
Alan Dugan
Tess Gallagher
Jorie Graham
Seamus Heaney
Lyn Hejinian
Ted Hughes
Ellsworth Kelly
Jhumpa Lahiri
David Mamet
Harry Mathews
Thomas McGuane
Czeslaw Milosz
Les Murray
John Updike
Helen Vendler

Harvard Review

POETRY, FICTION, ESSAYS, DRAMA, GRAPHICS, AND REVIEWS

SUBSCRIPTION RATES

(TWO ISSUES/YEAR):
One Year: $16
Three Years: $45
Five Years: $70
Foreign (air mail only): $28

Subscription forms can be
downloaded from:

http://hcl.harvard.edu/
houghton/departments/
harvardreview/
subscribe.html
or contact us:

HARVARD REVIEW

Lamont Library, Level 5
Harvard University
Cambridge, MA 02138
Ph: 617-495-9775
Fax: 617-496-3692
Email: harvrev@fas.harvard.edu

I have always wondered why short stories aren't popular in modern America. We are such busy folk, you'd think we'd jump at the chance to have our literary wisdom served in doses that fit between taking the trash to the curb and waiting for the carpool. We should favor the short story and adore the poem. But we don't. . . . Why should this be? . . . Good fictional tales will always be my pleasure, my companionship, my salvation. I hope they're also yours.

—Barbara Kingsolver

(From "What Good Is a Story?" in *Small Wonder*, used with permission of the author and HarperCollins Publishers)

Need something good to read between the trash and the carpool?

We have it all—fiction, poetry, essays, art, and reviews—and can deliver it to your door four times a year for only $24.

Subscribe for two years ($40) and get a large cotton tote bag with our new logo imprinted in white on your choice of colors: black, royal blue, navy, teal, or burgundy.

THE GEORGIA REVIEW

The University of Georgia, Athens, GA 30602-9009
(800) 542-3481 • www.uga.edu/garev

THE GREENSBORO REVIEW

For Over 35 Years
A Publisher of Poetry & Fiction

Works from the journal have been anthologized or cited in *Best American Short Stories, Prize Stories: The O. Henry Awards, Pushcart Prize, New Stories from the South,* and other collections honoring the finest new writing.

Recent Contributors

A. Manette Ansay
Julianna Baggott
Stephen Dobyns
Brendan Galvin
Rodney Jones

Jean Ross Justice
Jesse Lee Kercheval
Thomas Lux
Jill McCorkle
Robert Morgan

Dale Ray Phillips
Stanley Plumly
Alan Shapiro
George Singleton
Eleanor Ross Taylor

Subscriptions

Sample copy—$5   One year—$10   Three years—$25

The Greensboro Review
English Department, UNCG
PO Box 26170
Greensboro, NC 27402-6170

Visit our website
www.uncg.edu/eng/mfa
or send SASE for deadlines
and submission guidelines

Produced by the MFA Writing Program at Greensboro

For 77 years
Prairie Schooner
has published the
names we all
know. Be sure that
the next genera-
tions of writers are
even now being
published in our
pages.
– Hilda Raz, in
Current magazine.

Published four times a year
$26 for one year
$45 for two years
$60 for three years

To subscribe,
WRITE: *Prairie Schooner*
201 Andrews Hall
University of Nebraska
Lincoln NE 68588-0334
CALL: 1-800-715-2387
VISIT: www.unl.edu/schooner.psmain.htm

ReadtheFuture

other voices

FICTION FROM *OTHER VOICES* WAS INCLUDED IN *BEST AMERICAN SHORT STORIES OF THE CENTURY*, EDITED BY JOHN UPDIKE AND RECENTLY CITED IN *THE NATION* AS A LEADING FORUM FOR WRITERS OF COLOR.

"LOOKING FOR THE BEST IN SHORT FICTION? [*OTHER VOICES*] CHALLENGES JUST ABOUT ANYTHING YOU WILL FIND IN BETTER-KNOWN COMMERCIAL MAGAZINES."
–Library Journal

"NATURAL, IMPULSIVE, THE ANTITHESIS OF SELF-CONSCIOUSNESS, THESE ARE AFFECTING AND ACCESSIBLE STORIES WITH A STRONG DRAMATIC TENSION AND NARRATIVE DRIVE." *–Small Press Review*

"*OTHER VOICES* IS A CACOPHONY OF EVERY KIND OF VOCALIZATION, FROM LOVING WHISPERS TO MURDEROUS SCREAMS, FROM MURDEROUS MUTTERINGS TO PASSIONATE SCREAMS, FROM HUMMING TO OPERATIC SOPRANO, FROM MONOTONE TO SYMPHONIC CLIMAX TO A SINGLE BUGLE BLOWING TAPS." *–Cris Mazza*

DIVERSE, ORIGINAL FICTION BY PAM HOUSTON, AIMEE BENDER, JEFFREY RENARD ALLEN, STEVE ALMOND, JOSIP NOVAKOVICH, DAN CHAON, WANDA COLEMAN, MOLLY GILES... IN-DEPTH INTERVIEWS WITH JUNOT DIAZ, MICHAEL CUNNINGHAM, ALICE SEBOLD/ GLEN DAVID GOLD, IRVINE WELSH...

4-issue (2-year) Subscription

❑ Individual: $24   ❑ Library/Institution: $28

❑ Canada: $26   ❑ Foreign: $34 (surface) $38 (air)

Start with issue #_____ (#1 is not available)

❑ **Sample Issue** (current #): $7.00 (includes postage)

Name_____

Address_____

City_____ State_____ Zip_____

Enclosed is my   ❑ check   ❑ money order for $_____

other voices

Department of English (MC 162)
University of Illinois at Chicago
601 South Morgan St.
Chicago, IL 60607-7120
(312) 413-2209

Feminism/Femininity in Chinese Literature.

Edited by Peng-hsiang Chen and Whitney Crothers Dilley.

Amsterdam/New York, NY 2002. X,219 pp. (Critical Studies 18)

ISBN: 90-420-0727-3   € 55,-/US-$ 61.-
ISBN: 90-420-0717-6   € 25,-/US-$ 28.-

The present volume of Critical Studies is a collection of selected essays on the topic of feminism and femininity in Chinese literature. Although feminism has been a hot topic in Chinese literary circles in recent years, this remarkable collection represents one of the first of its kind to be published in English. The essays have been written by well-known scholars and feminists including Kang-I Sun Chang of Yale University, and Li Ziyun, a writer and feminist in Shanghai, China. The essays are inter- and multi-disciplinary, covering several historical periods in poetry and fiction (from the Ming-Qing periods to the twentieth century). In particular, the development of women's writing in the New Period (post-1976) is examined in depth. The articles thus offer the reader a composite and broad perspective of feminism and the treatment of the female in Chinese literature. As this remarkable new collection attests, the voices of women in China have begun calling out loudly, in ways that challenge prevalent views about the Chinese female persona.

USA/Canada: One Rockefeller Plaza, Ste. 1420, New York, NY 10020,
Tel. (212) 265-6360, Call toll-free (U.S. only) 1-800-225-3998,
Fax (212) 265-6402
All other countries: Tijnmuiden 7, 1046 AK Amsterdam, The Netherlands.
Tel. ++ 31 (0)20 611 48 21, Fax ++ 31 (0)20 447 29 79
Orders-queries@rodopi.nl   **www.rodopi.nl**
Please note that the exchange rate is subject to fluctuations

THE VIRGINIA QUARTERLY REVIEW

A National Journal of Literature and Discussion

VQR

SPRING 2003   *Volume 79, Number 2*

FIVE DOLLARS

The Rotunda: Symbol of American Higher Education

WHAT'S WRONG — AND RIGHT — WITH
AMERICAN HIGHER EDUCATION? *James Axtell*

THE NEW LOOK — AND TASTE — OF BRITISH CUISINE *Richard Jones*

POLIO SUMMER *Mariflo Stephens*

FICTION *K. A. Longstreet, Roberta Silman, Jane R. Shippen, Mark Vollmer*

POETRY *Charlie Smith, Edward Bartók-Baratta, Brian Teare,
John McKernan, Elisabeth Murawski, David Ray*

THE GREEN ROOM • NOTES ON CURRENT BOOKS

THE VIRGINIA QUARTERLY REVIEW, ONE WEST RANGE, CHARLOTTESVILLE, VA 22903
SUBSCRIPTION RATES: INDIVIDUAL $18.00; INSTITUTIONAL $22.00

The Iowa Review

PRESENTS THE SECOND ANNUAL

The Iowa Award

POETRY, FICTION & NONFICTION

Judges to be announced

$1000 TO EACH WINNER

Plus publication in our December 2004 issue

SUBMIT DURING JANUARY 2004

1. Submit up to 25 pages of prose or 10 pages of poetry (whether one poem or several). Multiple submissions are fine assuming you advise us of acceptance elsewhere. All submissions will be considered for publication in *The Iowa Review*.
2. Manuscripts must include a cover page listing author's name, address, e-mail address and/or telephone number, and the title of each work, but names should not appear on the manuscripts themselves.
3. Enclose a $15 ENTRY FEE (checks payable to *The Iowa Review*).
4. Up to three entries may be offered in each category by adding $10 for a second submission and $5 for a third.
5. Label your envelope as a contest entry—for example: "Contest: Fiction."
6. Postmark submissions between JANUARY 2 & JANUARY 31, 2004.
7. Enclose a #10 SASE for final word on your work. Enclose a SAS postcard if you also wish confirmation of entry receipt. Manuscripts will not be returned.
8. NO ELECTRONIC SUBMISSIONS.

THE IOWA REVIEW   308 EPB   IOWA CITY, IOWA 52242-1408

JOHN IS NOT REALLY DULL HE MAY ONLY NEED WEST BRANCH

W.P.A. Federal Art Project, LOC Call Number POS-WPA-NY .01.J64, no.1. Content altered from original state.

POETRY · FICTION · ESSAYS · REVIEWS
BUCKNELL HALL, BUCKNELL UNIVERSITY, LEWISBURG, PA 17837
www.bucknell.edu/westbranch

The Southern Quarterly

A Journal of the Arts in the South

The Southern Quarterly has been published by the University of Southern Mississippi since 1962 and was the first scholarly journal devoted entirely to the interdisciplinary study of the arts and culture of the southern United States. Over the years, *SoQ* has published special issues and features on a wide variety of themes and individual artists, including: The South and Film, The Texts of Southern Foods, The African American Church, Southern Cemeteries, Race and Gender, Country Music, Contemporary Theater, Southern Identity, Southern Novelists on Stage and Screen, The South and the Sixties Counterculture, Walker Percy, Tennessee Williams, Eudora Welty, Cormac McCarthy, Lee Smith, Robert Penn Warren, Zora Neale Hurston, Caroline Gordon, Katherine Anne Porter, Anne Tyler, Ellen Douglas, Conrad Aiken, Lillian Smith, Bill Russell . . . and Elvis.

Recent *SoQ* special issues and features: Harry Crews, Tennessee Williams: The Non-Dramatic Work, Peter Taylor, Cormac McCarthy's Border Trilogy, Outsider Architecture, The South in Film, Donald Harington, Robert Hazel, William Gilmore Simms, Lewis Nordan, The Souths: Global and Local.

Upcoming in *SoQ*: General Issue (Winter 2004).

Regular *SoQ* departments: book, film, exhibition, and performance reviews, interviews, artists' portfolios, and, since 1989, the annual Bibliography of the Visual Arts and Architecture in the South.

To subscribe:
> Individuals $18/year. Institutions $35/year.
> Add $5 for international mailing. $7 for a sample issue.
> Back issues list and submission guidelines available.
> Make checks payable to *The Southern Quarterly*.

Address all correspondence to:
> The Editor
> *The Southern Quarterly*
> Box 5078 - The University of Southern Mississippi
> Hattiesburg, MS 39406-5078

www.usm.edu/soq

Cimarron Review

A Quarterly Review
$7.00 per issue
$24.00 per year

Standard Guidelines; No Themes
http://cimarronreview.okstate.edu

Gobshite

Quarterly

*Your Rosetta Stone for the
New World Order*

Issue 3 now available

Gobshite Quarterly
Baptized in legible fonts!

COMING AT YOU MULTILINGUALLY AT
BOOKSTORES & NEWSSTANDS IN THE U.S.,
CANADA, U.K., AND ELSEWHERE.
ISSUE THREE, AUGUST 2003
ISSUE FOUR, NOVEMBER 2003
WWW.GOBSHITEQUARTERLY.COM

Dalkey Archive Press

NEW RELEASES

Heartsnatcher
by BORIS VIAN

My Paris
by GAIL SCOTT

Garden, Ashes
by DANILO KIŠ

A Bad Man
by STANLEY ELKIN

Heartsnatcher

Boris Vian

Foreword by Raymond Queneau
Introduction by John Sturrock
Translation by Stanley Chapman

French Literature Series
A Novel
$13.95 / paper
ISBN: 1-56478-299-9

Set in a bizarre and slightly sinister town where the elderly are auctioned off at an Old Folks Fair, the townspeople assail the priest in hopes of making it rain, and the official town scapegoat bears the shame of the citizens by fishing junk out of the river with his teeth, *Heartsnatcher* is Boris Vian's most playful and most serious work.

The main character is Clementine, a mother who punishes her husband for causing her the excruciating pain of giving birth to three babies. As they age, she becomes increasingly obsessed with protecting them, going so far as to build an invisible wall around their property.

All of these events are observed by Timortis, an elegant psychiatrist who is appalled by the town's oddities and searches for someone to psychoanalyze in order to fill the void in his own personality. Unsuccessful, he settles for a neutered cat and a maid who thinks "psychoanalyze" is a euphemism for sex.

"Boris Vian has written fine, beautiful books." —*Raymond Queneau*

"To Americans, Boris Vian has long been one of the hidden glories of French literature." —*Jim Krusoe*

——— *Now Available* ———

My Paris

GAIL SCOTT

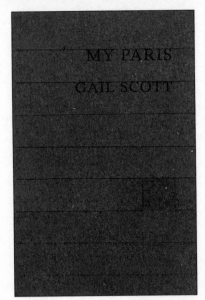

Canadian Literature Series
A Novel
$12.95 / paper
ISBN: 1-56478-297-2

In *My Paris,* a Canadian woman keeps an extraordinary journal of her time in a Parisian studio. Not a real tourist, she prefers indoor spaces, seeing Paris go by on TV or watching from her window the ever-changing displays of men's designer clothing across the boulevard. Or she roams the streets and old arcades, caught between nostalgia and a competing sense of the present day, between Paris's rich cultural traditions and the realities of Western imperialism. Dismayed by the impossibility of reconciling these contradictions, and by her own part in perpetuating them, she assembles in her journal pieces of the present, past; of art, philosophy; of herself and of the world outside her, pulling them together on the page in a very personal act of subversion and creation.

"Gail Scott moves through the ghost world she calls Paris with grace and intelligence in this troubling and poignant book of shadows and their elaborations."
—Carole Maso

"My Paris *is a tour de force of technique, style, and soul.*"
—Brad Hooper, Booklist *(starred review)*

——— *Now Available* ———

Garden, Ashes

Danilo Kiš

Introduction by Aleksandar Hemon
Translation by William J. Hannaher

Eastern European Literature Series
A Novel
$12.95 / paper
ISBN: 1-56478-326-X

Garden, Ashes is the remarkable account of Andi Scham's childhood during World War II, as his Jewish family traverses Eastern Europe to escape persecution. As the family moves from house to house, the novel focuses on Andi's relationship with his father; he recounts the endless hours his father poured into the creation of his third edition of the *Bus, Ship, Rail, and Air Travel Guide,* the bizarre sermons he delivered to his befuddled family, and his eventual disappearance and assumed death at Auschwitz. Despite the apocalyptic events fueling this family's story, Kiš's writing emphasizes the specific details of life during this period, constructing a personal account of a future artist growing up under the shadow of the Nazis and in a world capable of containing a person as unique as his father.

"In Kiš's case . . . it is the consistent quality of the local prose that counts. It is how, sentence by sentence, the song is built, and immeasurable meanings meant. It is the rich regalia of his rhetoric that leads us to acknowledge his authority. On his page, trappings are not trappings, but sovereignty itself."
—William H. Gass, New York Review of Books

——— *Now Available* ———

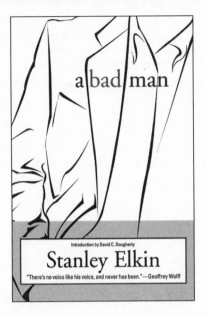

A Bad Man

STANLEY ELKIN
Introduction by David C. Dougherty

American Literature Series
A Novel
$13.95 / paper
ISBN: 1-56478-332-4

Sentenced to a year in jail for providing his customers with everything they needed—drugs for the nervous, abortions for the unintending, guns for the crazed—department store owner Leo Feldman finds himself in a Kafkaesque prison. Labeled a "bad man," Feldman is treated as a fool, made to wear a clownish version of his business suit with button holes too big for the buttons and miscut legs and pockets. While incarcerated, he's forced to come to terms with his criminal self—a man always on the make, one who can't avoid overselling to the poor and lying to the trusting—in this grey-stone purgatory run by a sadistic prison warden who enforces a set of elaborate, ever-shifting rules.

"*A Bad Man puts Stanley Elkin in the same league with the smartest, most imaginative and verbally gifted novelists working in America today.*"
—Washington Post

"*One can almost thumb through this new novel at random and find fanciful diction, boffo wit, prize punning, razzle-dazzle mimicry, picturesque conceits and one-handed insights. . . . I know of no serious funny writer in this country who can match him.*"
—New York Times

—— *Now Available* ——

ORDER FORM

Individuals may use this form to subscribe to the *Review of Contemporary Fiction* or to order back issues of the *Review* or Dalkey Archive titles at a 10-20% discount.

Title	ISBN	Quantity	Price

(10% for one book, 20% for two or more books)

($4 domestic, $5 foreign)

Subtotal_____

Less Discount_____

Subtotal_____

Plus postage_____

1 year individual subscription ($17 domestic, $20.50 foreign)_____

Total_____

Ship to _____

_____

_____

_____

mail or fax this form to:

Dalkey Archive Press

ISU Campus Box 8905

Normal, IL 61790-8905

fax: 309.438.7422

tel: 309.438.7555

Credit card payment   ☐ Visa   ☐ Mastercard

Acct #_____   Exp. Date_____

Name on card_____   Phone Number_____

Please make checks (in U.S. dollars only) payable to *Dalkey Archive Press*